DEATH AT BRIGHTON PAVILION

CAPTAIN LACEY REGENCY MYSTERIES BOOK 14

ASHLEY GARDNER

JA / AG PUBLISHING

CHAPTER 1

July 1819

I woke, or seemed to. I was on my feet, fully dressed in my evening clothes. My head ached, blood pounding in my temples, my eyes hot. Every limb was on fire but stiff, the old injury in my knee throbbing in quiet agony.

I rubbed finger and thumb into my eyes, trying to clear them, and moved my tongue in my dry mouth. The taste I met was foul, sticky and sweet, and at the same time rancid.

I had no idea where the devil I was. A cautious glance showed I stood in a massive but unfinished room, dim and silent. Cloths draped a bare wood floor, and a ceiling soared overhead, gray light leaking through tiny windows at the top.

Something caught my attention at my feet, and I rubbed my eyes again as I bent to peer blearily at the object.

It was a man, sprawled on a dust sheet, limbs askew. I stared at him in a daze, barely able to comprehend what I was seeing.

He was dead—I knew that immediately. His face was gray, open eyes unseeing, chest still. A blue uniform coat gaped to show a white shirt now stained with dark blood. The sword that had killed him, also coated with blood, was clenched in my hand.

It was a cavalry saber, well-balanced with a thick hilt and a curved blade. It wasn't the sword from my walking stick—that one was straight, and the stick lay on the floor at my side.

I had no idea how I'd come to be here, or why I stood over the body of a dead man with a bloody sword in my cramped grip.

My heart beat thick and fast, senses returning slowly, but no memories. The chamber was utterly silent, no running footsteps of someone hurrying to investigate a fight, no shouts of horror or dismay. Only quiet, until a breeze outside carried to me the lone, shrill cry of a seagull.

I realized as awareness trickled into me that I stood in the Prince Regent's house in Brighton. Half of what the prince called his Pavilion was unfinished, the other half already a confusion of styles, much like Carlton House, but on a more whimsical scale.

I'd dined here tonight with Grenville, my wife, and several other guests, including the man on the floor, hours ago it must be. Dawn's light above confirmed that it was likely four or five on this summer morning.

I passed my tongue over paper-dry lips, panic a dim thing shouting inside me. My head hurt like fury, my stomach burned, and renewed pain flowed through my blood as bits and pieces of the night swooped at me like visions from a nightmare.

The man on the floor was Colonel Hamilton Isherwood of the Forty-Seventh Light Dragoons. I'd encountered him on the Peninsula, at Salamanca, seven years ago, where he'd despised me, and I him. Those memories were sharp and clear, as bright as the Spanish sky and the dusty, hard hills around it. Far clearer than the hours between supper and now.

Tonight, Isherwood had behaved, at the meal at least, as though we'd been briefly acquainted during the war, nothing more.

I had absolutely no memory of killing him.

Or of trudging back to the Pavilion after I'd left it last night. I should be at home in the bow-windowed house we'd hired, asleep next to my wife. Not in an unfinished room with a bloody sword in my hands, an old enemy dead at my feet.

I shook, my palms sweating in my gloves. I wanted to heave up the Regent's excellent supper and fine port, but my throat remained closed.

Lay down the sword and depart, my common sense told me. *Walk back home. Do not be found here.*

Wise advice. I began to place the sword on the floor when I heard a gasp, loud in the silence.

I jerked around to see a young man in the wide doorway, a flickering candle in his hand. He wore a dressing gown, but he was not a guest. I'd seen his face earlier this evening, but it had been blank with deference as he'd served me port in the prince's drawing room.

He was a footman, slim and tall, his skin black. He'd worn a turban while he carried trays about, as it was the fashion to have one or two "Moorish" servants in attendance, but the lad was no more Moorish than I was.

He stared at me as I slowly straightened, the candlelight showing his dark eyes wide with shock. He opened his mouth, drawing breath to shout.

"No!" I cried in a fierce whisper as I moved a shaky step toward him.

His face took on a look of abject terror, and I realized I still had the sword in my hand. I dropped it, but the lad turned and fled from the madman with the bloody weapon. He dashed through a doorway and was gone.

"Damnation."

I snatched up my walking stick, having to brace myself on it to regain my feet. I could barely move as I turned to search for a another way out of the room, one that would take me in the opposite direction the footman had gone.

The door through which he'd disappeared was open—in fact, the door had not been hung yet and leaned against the wall. I must be in one of the chambers the builders were over-hauling in their frenzy to redesign and expand the Prince Regent's Pavilion.

Drapes covered the soaring walls to protect them, the plas-terwork on the arches still wet. The scent of paint, plaster, and dust hung heavily in the silent air.

I stumbled to the far end of the chamber, expecting at every step to hear men pounding after me. The footman would no doubt raise the alarm.

I pawed at the drapes until I found a chink in one and lifted it to slide behind it. The cloths hung about a foot out from the edges of the room, creating a tunnel between fabric and unpainted wall.

I groped my way along this this for a while before I came upon a smaller door, closed but unlocked. I ducked through the narrow portal and along a short hall only to emerge in another enormous room.

This chamber had whitewashed walls, several massive fire-places, and tables covered with pots, bowls, baskets, boxes, and haphazard piles of fruits and vegetables. Plucked fowls on one table leaked juices into a mound of flour.

It was far too early to find anyone in the kitchen, to my relief—and dimly to my distress. Something behind my panic did not like to see the comestibles out in the open with mice enjoying a small feast on the corner of a table.

I moved haltingly through the room, ignoring the smell of overripe fruit and aging fowl, but there seemed to be no way out of the infernal kitchen. At last I discovered another door the shadows of a cupboard, and I entered another corridor, my entire body beginning to shake, as though I had an ague.

The passageway was plain and unadorned, the walls flaking plaster. A servants' route through the lavish house.

I heard a step and flattened myself against the wall, as though that would make me unseen. Whoever it was loped toward me without trying to be silent, obviously not expecting to meet anyone back here.

When he was a few paces away I saw by the light of his candle that it was the same footman, probably on his way to alert someone about the murder. He jerked to a halt when he saw me, and I took advantage of his shock and seized him before he could run again.

He struggled. He was half my age, and very strong, but I was an experienced fighter, and in spite of my current infirmity, I held him in a firm grip.

"Stand still," I commanded in a fierce whisper. "I did not kill that man. I found him there."

Hadn't I? I wished like the devil I could remember.

"I promise you," I said. "I give you my word." The phrases stung my throat and I hoped they were true.

The young man's frightened breath made a wheezing sound in the stillness. "You're Mr. Grenville's friend, ain't ya?"

His accent put him from somewhere in south London. He had no question about my identity, but the servants would know who was in this house at any given time and what they meant to the Regent.

"Yes," I answered breathlessly. "Mr. Grenville will vouch for me. My wife will too—though that rather depends on her mood."

The young man only stared at me as I made my feeble joke, ready to spring and run the instant I released him.

"What is that room?" I asked, waving vaguely behind me. "Where Colonel Isherwood ..."

"Banqueting room. Sir."

"What the devil was he—?" I broke off, knowing the question was a futile one.

I considered for a moment that this young man had murdered Colonel Isherwood, but I could see no evidence of it. The death had been a messy business, and the lad did not have a splash of blood on his white shirt or the dark blue dressing gown. I unfortunately, had a streak of blood starting at my right knee and ending in the middle of my coat, as though the dying man's blood had smeared me.

"Show me the way out," I said. "Unless you have a mind to run for a watchman. If so, you'd better go now."

The young man swallowed, his slim throat showing a prominent Adam's apple. "This way, sir."

Whether he'd decided to trust me or would lead me straight to said watchman I could not guess, and truth to tell, I did not much care. I only wanted free of this place.

I released him cautiously. He did not bolt but started through corridor, I staggering on his heels. The hallway's blank walls were broken only by plain doors that would lead to the chambers of the Regent's luxurious hideaway, each door identical.

My guide moved unerringly, leading me around turns and down short staircases until I was completely lost. I half-fancied we'd emerge once more into the room where the dead man lay, with twenty watchmen and a magistrate waiting to arrest me.

We descended yet another set of stairs, and the footman slowing for my hobbling steps, and opened a door at the bottom. I had so convinced myself we'd return to the banqueting room or a similar chamber that I was surprised to feel cool, damp outside air and hear the sea in the distance.

The narrow door, opening to a tiny and noisome passage, must be meant for those removing slops or night soil, the parts of life one did not want marring a beautiful palace. A path led around a wall and past a bit of shrubbery that screened it from the house.

"Gate at the end," my guide said. "Turn right. Lane will take ya to Great East Street."

"Thank you," I said sincerely. "What is your name, lad?"

I expected him to say "John," or another common moniker Englishmen gave their servants. He stared at me and answered, "Clement."

"Clement," I said. "Again, I thank you."

I held out my hand. He gazed at it in amazement and fear, as though I were handing him a snake.

I gave him a weak smile, let my hand drop, and made a weak bow. "I am most grateful. I swear to you, I did not kill Colonel Isherwood. You ought to send for a magistrate, no matter what you think of me, because *someone* murdered him."

"Yes, sir," Clement said, but I could not tell whether he'd obey me.

I left him and moved down the muddy path, which did indeed lead to a cesspit that stank in the damp air.

I looked back before continuing along the tall box hedge that separated the privies from the main house, and saw that Clement had disappeared. Now to discover whether he'd aided me or would betray me.

The wall led to a gate, as Clement had promised, and the gate opened to a walkway. I followed this to Great East Street then turned my steps south, or thought I did, trying to make for the promenade that fronted the town above the sea.

My head had not yet cleared, however, and I easily grew disoriented in the dawn light. I took a wrong turn and stumbled about in the back lanes, until I begged a flower seller to tell me the way out.

With a nosegay pinned to my lapel—the price of the information—I eventually reached Bedford Row and headed west under a misting rain, my body aching with each step.

I passed the artillery battery that faced the sea and turned to the new square which held the house my wife had hired for our summer stay in Brighton.

I found the front door locked. As I leaned heavily on the doorpost, wondering whether the cook had unbolted the back way in, the door was opened with a wrench. I nearly fell inside and into Bartholomew, my valet, who'd come to see who was trying to get into the house.

The belligerent look he'd assumed for an intruder vanished to be replaced by astonishment.

"Sir?" He blinked. "Were you walking all night? We thought you'd put up at Mr. Grenville's."

I had no strength to answer. I pushed past him, ill and weary, needing my bed.

Before Bartholomew could close the door, there was a rush of footsteps, and Thomas Brewster charged in from the street.

"Where you been, guv?" Brewster glared at me, out of breath, his clothes mist-spotted and mud-splotched. "I've been scouring this town for hours looking for you. You slid off from Mr. Grenville in the park, and I lost ya in the dark. I've been running around since searching for ya, getting all wet in this blasted fog. Where the bloody hell did you get to?"

CHAPTER 2

"The Royal Pavilion," I made myself say as Bartholomew closed the door, shutting out the morning. My voice rasped, and I braced myself blearily on my walking stick. "So it seems."

"What the devil did you go back *there* for?" Brewster demanded. "Couldn't get your fill of the place?"

Bartholomew gazed at me as well, waiting for me to explain. My temper began to fray under their scrutiny, because I had no idea what to tell them.

"Where I walk in the middle of the night is my own business," I said stiffly. "Now I'm off to bed before I drop."

Bartholomew, though curious, was well-trained enough to clamp his lips closed over more questions and begin to help me from my coat.

Brewster, on the other hand, had never been trained to be anything but rude.

"'Tis *my* business what you get up to. I'm only in this benighted town full of dafties who think swimming in the sea will cure them of all ills so I can keep you from harm. When ye wander off in the middle of the night and come home looking like the devil is after ye, I want you to stand still and tell me what it's all about."

If Brewster had worked for me, I could tell him to calm himself and go home, but he answered to another authority. His employer was James Denis, a man who'd decided he had the power of life and death over me. At the moment, Denis was interested in keeping me alive, and so Brewster had been sent along on this jaunt to Brighton to watch over me.

"Very well." I had to wet my parched mouth before I could continue. "I have no memory of parting from Grenville. I came to myself at the Pavilion, and returned home." I cleared my throat as Brewster and Bartholomew regarded me in dubious silence. "Also, Colonel Isherwood has been killed. Good night, gentlemen."

I turned and headed for the stairs. Brewster was beside me before I'd taken two steps, putting himself between me and the newel post.

"Ye don't get away that easy, Captain. Chap's been killed? By you, do you mean?"

I tried to shrug. "As to that, I could not say. I found him dead, but I will have to speak to you about it later."

The truth was, I could barely stand. I might appear cool and collected, but I shook deep inside myself and my stomach roiled.

Bartholomew's mouth fell open. "'Struth, sir."

"Bloody hell," came Brewster's rumble. "This is why I don't ever let you out of me sight. You always find trouble."

"So it seems," I managed to say. "But I am to bed, and we will speak later. Please do not wake her ladyship, and do not mention this to the rest of the household."

Bartholomew, though he remained worried, nodded. "Yes,

sir." He stood back to let me climb the stairs.

Brewster scowled and plunked himself upon a delicate bench in the cream-colored front hall. "I'll wait."

I left him there, too weary to argue. I sensed Bartholomew full of questions as we ascended to the upper floor, but as I was growing more ill by the moment, I could not rationally discuss anything.

I'd scarcely reached my chamber at the top of the stairs before I vomited all I had into the basin in the corner. Bartholomew did not hide his dismay, but he was there with a towel before I could soil my clothing.

He had me undressed quickly and bundled into bed. For the first time since we'd arrived, I was grateful my wife had insisted on separate bedchambers, though I suspected her need for privacy stemmed the fact that I rose too early for her liking and had a tendency to snore.

Bartholomew shoved a goblet under my nose and told me to drink. The last thing I wanted was brandy, but I obeyed, conceding that the burning liquid eased my stomach a trifle.

Only a trifle. I was still queasy when Bartholomew settled the blankets over me, but also exhausted. I dropped off quickly, and dreamed of the dead Colonel Isherwood pursuing me through garish rooms of the Pavilion with a bloody sword.

I HAD NO IDEA HOW LONG I SLEPT. I DRIFTED IN AND OUT, MY dreams troubling.

I fancied I saw faces above me after Isherwood's faded— Bartholomew mostly, but then Grenville, Brewster, and Donata.

Beautiful Donata. I reached for her, reasoning I'd feel better against her softness. She wore a large cap, very unlike her usual affairs, but it looked fetching on her. Before I could touch her, however, her hair changed to long locks of lush gold, her smile wide and unreal. That face became the one of the actress Marianne Simmons, who'd once lived upstairs from me, her sharp eyes holding disapproval.

You're a lazy lie-abed, you know, she informed me. *What are you going to do about this, Lacey?*

When I at last swam to my senses, the light in the windows was weak, but my head had cleared somewhat. I sat up.

At once, Bartholomew swiftly entered the chamber. "Feeling better, are we, Captain?" he asked in overly bright tones.

I rubbed my chin, finding it rough with whiskers. "I am, thank you. Restless night, but I might as well rise. What does my wife have scheduled for me to do this morning?"

Bartholomew gave me a startled glance but moved to the basin and began clinking shaving things onto a tray. The sound was loud to my addled brain—I must have imbibed far too much the night before.

"It's long past morning, sir," Bartholomew announced. "Well into afternoon."

"I've slept all day?" I glanced at the window in disbelief, but I saw only gray skies and had no idea where the sun lay. "Why didn't you wake me?"

"Why not indeed, sir?" Bartholomew finished piling his tray and waited for me to climb from bed and don my dressing gown. "You couldn't be waked, is why, though we all tried. Mr. Grenville wanted to send for a physician, but her ladyship don't trust them. Her ladyship is back in bed, as she was spent from looking in on you all day. When you started snoring hard, she said you would be all right and retired to her chamber. She convinced Mr. Grenville to go home and sleep too."

I remembered the changing faces from my dreams—my friends and family must have been hovering over me to see whether I lived or not. Rather embarrassing.

"Do not disturb her then," I said, hiding my discomfiture. "I appear to be right as rain." I swayed, giving the words a lie, but I'd been hungover before. The only thing to do was wait it out. I dropped into the chair before the fire and tilted my head back, ready to be shaved.

"Mayhap." Bartholomew looked dubious but lathered my face with warm soap and poised the razor over my throat. "After you arrived home at dawn looking like demons were chasing you I agree with Mr. Grenville that perhaps you need a dose of something."

I blinked at him. "What are you talking about? I slept soundly in my bed all night, after apparently drinking far too much at dinner at that blasted Pavilion. I hope I didn't mortify my wife and Grenville."

The razor hesitated. "You don't remember coming home with a posy on your coat saying you'd been back to the Pavilion but don't remember why? And that a colonel had been killed."

I started, and Bartholomew quickly lifted the razor away. "What colonel?"

My first thought was of Colonel Brandon, with whom I'd had an uneasy friendship since we'd returned from the Peninsular War. Brandon, dead? An icy pain struck my heart, the intensity of which surprised me.

"No, sir. Chap with a funny name. Isher. Something like that."

Amid relief that Brandon was well and whole, memories slammed into me, not nice ones. "Isherwood? Good God."

Colonel Hamilton Isherwood of the Forty-Seventh Light Dragoons, the cavalry regiment who'd served alongside the Thirty-Fifth—my regiment—at Salamanca. He'd had the rank of major then, and I hadn't seen him again until he'd walked into the supper room at the Pavilion last night.

"He's been killed, you say?" I asked in amazement.

Bartholomew gave me an odd look. "You told *us,* sir. When you returned early this morning."

In a chill, I sank back, searching the haze of my memory, but I found nothing but a blank.

After the tedious supper with the Regent and his aristocratic acquaintances, from which the Regent had excused himself fairly early, Donata had gone on to another outing with friends, and Marianne had departed to visit some theatrical acquaintances. I vaguely remembered Grenville and I strolling together after that in the dark in the Steine—the park near the Pavilion—and the taste of a cheroot. But I had no recollection of returning to the Pavilion, or wandering about Brighton after that in the small hours.

"You must be mistaken," I said uneasily.

"No, sir." Bartholomew came at me with the razor again, and I made myself subside so he could work. "You said and did all I have related."

He shaved me swiftly and competently, and when he finished, I snatched up the towel he handed to me and dried off my face. "I must have been far deeper in my cups than I thought, but Brewster will know what happened. He follows me about like a damned hound."

Bartholomew moved off to clean up the shaving things. "He

was as confounded as me, sir. It appears you eluded him in the dark."

I emerged from the towel. "Send word to him, will you, Bartholomew? I'll need to speak to him."

"He's downstairs, sir. Wouldn't move, even when his wife came to fetch him home. *She's* worried about you too."

Mrs. Brewster, a minuscule woman, had a strength about her that could unnerve the strongest man. She certainly had the brutish Brewster under her thumb.

"I'd better be dressed then," I said.

Not long later, I indeed found Brewster waiting for me in the lower hall, seated on a bench near the front door. I forestalled his growled questions by bidding him to follow me into the dining room.

Brewster never liked entering the main rooms of the house, feeling uncomfortable in luxury. He took a few steps into the chamber and halted, standing like a stone. Bartholomew discreetly vanished, closing the door behind him.

"Before you shout your disapprobation at me," I said as he drew a breath, "tell me exactly what happened last night. My memory is vague."

Nonexistent, in fact, as though I'd been drunker than I'd let myself become in a while, but I wanted to hear Brewster's version of the tale.

"Huh." Brewster wiped his nose with the back of his hand. "If I've caught a chill chasing you about … After you come out of the Pavilion once your supper was done, you and Mr. Grenville decided a walk in the dark under the trees would be entertaining. The pair of you wandered about that Steine place, then Mr. Grenville said he'd been invited to a soiree in one of the fine houses on the Grand Parade. You decline to go and headed past the Regent's stables once you parted from him. It was dark as a tomb back there, and all of a mist too. You took a turn I missed and vanished like smoke. I searched up and down, but never saw you again until I caught sight of you coming out of the market down by the sea, sweet as you please, the church clocks striking five." He finished, scowl firmly in place.

"Ah." I moved to the sideboard, hoping to find breakfast, but it was empty, and I remembered it was evening, the morning meal long since finished. "Well, it appears I am unharmed," I said, trying to speak lightly. "No need to report to Mr. Denis."

Brewster sent me an aggrieved look. "He'll want to know anything odd. You turning up out of nowhere bleating about this Isherwood bloke being dead is right odd."

Memories of the Peninsula rose again, of Salamanca, with the domes of its cathedral golden in the sunlight, the roar of men converging on the battlefield, the high heat of July, the screams of the dying. The aftermath, the exhaustion, giddy victory, the celebrations, the warm sun in a high room inside the city's walls.

Isherwood had turned up at supper last night, resplendent in his uniform. I'd regarded him in surprise and dismay, and he'd done the same to me. Not a happy reunion.

I shut out the thoughts. "I should begin with Isherwood, then. To discover whether he is alive and well. If he was killed, surely there'd be a mention in the newspapers?" Several had been left for me on the table, but a quick glance at the first pages showed no report of a murder at the Regent's Pavilion.

"Wasn't in any papers I read as I was awaiting for you to wake, and her ladyship or Mr. Grenville didn't know nothing about it. Would be all over town, wouldn't it? If a dead body turned up at His Royal Highness's house?"

He had a point. It would be too much of a sensation, and Brighton, and soon the rest of the country, would be abuzz.

"I might have dreamed his death," I said uncertainly. "My mind is in such confusion I can't be certain. So let us find out whether he is alive or dead."

"How do you intend to do that?" Brewster demanded. "Walk about the town and shout his name?"

"Go to the Pavilion and find out what I can." I spoke as though this would be a simple matter, cleared up in an hour.

Brewster continued to glower. "My advice? Which I know you will not take." He hardened his glare. "Leave it."

"Pardon?" My mind had drifted again. Meeting Isherwood last night after seven years almost to the day had been rattling.

Isherwood had remembered me well—I'd seen it in his eyes. He'd chosen to ignore that fact and pretend we'd never met. He'd kept up the pretense until after supper when we'd shared port … Not so much shared it as drunk it while he snarled invective at me in a heated whisper.

"I said leave it," Brewster repeated. "Go with your wife and wee ones to the sea and forget you went strolling about Brighton in the middle of the night bleating about dead colonels. Let that be the end of it."

"Do not stir things up, you mean?" I considered this. "Perhaps you are correct. Perhaps I only dreamed it."

"That's right, guv. Ye were restless and wandered about to clear your head. Came home and fell asleep so hard you don't remember none of it."

What he said was possible. Also untrue.

I knew that if I consulted with Donata and my friends before I departed to look for Isherwood, they, like Brewster, would try to stop me. Brewster had a point—I'd come to Brighton as Grenville's guest, to celebrate his happiness in his new marriage. My two daughters and my stepson were with me, and I wanted this time to embrace my family.

I equally knew the missing hours would haunt me until the end of my days and that I wouldn't be able to rest until I pieced together what had happened.

I left the dining room, still hungry, fetched my hat and coat, and stepped out the front door. Brewster, heaving an aggrieved sigh, followed.

It was an easy walk from our hired house along Bedford Row that skirted the sea, even for me with my injured leg. The mist of the previous night had gone. Daylight lingered for quite some time in midsummer, and Brewster and I moved through a golden evening toward the avenue that would take us into the main part of Brighton.

I had decided to begin at the Pavilion, to discover if anyone had reported a death, before I moved on to Isherwood's house if I found no news. I knew where Isherwood lived, because he'd boasted of it at supper, but I was in no hurry to encounter the man again if he were still alive.

Had I not been so uneasy, I would have noted what a lovely hour it was. The sea, a hue of gray-blue, stretched away at our right hand, and a brisk wind cooled what heat the day had brought. Out on the water were fishing boats, and among them, twisting and turning in the wind, glided the pleasure sailing craft of gentlemen.

Walkers had emerged to take advantage of the fine weather, husbands strolling with wives and daughters, gentlemen wandering in search of entertainment, and women walking together, followed closely by a servant or two. Plenty of taverns fronted the sea, along with restaurants for families—many such places has sprung up now that the Prince Regent had made Brighton fashionable for a seaside holiday.

I decided to head north up Ship Street instead of continuing along the sea walk. There were plenty of crowds along the waterfront—easier to cut through the town than follow the shore, or so I told myself. However, when I reached the small brick cottage that housed the Quaker meetings, I paused, something nagging at me.

I had learned since our arrival in Brighton that this cottage had been built fifteen years previously when the Regent had decided to tear down houses and close off streets to expand his Pavilion. One of those houses destroyed had been the meeting place of the Society of Friends. They'd been given no choice but to move, and they'd built this new cottage on grounds owned by one of the Quakers.

"I was here," I said to Brewster after some moments of indecisiveness. "I think."

Brewster scowled. "Turned Dissenter, have ye?"

"No." I was too impatient to banter with him. "I do not mean I attended a meeting, but I was here." I tapped the pavement. We stood outside a gate that led to a garden laid out in neat rows, the green tops of vegetables bright against the soil. "I spoke to someone."

The Meeting House was quiet now, its small windows unlighted, but I saw movement in the open doorway. As I peered through the garden, a man emerged and paused on the doorstep to regard me. He was small in stature, wore a plain gray coat and knee breeches, and held a wide-brimmed hat.

As though making up his mind, he set the hat on his head

and walked briskly out of the house and down the path to me, bathing me in a kind smile.

"I am pleased to see thee well again, Gabriel," he announced. "We won't have a meeting this evening, but thou art welcome to sit quietly in the lecture room and reflect."

CHAPTER 3

*A*gain?" Brewster gazed at me incredulously as the Quaker man nodded at us. "Give me strength. You *have* been here, guv."

The man turned to Brewster with no less deference than he had shown me. "Indeed, Gabriel Lacey and I spoke last night. He was quite disturbed about something but looks much better this evening."

I gazed hard at the man, nonplussed. "I spoke to you?"

"We spoke together." He addressed me gently, as though not wishing to startle me. "I met thee in the Steine as I took a moonlight stroll, and thou walked here with me. Thou had much agitation."

I chewed my lip, my stomach knotting. "I have no memory of this."

The man nodded. "I thought thou wert inebriated and looked regretful for it."

"You know my name."

"Thou gave it to me. And I gave thee mine. Clive Bickley."

The fact came to me that Quakers never used titles, preferring to address each other by first names. I had probably told him I was Captain Gabriel Lacey. Any other Englishman would refer to me as *Captain*, or *Lacey* if we were friends. It felt odd to hear my Christian name from the lips of a man I didn't remember meeting.

Odder still was the way the man looked at me, as though he knew everything that was in my heart when I did not.

"This question may sound strange to you, sir," I said. "But why did I come here with you? Did you ask me to walk you home?" It was safe enough in these parts, but perhaps I'd worried that a soft man, alone at night, might come to harm.

"Thou wert quite troubled, as I say," Mr. Bickley answered, his expression serious. "Thou told me of a momentous decision before thee and that though had much confusion about it. I begged thee to come to this place and rest until thou wert calm—we keep the cottage open for any friends who need a place to sit quietly. Thou came inside with me but stayed only a few minutes before rushing off again."

I was no stranger to losing hours or a night to drink, though I had not done so in a long time. In the army, after victorious battle—or after a disastrous one—I had joined fellow officers in becoming insensibly drunk, rising in the morning with an aching head and very little memory or what had happened the night before.

The problem was, I could not recall drinking much at all last night, save the wine I'd taken at supper at the Pavilion and the port afterward, which I'd not finished.

"I beg pardon if I was rude to you," I said.

"Not at all." Mr. Bickley gave me a warm smile. "If thou cannot find an answer to your worries, Gabriel, thou art always free to seek a quiet space here." He turned his gaze to Brewster. "Thou as well, Friend Thomas."

I came alert at the same time Brewster said, "'Ere. 'Ow'd ye know my name?"

Mr. Bickley reddened. Brewster began to close in on Bickley with his pugilist belligerence, but I held up my hand.

"Tell us," I said. "He was not with me last night, he says."

Mr. Bickley looked abashed. "He was not. We were curious about thee, Gabriel. We have seen thee walking through Brighton with thy wife and children. We sought gossip and learned thy names." The thorough shame with which he said the words would have been amusing any other time.

"In that case," I said, "I would be foolish not to take advantage of your knowledge. Did you see me speaking to anyone last night?"

"I do not believe so. Thou walked away into the darkness when thou left us, and we did not follow thee."

"You say *we*." I glanced at the house. "Do you mean other, er, friends?" I was not certain what Quakers called members of their congregation.

As though she'd been awaiting a cue, a woman left the house and approached us. Though her gown had a fashionably high waist and flowing skirt, the fabric was gray worsted, and the frock bore no ribbons, lace, or any other adornment. She wore a bonnet of plain linen, and beneath its shade I saw that her brown hair held threads of gray, but her face, surprisingly pretty, was unwrinkled except for a few lines about her eyes.

"Welcome, Gabriel," she said. She neither curtsied nor held out a hand for greeting. "As Clive hast told thee, we formed an interest in thee. Perhaps not polite or even wise, but thou interested us. Thou art not the same as most London men who travel to Brighton for the waters."

"'Struth," Brewster muttered.

"Indeed, Friend Thomas, it is God's truth," the woman said

giving him a gentle look. "I am Matilda Farrow. Has C¹ spoken to thee of why we had such an interest?"

Mr. Bickley, flustered and embarrassed, took a small step back as though letting Mrs.—or perhaps Miss—Farrow commandeer the discussion.

The trouble with a person being introduced with only their given names was that I could not tell what status they were— married, unmarried, gentleman or gentlewoman, aristocrat, of military rank, or anything else about them.

That was the idea, I gathered. From what little I knew of Quakers, I understood they considered all people to be of equal station, with no class demarcations. Their leaders, called elders, were chosen from among themselves, regardless of their status in the rest of the world. Quakers, like many other Dissenters, wanted to rid themselves of the grandeur and hierarchy of the more formal Church of England.

While I could not blame them—I'd met too many pompous bishops for my taste, including an overly arrogant one at supper last night—it currently made things difficult for me. I tried to be as polite as possible to everyone, but to do so, I had to know what to call them.

"Madam." I settled for this honorific as I bowed to her. "I am flattered by the interest of you and your colleagues."

Matilda smiled. "No, thou art not, Friend Lacey. Thou art unnerved, as thou ought to be, and most curious in return." She sobered. "We learned about thee, and spoke about it. We have heard that thou hast knowledge of men of law. And that thou has brought bad men to justice."

I acknowledged this cautiously. My exploits were generally not looked upon with benevolence. The opinion of most was that I should keep my long nose out of others' business.

"I will speak bluntly with thee, Friend Lacey," Matilda

continued. "A few of our members have vanished. Perhaps *vanished* is too strong a term, but we do not know where they are. As thou art skilled in these matters, we thought perhaps thou might find them for us? Not to drag them back into the fold—if our Friends wish to leave us, that is for them to decide. We will naturally be disappointed and sorrowful, but what we most want is to make certain they are well."

I understood. I read worry in Miss Farrow's eyes, and in Bickley's as well.

"I could make inquiries," I said hesitantly. "But I am not anything like a Runner. I cannot guarantee I will find anyone."

"Whatever help thou canst bestow us will be welcome," Matilda said. "Their names are Katherine Purkis and Joshua Bickley."

I raised my brows and shot a look at Mr. Bickley. He nodded, morose.

"My son."

"Ah." I cleared my throat. "Could it not be, sir, madam, that this young gentleman and lady left ... together? To marry, perhaps?"

Or to simply be together away from the watchful eye of the pious Quakers. I decided not to say this out loud.

Miss Farrow surprised me by laughing. "Indeed no, Gabriel. Katherine is over sixty, Joshua twenty. They *might* have eloped, but I rather doubt it. And they did not disappear at the same time." She regarded me with mirth, finding my conclusion hilarious. "Katherine has been gone for a week, Joshua only since Sunday after meeting. He might simply be visiting friends, as his father suspects, but we would rest easier knowing."

"I see." I bowed. "My apologies. I did not mean to make light of your concern."

"An excellent question and a natural assumption." Matilda lost her smile and folded her hands. "Wilt thou help us, Gabriel?"

They were kind, and they were worried. I could only agree.

BREWSTER WAS NOT AS SANGUINE AS WE LEFT THE MEETING House and continued our journey to the Pavilion.

"Unnatural," he muttered as he walked beside me. "All *thees* and *thous*. What a daft way to talk."

"They call it Plain Speech." I ducked around a low awning of a butcher's shop, the stench of raw meat and blood strong.

"Nothing plain about it. Sounds like one of them plays by Mr. Shakespeare you like."

"Or the Bible." I moved down a lane, a narrow artery that contained a bookseller, a wagon office, and a coffee house. The coffee house was lively at this hour, with gentlemen conversing loudly over what Orator Hunt was going on about these days. On any other evening I'd have been tempted to join them.

"Did ye truly speak to the Quakers last night?" Brewster asked as we made our way past holiday-makers, along with pickpockets and ladies who hung on the fringes, waiting for opportunities. "Or did they say such to coax you to help them today? They knew all about *you*."

"I must have done. It is Quaker teaching never to lie." I squeezed around a cluster of rather rotund gentlemen in frock coats who were pontificating with wild gestures.

One of the men, slimmer than the others, wore a cavalry uniform. Preston Barracks, housing light cavalry regiments, lay only a few miles from the center of town, and officers often ventured into Brighton, some residing there.

This officer threw me a sharp look was we passed. I thought he would speak to me, but at the last minute, he turned his head and resumed his part in the discussion.

"How do ye know Quakers don't lie?" Brewster growled as he pressed through the crowd. "A man can say he tells only the truth, but how can ye know he ain't lying when he says it? A man who claims he never lies can't be trusted, guv."

He had a point, but I hadn't read duplicity in Mr. Bickley or Miss Farrow. Chagrin and distress, but no slyness or cunning. They truly had been worried about the two Quakers who'd gone missing.

We emerged into Great East Street, which held more coaching offices, a bank, and several boarding houses. A passageway meandered past a tavern to the Steine, which was a wide green space in the middle of the bustle. The road skirting the Steine led to the Pavilion, its domed rotundas an incongruity with the straight brick exteriors around it.

Plenty of people strolled through the Steine gardens, as it was a fine evening, a breeze from the sea sweeping away both mist and heat. The long twilight let the sunshine linger well into the late hours, which meant more time for walks under an azure sky.

I'd hoped my memories of the previous night would leak through as I approached the Pavilion, but nothing came to me. The blankness was unnerving.

"How far did you follow me?" I asked Brewster. "Before losing sight of me?"

Brewster pointed. "Ye went up to the north side of the Pavilion, around the stables, then snaked back down through the town. That's when I couldn't find ye. I passed the Quaker house but I didn't notice you chatting in the garden with no Dissenters. Couldn't see you at all. You must have been inside the house with them, but how was I to know? I cursed you something fierce."

"I imagine you did. You didn't happen to note what sort of spirits I imbibed to erase all knowledge of my actions, did you?"

"Chance would be a fine thing. You and Mr. Grenville strolled out from the Pavilion once your ladies were off, and you weren't drinking anything then. Mr. Grenville could have given you a nip from his flask, but in that case, he'd be laid as low as you today. It must have been whatever you swallowed at supper or right after, unless you dropped into a tavern and drank bad gin."

I slowed my steps, the beauty of the park doing nothing to soothe my senses. "I never drink gin—I don't like the stuff. I've been hungover from port and brandy before, but never like this. Nor have I walked in my sleep, as far as I know. But perhaps a person can take it up."

Brewster looked aggrieved. "If so, I'll tell His Nibs I can't be your nanny anymore. It's enough to keep up with you when you're awake."

I'd spoken lightly but felt a chill. If I *had* walked in my sleep last night, I might have killed Isherwood—done any number of things—and have no memory of it at all.

Something stirred in the back of my mind, however, something I did not like. I stared at the lavish Pavilion, the whimsical home of a spoiled prince, and knew the answer lay within its walls.

I COULD NOT SIMPLY RUSH TO THE DOOR OF THE ROYAL PAVILION and demand entrance. For that, I'd need an appointment, and for that, I'd need Grenville.

Bartholomew had told me Grenville had gone home to sleep after looking in on me, and I did not want to disturb him. But if a murder had occurred at the Regent's summer house, I would expect a flurry of activity, with journalists vying to get in, as well as the curious residents peering into the windows. Sensations always drew a crowd.

But the Pavilion looked quiet and peaceful, late evening light glittering on its windows and brushing the new, Eastern-looking domes. All was calm—I had seen far more activity when we'd arrived for supper last night, lights glowing from every room.

"Perhaps I did dream it," I murmured.

"Would be a leg-up if ye did," Brewster agreed.

"There is no sign anything occurred here at all," I said as we turned our steps from the Pavilion. "Let us continue to the colonel's abode. He told us last night that he is stationed at Preston Barracks but lives in a house in town. Which would be just like him. He never associated with those of a lesser rank. He either commanded them or ignored them."

"Knew him well, did ye?"

I glanced away, uncomfortable. "It does not take long to discover a man's character."

Brewster accepted my evasive answer at face value and asked no more.

Isherwood had proudly stated that he'd taken a house in the Royal Crescent. The curved row of houses built at the end of the last century lay east of the center of Brighton, on the Marine Parade. All the houses faced the sea, giving each a fine view out its front bow windows.

I knew about this view because my stepson, Peter, as Viscount Breckenridge, owned one of the houses. His father had purchased it twelve years ago to tuck a ladybird into—so Donata had informed me in the disgusted tones with which she always spoke of her late husband. He'd still possessed the house when he died, and Peter, his only child, had inherited it.

We were not staying in that house because Donata had decided to take the opportunity of our holiday to have it thoroughly redecorated. Peter, upon his majority, could choose whether to keep the house or sell it, but for now, he—or the Breckenridge man of business—could always let it out.

I understood Donata's reluctance to live in the house and did not argue with her reasoning. For us, she'd hired one of the newest residences in town, in what was quickly becoming a highly fashionable square. I was pleased with her choice, liking the small house with its clean lines and ivory-colored paint.

The Royal Crescent was elegant, I had to admit as we approached it, with its dark gray brick, uniform white doors, and decorative railings on the first-floor windows. The crescent was nowhere near the size and magnificence of the one in Bath where we'd stayed last year, but the smaller stature of the houses fit the more intimate nature of Brighton and the town's proximity to the sea.

Though Isherwood had been pleased with himself for residing in one of these houses, he hadn't mentioned its number. I strolled along the Marine Parade, gazing at the curved row, wondering which was his.

Number 6 had all its draperies and blinds shut tight. Either no one was in residence, or they'd had a bereavement.

After some consideration, I went to this house rapped on the door with my gloved hand—they'd removed the knocker, which could indicate they were not in town or did not wish to be disturbed.

A footman answered after some time. He wore red livery and a white wig and did not look pleased to see us.

"Colonel Isherwood?" I asked.

"I will inquire, sir." The footman closed the door, leaving us on the doorstep.

"Bloke ain't dead then." Brewster announced this in profound relief. "Be no one to inquire to if he were."

Not necessarily. Footmen were trained to not reveal the circumstances of the family within. The only thing I could be certain of was that I had found the correct house.

The footman returned after a quarter of an hour. With no apology for making us stand on the doorstep for so long, he bade me follow him inside.

Brewster turned and walked unhurriedly down the stairs from the street to the kitchen doorway as I entered the house. I knew he'd gone to pry things out of those below stairs while he waited for me.

The footman led me to a library. The room, lined with bookcases, was lit by a tall bow window that looked out over the Channel, a lovely view indeed. The sea was gray-blue under the darkening sky, scattered clouds lined with pink from the lingering sunset.

Two men straightened from bending over a desk. I recognized one as an officer called Forbes—Isherwood had been mentoring him when we'd been in Salamanca—but the other's appearance made me start. It was Isherwood, but Isherwood with twenty years removed from him.

"You're his son," I stated.

Forbes looked haughty, but young Isherwood bowed. "I am

Colonel Giles Isherwood. I know you are Captain Lacey. Forgive our rudeness, but we are much agitated today."

He spoke in quick, polite tones, very unlike his father, who had shouted his opinions to anyone near.

Forbes gazed at me with dislike. He knew my brief history with Isherwood and had always despised me.

I'd removed my hat as I entered the house, but the footman had not taken it, and I turned it around in my hands. "Your father?"

"Dead," Forbes snapped before Giles Isherwood could answer. "He's been murdered."

CHAPTER 4

I watched them as Forbes's words ended my hopes. "How?" My voice went weak.

Forbes glared in outrage at the question, but Isherwood answered with calm readiness. "He was found at the Pavilion. Stabbed through the heart, with his own cavalry sword."

I began to shake. "My condolences for your loss," I made myself say.

"What is your purpose here, Captain?" Forbes snapped. "Come to sneer at this sordid business?"

"To offer my assistance." I groped for a plausible reason. "I heard a rumor of his death, and I wanted see if it was true." Not a lie. I absurdly wondered what Mr. Bickley the Quaker would think of my evasion.

"A rumor?" Forbes remained suspicious. "From where? The Regent's majordomo promised no one would know."

Isherwood moved past him to me and extended his hand. "It is kind of you to inquire," he said. "Well met, Captain. You were at supper with my father only last night, were you not?"

Forbes' words explained why the death hadn't been in the

newspapers, but his expression stated he didn't agree the murder should have been contained. He'd blurted the news to me without worry, perhaps because he believed I'd committed it. Forbes had always thought the worst of me.

I ignored him and shook young Isherwood's hand. He had a firm grip, which went with his rather hard face, close-cropped dark hair, and gray eyes that brooked no fools. He greatly resembled the older Colonel Isherwood but had a cool evenness about him that his father had lacked.

"We did indeed request the majordomo, who sent for me this morning, not to broadcast the murder to the newspapers," Isherwood said as we withdrew. "He readily agreed, as he did not want gossip to surround the Regent and the Pavilion. I did speak to the magistrate, who promised to investigate quietly, though I do not know how long that can last. We will prepare my father for his funeral, regardless. Is there anything you can tell us about this business, Captain? I am distressed, as you can imagine."

The speech was delivered without much inflection, but I saw the pain in his eyes. A man who grieved but would never openly show it.

I forced myself to think through what I could remember. "I dined with your father last night, with my wife, my friend Mr. Grenville, and several other guests. The Prince Regent graced us with his presence for a time, but he left early. Lord Alvanley was there ..." I trailed off, trying to remember. "Mr. Grenville would know better than I who was who."

"Did he quarrel with anyone?" Isherwood's thin lips curved into a smile. "I know my father, Captain. He was apt to enjoy a good quarrel."

"With me, in fact," I said, though the memory was vague. "Old soldiers, you know, reliving battles."

Forbes scowled, no doubt guessing what the argument had been about. "The colonel was never happy with *you*, Captain Lacey. I am surprised he sat down at the same table with you. Did *you* run him through?"

I had no idea, and this made me sick inside. "Not that I recall, Captain Forbes," I managed.

"It's Major now," he snarled. So, at last he'd been promoted, no doubt with Colonel Isherwood's help.

Young Isherwood took my reply for a jest, if one in questionable taste. "My father came home after the meal, or so I assumed. I was on duty at the barracks and not here. Why he returned to the Pavilion in the middle of the night, and who he met there, I do not know."

"What does his batman say?" I asked, hiding my worry about the answer. "Did anyone observe him leaving?"

Major Forbes' face pinched. He was of an age with the deceased Colonel Isherwood, which put him about fifty. Gray streaked his dark hair but his skin was smooth, only a few lines etched into it by sun and weather.

"None did," Forbes said. "That is what the servants claim. The footman on the door should be whipped."

Young Isherwood did not look pleased with this. "My father did as he liked and none could stop him. If he slipped out, he had reason. We simply do not know what that reason is."

"If the pair of you lived at the barracks, this would never have happened," Forbes growled. "Why you need a fancy house on the edge of town ..."

Isherwood held up his hand, and to my surprise, Forbes clamped his mouth closed. The young man, a colonel like his father, outranked him, yes, but from what I remembered,

Forbes had never been the obedient sort. Young Isherwood must have commanded his respect.

"As I say, we have not—and those at the Pavilion have not—announced he was murdered," Isherwood went on. "It would cause a sensation that the Regent cannot afford, and neither would the regiment want it. Nor do I." Isherwood gave me an apologetic look. "We have put about that he felt unwell in the night and died of a sudden illness."

"Should send for the Runners," Forbes muttered. "Villain is probably far out to sea by now."

"I can only believe it was some ghastly accident," Isherwood said. "My father could be ... prickly. Perhaps he quarreled with a man, or did something as foolish as challenge him to a duel, and was run through in the heat of the moment."

"And the blackguard fled," Forbes said. "Heading for Paris or Amsterdam, never to be seen again."

"In that case, little we can do." Isherwood's voice hardened. "I will, of course, if the villain can be found, prosecute and bring him to justice. But damned if I'll let my father's death be fodder for the newspapers or the morbid masses, who enjoy flocking to scenes of murders. Not what I want marring my father's memory."

"I understand," I said. He was not wrong—when murders occurred, especially in out-of-the way places, people swarmed to the scene of the grisly crime to gape at the scene and take small things, even pebbles or nails, as souvenirs.

The Prince Regent would hardly want a mob to surround the Pavilion and worse, try to enter and take whatever they found. With the renovation going on, there would be plenty of costly building supplies lying about and not enough men to guard the doors.

I moved uneasily. The scenario young Isherwood described

—his father quarreling heatedly, the man he argued with lifting the nearest sword and impaling him in anger—I could have done exactly that. If I'd lost my temper, as I was wont, and been far gone on drink ...

And why could I remember nothing? Even the events of the supper and after were blurry. I'd always considered my father teetering on the edge of insanity—perhaps he truly had been, and now that madness had trickled to me.

"Captain Lacey, I have heard from others that you sometimes assist the Runners," Isherwood said. "Discreetly. I wonder if you can help?"

He put it as a question, but I had a feeling that this young man had made up his mind and was close to making it a command. He had a natural air of authority that not every officer achieved. I'd made my men obedient with my loud shouts and hot temper, but I imagined Giles Isherwood rarely had to raise his voice.

I could not very well refuse. What else could I tell him? That I would not help, because I had to suspect myself?

I gave him a bow. "I will be happy to assist in any small way I can."

Isherwood acknowledged this with a nod. "Thank you, Captain." He clasped my hand. "Nothing to be made public." His handshake firmed as he said the words.

"I agree," I said.

Isherwood looked into my eyes, his own so like his father's, and released me.

We said good evening—nothing more to do—and I departed. Major Forbes's only farewell was a growl.

BREWSTER LEANED AGAINST THE RAILINGS AT THE END OF THE crescent, surveying the curve of houses as he waited for me.

"Easy pickings," he remarked as I joined him.

"I beg your pardon?" I paused to catch my breath, still nonplussed by the interview.

Brewster waved at the houses. "Windows close to the ground, none but seagulls to see a thief from the other side of the road. Residents probably don't even lock up their valuables, thinking all is safe because they're on holiday." He sounded disapproving.

"Please curb your tendencies," I said. "I have enough troubles without having to save you from arrest."

Brewster blinked at me in surprise. "I don't need to do them over. Just observing. Professional like. His Nibs would have me balls if I did some thieving on me own."

"What about the Pavilion?" I began walking along the seafront in the direction of our lodgings. "What is your professional opinion about *it*?"

"As it's covered in scaffolding inside and out? Easy pickings again, guv. Valuables would be locked away, but I'd wager they're in boxes, what are convenient for carrying."

"So a man could get into and out of the Pavilion unseen? Including Colonel Isherwood and myself, it seems. A man could meet him, stab him to death, and be gone again, with no one the wiser."

"That's what happened, most like," Brewster said. "Lots of holes where doors and windows should be. Bloke could slip in with the workmen. Hide. Wait. Stab, and be out." He glanced up the road that led to the Pavilion as we passed it. "Shame. All those costly trinkets just sitting there. A man could have enough to make a killing at the next Nazareth, without having to kill in truth."

"I doubt a robber murdered Isherwood. An interrupted thief would have dropped his loot and run, I'd think. Too risky to tussle with Isherwood, a trained and experienced soldier. Also, I believe the Regent would kick up a fuss if any of his things went missing."

"You may be right," Brewster conceded. "The downstairs at Isherwood's don't know much. Young colonel lived in the house with his father, but sometimes they spent nights at the barracks. Kitchen couldn't praise the son enough. A true gentleman, they say. Won't miss the father much, I'm thinking."

"Did any of them see him leave last night?" I asked.

"No, more's the pity. Master came home after his night with the Regent and went up to bed. So all the staff toddles to bed after. Scullery maid swears she heard a door open around three in the morning, but she's not a reliable sort. Soon as cook told her she couldn't have heard nothing of the kind, and then the maid says, no, she didn't."

Which meant she might have heard the door but hadn't been instructed in time to keep quiet about it. Or she hadn't heard at all and the cook was correct that the scullery maid liked to invent things.

"My wife's servants are utterly loyal to her," I mused. "Would lie themselves blue to help her."

"They would," Brewster agreed. "Right pompous about it, are her ladyship's slaveys. Not sure the colonel's would, but they're loyal to the son, I can see. Raised him, some of them did. His mum died when he was a wee tyke."

I'd known that. The wife who'd accompanied Isherwood on the Peninsula had been his second, and his son hadn't been there or even mentioned. Giles might have been at university or working on his own army career elsewhere at the time.

"If they thought they needed to protect the son, they'd lie, do you think?" I asked Brewster.

"That they would, guv. 'Tis my humble opinion."

Were the servants, in fact, protecting young Isherwood? If Giles had followed his father and killed him, for whatever reason, he would have strong incentive to keep the murder from being generally known. But if true, why ask me to help?

"What did you learn from the upstairs?" Brewster asked as we passed the fish market. It was shut for the day, as most of its business happened in the morning, but strong odors lingered in its shadows.

"That Captain—no, Major—Forbes remembers me from Salamanca and was not pleased to see me."

"Mmm. Not good news, I'm thinking."

"Not really, no. I also learned that young Isherwood is indeed a gentleman and can cow Forbes easily."

Brewster's brows twitched. "What terrible things did you do to the major at this salamander place?"

"Salamanca," I said. "In Spain, near the border of Portugal. We chased a French regiment about the hills there. Wellington was ready to turn for Portugal when he saw that the French lines had become scattered, and he turned and struck. Quick battle, definite victory, quite the coup for Wellington. Isherwood and Forbes were in another cavalry regiment, but we'd camped together and then stayed in Salamanca once we kicked the French out of their strongholds."

Brewster listened in skepticism. "Did you embarrass this Forbes or Colonel Isherwood in battle or some such? Fought better than they did? No idea what goes on in the army, guv."

He finished without apology. Brewster thought soldiering a mad game and had told me so on many occasions.

"I never saw them during the actual battle. Had my own

men to look after." What I mostly remembered was July heat, dust, noise, screaming, shouting, strength surging as I cut with my saber. I'd been a whole man then, not supporting my shattered knee with a walking stick.

"Well then?" Brewster was not going to let go of it.

"My quarrel with Isherwood was after the battle," I said carefully. "It was a drama of army life and finished long ago."

Brewster waited, but when I was no more forthcoming, he gave me a narrow look. "You mean both Isherwood and Forbes would cheerfully have killed *you*. Can't say I blame them. I'm sure you did *something* to get right up their backs, and knowing you, it were something bad." He shook his head and gazed out to the gray sea. "I truly don't know how you've lived this long on your own."

"Neither do I." I studied the sea with him, wishing I were on it, heading back to Egypt or another exotic and warm place. "Nothing for it, Brewster. I will have to prove that I did not— or perhaps did—run Isherwood through. If I did ..."

Brewster pulled me to a halt, his grip hard, and spoke in a quiet but fierce voice. "If ye did kill the man, you'll *not* be throwing yourself at the magistrate, confessing such and getting yourself strung up to dance on the wind. You'll let His Nibs sort it out and take you off somewhere safe. Won't do your wife and kiddies no good if you kiss the hangman."

He was right. Donata could be ruined if it turned out she'd married a murderer, and neither would my daughters live it down. In our world, scandal stuck and could destroy entire families. Peter might survive it—he was not my true son, and he was a peer, if in his minority at the moment. Peers weathered their unfortunate relations better than the rest of us. Donata would find protection at her father's house, and Gabriella could return to France to her mother and stepfather, but Anne would always be tainted by my misdeeds.

I sighed and resumed the walk. "If it turns out I am guilty of this crime, I will have to swallow my pride and everything I believe right, and throw myself on the mercy of His Nibs."

Brewster gave me a dumbfounded look. "Fatherhood has changed you, guv."

"It has. It did both times." I thought of Anne and how she'd given me her baby smile when I'd looked in on her before I'd left this afternoon. "I wouldn't trade that for the world."

WHEN WE REACHED HOME, DONATA APPEARED ON THE UPPER landing of the staircase of our rather dainty house. She wore a loose gown with her hair caught in a simple knot—I knew from experience she'd been at her evening toilette and must have exited her chamber when she'd heard me come in.

"There you are," she said with obvious relief. "I thought perhaps you'd disappeared again."

"Not with Brewster to look after me." I tried to sound unworried, but she was not reassured.

Brewster had already ducked down the back stairs for a cup of something, leaving me to Bartholomew, who busied himself putting away my coat and hat.

"Mr. Brewster didn't look after you last night," Donata said as I climbed to her.

"Not his fault. If I remain stolidly at home tonight, I will give him the evening off. He deserves the rest."

My wife sent me an impatient look. "You cannot remain stolidly at home—we have already planned to attend the lecture. Grenville and Marianne are meeting us, as are several of my acquaintances. The entertainment is a bit provincial, I know, but I did promise." She babbled a bit, her nervousness apparent.

I reached her, took her firmly by the shoulders, and stopped her words by firmly kissing her mouth. Donata gave me a startled look as I pulled away, and I continued past her up the stairs.

"Gabriel ..." Her voice was faint behind me.

"I will prepare to go out, have no fear." I reached my chamber, the first room at the top of the stairs. "But I want you with me all night. No going off on your own."

Without further word, I entered my chamber and closed the door. I wondered, as I pulled off my cravat, if I meant she should stay near me for her protection or for mine.

I HAD BARTHOLOMEW TURN ME OUT IN MY REGIMENTALS. Tonight, for some reason, I wanted to appear as myself, not in the highly fashionable suits Grenville's tailor made for me and Donata paid for. I usually allowed them to dress me as they saw fit, having no wish to embarrass my friends, but some days I wanted to put off the costume and resume my own skin.

Donata gave me a sharp look as I appeared in my cavalry blues, with its white facings and silver braid, my boots—the only concession I made to a new item—gleaming with polish.

She said nothing, however, only took my arm so I could lead her downstairs. She was in a light gown for summer, a gauzy affair of green and blue. A single feather stuck straight up from the small turban she wore over her midnight hair.

The carriage awaited. Brighton was a small enough city that even I could walk across it in little time, but we needed to arrive in style. Jacinthe, Donata's lady's maid, rode stiffly upright on the top of the carriage, carrying Donata's slipper box and a bag with anything she might wish while she was out of the house.

We traveled northward to Church Street and then east to Marlborough Place, which lay north of the Pavilion. I glanced at the building whose scaffolding was now vanishing into the late twilight, expecting a shiver of horror or perhaps a slap of memory, but nothing came to me. The Pavilion was simply a great house with odd domes shimmering in the rising moonlight.

The coachman let us out in front of a private home, where we would listen to a lecture. Gabriella would meet us here, under the chaperonage of Lady Aline Carrington. Anticipating my daughter's presence was the one reason I had not argued with Donata about going out tonight.

Our hostess was an old friend of Donata's. She had married an army officer who'd been a commanding general on the Peninsula. He hadn't been in charge of my regiment, but I remembered the general as a man with a sensible head on his shoulders.

I greeted him and his wife, the four of us mouthing politenesses. I would have enjoyed a good long talk with the general, but for now, we could only give each other a "Good Evening," mention the weather, and move into the drawing room.

"Father." My daughter hurried to me eagerly, never shy, and kissed my cheek. "Are you well?"

She peered at me anxiously. She'd spent the day with Lady Aline, who now followed her slowly. The two ladies must have speculated about my strange affliction and disappearance in the night.

"I appear to be," I said. "A commotion over nothing. It seems I imbibed a bit too much at supper."

"Not like you," Gabriella said in concern.

She was kind. I tended to moderate myself while my children were in the house, but there had been times in my life when I'd been roaring and most obnoxiously drunk. I was a merry fellow when heavily in my cups, but still nothing I wanted my daughter to see.

"A man can grow immoderate when he is enjoying himself," I said. "But I will take care not to let it happen again."

Gabriella nodded, but continued to regard me in worry.

I bowed to Lady Aline and remarked upon how fortunate I was to lead two such lovely ladies to their seats.

"You're a liar, but a charming one," Lady Aline said, giving me a smile. "So pleasant to see you, dear boy."

Grenville arrived while we exchanged compliments, Marianne on his arm. All eyes turned to them, the sensation of Grenville having actually married his actress mistress removing any attention from me.

Newspapers and magazines had already thoroughly lambasted Grenville for his misalliance, which he'd taken with aplomb. His true friends, however, had been far more forgiving. Those who'd decided to shun him had lost popularity and so were beginning to toady up again.

Marianne, for her part, had taken on her role as Mrs. Grenville with enjoyment, acting the benevolent matron with thorough enthusiasm. Her new demeanor unnerved me, but I knew that beneath it lay fear she'd embarrass Grenville. She cared about him enough, I could see, to try to charm all in his circle.

Grenville and Marianne moved among the guests with great dignity, as though they were royalty greeting the masses.

Marianne had dressed in an elegant silver and blue gown, but the décolletage was modest, as was the skirt. Her days of wearing the thinnest muslin clinging to her every curve were at an end.

Behind Grenville came a bishop I recognized from the supper last night—Craddock, I believed was his name—a surly but robust man who'd expressed displeasure at the many Dissenters Brighton attracted. A man who would have been happier at a large church in the middle of London.

After him, unnoticed by all but the host and hostess, were a couple who had also been at supper.

Viscount … Armitage … the name came to me. And his lady wife. When I gazed at them, something tickled the back of my mind, a tickle that grew to thunder and began to bang hard inside my head.

CHAPTER 5

*M*y weak knee suddenly faltered. I barely caught myself on my walking stick, my leg twisting and sending fire up my limb.

"Are you all right, my boy?" Lady Aline asked in concern.

I scarcely heard her through the buzz in my ears. My daughter's eyes, a brilliant blue, came through the fog, and I anchored myself with the sight of them.

"My slippers pinch so," Gabriella said, hand on my arm. "Will you sit with me until the lecture begins?"

Bless her. She knew I was infirm but couched her words to imply I'd do her a favor if I got off my feet. I acquiesced and allowed her to tow me to a line of gilded blue damask chairs that had been placed against the wall.

As soon as I sat down and drew a breath, my dizziness passed. Unfortunately, so did the tantalizing hint of memory.

"What can you tell me about Lord Armitage?" I asked Lady Aline, nodding at the man and his wife. "I met them last night at the Pavilion but know little about them."

Armitage was not very tall, but he had a commanding presence, his hair crisp black, his face square and sharp, glittering eyes taking in the room. His wife was a beauty, though not a conventional one. Nothing fair and frail about her. She was the same height as her husband, with dark hair that gleamed in the lamplight. The gold net of her gown caught the same light, as did the diamonds in her hair. They made a striking pair.

Lady Aline Carrington, daughter of an earl and proud to be a spinster, knew everything about everyone in Britain. Gossip she did not know was not worth learning.

"I forgive your ignorance because you lived so long away from home," Lady Aline said. "It was quite a scandal in its day, but people have forgotten, as you can see."

She gestured with her lorgnette at the throng around Grenville and Marianne, everyone exquisitely polite, of course, but avidly curious about her. Lord and Lady Armitage were greeted courteously but all attention tonight was on Grenville and his new wife.

"Lady Armitage was Miss Elizabeth Randolph, niece of an ambassador from the American states to Austria fifteen years ago," Lady Aline began. "Quite stunning she was, and she is still very comely. Lord Armitage was in Vienna, also an ambassador, during the wars with Bonaparte, and there he met Miss Randolph. So did a number of gentlemen, including Armitage's brother, who lived with him there. The Austrian Emperor's nephew was also much interested in Miss Randolph. There were duels and so forth. She flitted through it all quite happily, enjoying the attention."

My daughter listened with interest, but I did not send her away or tell Lady Aline to eliminate the sordid details. I preferred Gabriella to hear the truth about people instead of remaining in ignorance.

"But Miss Randolph married Lord Armitage," I observed as

Armitage and his lady drifted arm-in-arm through the crowd. "They seem to get on well. I assume she fell in love with him and forsook all others?"

"She fell in love with his *brother*," Lady Aline said with enjoyment. "*He* was good for nothing. A decent soldier, I hear, but a roué of the worst sort. Had half a dozen ladies on his string, both respectable women and those of the demimonde. He seduced Miss Randolph, it was rumored, and ruined her utterly. Her uncle tried to hush it up, of course, but everyone *knew*, and no announcement of an engagement was forthcoming. Lord Armitage, mortified, and possessing a few more morals than his brother, tried to insist the brother marry her. They came to blows over it." Lady Aline flapped her peacock-feather fan as though warm from the exciting tale.

"Good heavens," Gabriella said. "Did Lord Armitage marry Miss Randolph to save her reputation? That was noble of him."

"If he had done, it would have been a satisfying end to the tale," Lady Aline continued. "But life is not so tidy, Gabriella, dear. Miss Randolph decided that being ruined was a fine thing, as she no longer had to play the insipid miss—or so she said. She began a grand flirtation with the Austrian Emperor's nephew. He had no intention of marrying her, of course, and she was well on the way to becoming a courtesan."

"Then how did she come to marry Lord Armitage?" Gabriella asked.

Lady Aline leaned closer. "I am sad to relate that Miss Randolph discovered she was increasing. Disaster. Lord Armitage pressed harder on his brother to do the honorable thing, and his brother actually wavered, declaring he really did love the lady. He might have proposed, but then both men joined the Austrians at Austerlitz, to observe that battle. Unfortunately, the French bullets did not care that the two men had only come to watch, and Lord Armitage's brother was killed." Lady Aline lifted her fan to shield her face as she spoke the next words. "Some are uncharitable enough to say that Armitage himself killed his brother, to leave the way free to Miss Randolph. I don't *quite* believe that—he could have simply married her while his brother played the rogue. But apparently, Miss Randolph and Armitage's brother had been very much in love. They'd patched things up between themselves before he went to Austerlitz, and he looked forward to becoming a father."

"Poor Lady Armitage," Gabriella said softly.

Lady Aline gave her a fond look. "You are a kindhearted gel, my dear. Yes, Miss Randolph was quite grieved at his death. When Lord Armitage insisted Miss Randolph marry him to save her from utter ruin, she had little choice but to accept. She'd never been officially engaged to his brother, no settlements, so there was no impediment to her marrying Armitage. When her child was born—a girl, thank heavens—Armitage declared the child his. We all know better, of course, but no one challenges the statement. All was well, it turned out—Lord and Lady Armitage discovered after this hasty marriage that they rather liked each other. Armitage is wealthy and powerful in his circle, able to give Lady Armitage a luxurious life. He went to the Peninsula for a time, but since he's been home, the two have been inseparable."

"So it was a happy ending," Gabriella said, eyes shining.

"Eventually," Lady Aline conceded.

Our gazes went to the couple across the room, Lady Armitage in the act of disengaging from her husband to speak to several ladies. She had no stiffness in her, and the other women responded to her with ease—they clearly did not shun her. I wondered whether she'd had difficulty at first, an outsider with a scandalous history, being accepted into her husband's circle.

But then, she was an ambassador's niece, possibly connected to a highborn family—many in the American government could trace their lineage to British patriarchs— and she was charming. The Regent had invited her and her husband to the Pavilion last night, so Armitage at least must be one of the Regent's cronies. The Regent's friends tended to be a bit dissipated, but Armitage had seemed steady and forthright, if too blustering for my taste.

Had he been the upright diplomat in his youth, indignantly demanding his reprobate brother marry Miss Randolph? Or had Armitage been a reprobate himself but had simply hidden it well? After all, Armitage had ended up with the beautiful lady, and there were those who said he'd leveled the field for her.

And what had Lord Armitage's appearance made me begin to remember about the events of the previous night?

That, I would have to discover.

THE LECTURE TONIGHT WAS ABOUT THE ANCIENT ROMAN RUINS at Herculaneum, an interest of mine. The man who spoke had an excellent style of oration, and even those who might have nodded off at the subject remained bright-eyed and applauded loudly at the end.

We broke for refreshments. I greeted the lecturer and praised his knowledge, asking questions about the discoveries around the Bay of Naples. The discussion took my mind off my troubles for the moment, but when the host led the lecturer away to speak to others, I retreated to a smaller room where

I'd been told brandy was plentiful. A card room was also available, but I did not have the head for cards tonight.

I found Grenville already ensconced in the small chamber. He was pouring himself a brandy as I entered, and he held up the decanter in invitation. As I closed the door, he trickled a large measure into a goblet and handed it to me.

"To our wives," he said, raising his glass. "May they chatter to their heart's content."

I toasted the ladies and drank deeply.

"I hate to ask it," Grenville said after we'd settled into the quiet. "But are you quite well this evening? Bartholomew passed word to Matthias that you were up and walking about as usual but still looked peaky. Not to embarrass you, my friend," he added quickly. "We are concerned, is all."

I lounged into my chair and took a sip of the excellent brandy. I appreciated Grenville not hovering over me, too solicitous. A gentleman did not imply another was weak, even when that other could barely stand.

"I appear not to have had any terrible lapses in memory today, nor found anyone dead at my feet." I tried to keep my voice light, but the ordeal had been damned unsettling. Still was.

"You raved a bit in your sleep," Grenville said. "To be honest, we were worried you'd not recover."

I recalled my dreams of faces swooping over me, Grenville's included. Unnerving to think they'd seen me half insensible and looking like death.

"I have recovered, it seems," I said. "I feel perfectly as usual at the moment."

Grenville gave me an admiring look. "I envy you your constitution, Lacey. A lesser man might have had solicitors reviewing his will or deciding he was headed for madness."

"I do hope it is not madness. My father was certainly unstable, though I'd always attributed it to drink. But then—he possibly did kill Marcus's father."

"If your dear cousin is telling the truth," Grenville pointed out. "But I am working in the dark, my dear fellow. Donata, Bartholomew, and—reluctantly—Brewster told me the gist of things, but I have not heard the story from your lips."

I took the precaution of rising and confirming no one else was in the room with us or listening at convenient keyholes, then I resumed my seat and told him, in a low voice, everything I remembered. I included retracing my steps with Brewster today, meeting the Friends and Isherwood's son.

When I'd finished, Grenville sat limply. "Good Lord."

I wet my dry mouth with the brandy. "What I must discover now is whether I actually killed Isherwood."

"There is no certainty that you did," Grenville said with an assuredness I did not share. "The sword was not yours, but Isherwood's, his son told you. Isherwood was not a feeble man, and you would have had to fight him to wrest the weapon from him. He proved himself quite strong at supper, when he nearly strangled that footman."

I thought back but could not recall the incident. "Another memory denied me."

"I beg your pardon—I am not certain you had arrived yet. A footman of the Regent's was slow, in Isherwood's opinion, to fetch him a glass of hock. Isherwood took the young man by the lapels and shook him hard, poor lad. The boy's turban fell to the floor, which Isherwood thought hilarious. I was a bit terse with Isherwood after that."

"Turban." Another memory knocked at me.

"Yes. Tall young footman, too old to be playing a Moorish boy, but the Regent likes his costumes."

It came to me then, clear as a summer morning, the footman in his dressing gown, staring at me as I stood over Isherwood's body, the cavalry sword in my hand.

"Clement," I said.

Grenville blinked. "Pardon?"

"The lad's name. Clement. He told me."

"Oh? When was this?"

"When I found Isherwood. I remember now." I closed my eyes, hoping the rest of the night would come flooding back, but it did not. I recalled Clement helping me find my way out of the Pavilion, and my cold and stumbling walk back home, but nothing between being with Grenville in the Steine and finding Isherwood's dead body.

I told Grenville about Clement then studied my empty goblet. "I do not recall imbibing enough strong drink to take away my memory. I suppose I must have done, but usually when I overindulge, I simply fall asleep and wake feeling miserable. I have never wandered about town, had conversations with Quakers, and then dueled with a man, killing him with his own sword."

"It might not have been drink," Grenville suggested. "Another substance, perhaps."

"I had nothing but wine at supper and port afterward, all of which were excellent, and I was not the only one who drank them. I remember *you* enjoying them quite soundly."

"I did. Perhaps you took something else and you simply cannot recall it."

"Possibly," I conceded. "But what substance would affect me so? I use laudanum to combat the pain in my knee when it becomes too great, but again, if I take too much, I merely sleep."

"As to that." Grenville rose. "If you will sit here a moment, I will return in no time."

I helped myself to another brandy as Grenville slipped out, and was halfway through it when he returned.

He brought Marianne with him. I stood up politely as Grenville ushered her in and closed the door, but Marianne waved me back down. She drew a straight-backed chair next to my softer seat, sat down, and leaned to peer hard at me.

"What are you doing?" I asked her nervously.

"Studying your eyes." Marianne's were marvelously blue. She wore her hair in a matronly knot tonight, revealing the strong bones of her face.

"What is the matter with them?"

"Nothing." Marianne continued to stare at me. "A bit blood-shot. Your pupils look normal, but ..." She suddenly pushed her hand at my face.

Soldier's instinct made me grab her wrist, but I instantly gentled my touch and released her. Grenville had started for me when I'd latched my fingers around her arm, but he subsided, looking a bit abashed at his reaction.

Marianne resumed her scrutiny of my eyes. "You were slow to focus. Whatever substance you took is lingering, though mostly gone, I think. The wine and brandy you have drunk today will slow its dispersion, but I believe you will be well by morning. Have a good sleep tonight."

I was torn between amusement and alarm. "Are you now a physician?"

"My dear Lacey, in a theatre company, one learns all sorts of tricks—for keeping oneself awake, for example, or ensuring a sound sleep amidst noise and chaos. Laudanum or opium for relaxation. Belladonna to brighten the eyes. The magical gas that takes away pain and makes you silly. And of course, gin, when one wants to forget one's troubles."

"Could the gas have done this to me?" I remembered inhaling an odorless concoction at a gathering a few years ago, and the sudden and surprising absence of pain. But I recalled every moment of that day, no blurring of memory.

"Possibly. Possibly not. On the other hand, the opium eater sometimes forgets hours, or entire days, even the act of taking the opium itself."

"Does it cause bad dreams?" I asked.

"Yes, the dreams when one comes down can be awful." Marianne cast a quick glance at Grenville, who was listening intently. "Do not worry—I am not an opium eater myself. I've watched too many become a slave to it to wish to inflict that upon myself."

An opium delirium would explain both the memory lapse and the dreams last night, I decided. Also my fear that I was going mad.

"But look here," Grenville broke in. "Opium *might* be the solution, but how would an enemy get it into you, Lacey? I cannot imagine you tamely swallowing a bottle or smoking a pipe of the stuff at another's suggestion."

"Neither can I," I agreed. "But what if I thought the opium was something else?"

"The smell and taste are distinct and unpleasant," Marianne said. "You could not have mistaken it. I suppose someone *could* have dosed a strong enough tea or coffee and you might not notice it."

"It was late when we left the Pavilion. I rarely have coffee after midnight."

"You might have drunk it, nonetheless, and simply do not remember," Marianne said. "I have known actors who have lost entire weeks of their lives while they ate opium. They'd take the stuff even before a performance and muff their lines, which was most annoying for the rest of us."

"You met the Quaker fellow," Grenville reminded me.

"A man who takes no strong drink, not even coffee?" I shook my head.

"It might not have been opium at all," Marianne said. "There are other substances, not as well known, that have similar effects. Plants and medicines from China and India, for example. Sailors bring them back, as do soldiers."

"And there are plenty of soldiers in Brighton," Grenville put in. "And sailors. Large merchantmen unload at Portsmouth, not many miles down the coast. Smugglers land anywhere they can find a cove."

I sat back, more frustrated than ever. "Excellent. We are looking for smugglers who might have sailed here from anywhere in the world, with any exotic substance, who sought a former cavalry officer, dosed him, and set him off to either kill another officer or at least make him believe he did."

My friends exchanged a glance. "I do see the difficulties," Grenville said.

"Brewster advises me to leave it alone," I replied sourly.

Grenville gestured with his brandy glass. "I see his point as well. Why should you have anything to do with it? Let Isherwood's son try to find out what he can. You return to London and stay well out of it."

"I have a witness," I reminded him. "Clement. And you know I cannot go through my life wondering whether I've killed a man. A certain Bow Street Runner would joyfully arrest me on the speculation alone." I spoke of Timothy Spendlove, who waited for any excuse to put me in the dock.

"I know," Grenville said. "I did not believe you would leave it, and my suggestion was not wholehearted."

I glanced at Marianne. "What do you think, Mrs. Grenville?"

Pink stole over her cheeks—this was the first time I'd addressed her thus. "I agree with Mr. Grenville," she said. "You will investigate whether we believe it prudent or not."

She'd ceased referring to Grenville as *him*, I noted. I wondered if she called him *Lucius* in private.

"Exactly, my dear fellow," Grenville said warmly. "What do you propose we do to help?"

I let out a breath. "We must find out everything we can about Isherwood's enemies. You know the Regent, Grenville— why did he invite Isherwood at all? What about Lord and Lady Armitage? Lady Aline told me their history—what is it about them I need to remember?" I pressed my hands together. "In other words, please, my friends, use your connections and your penchant for persuading people to talk to you, and discover whether another did this deed or ..." I swallowed. "Or whether I truly am responsible and need to make amends."

***

WE LEFT THE GATHERING AT TWO IN THE MORNING, WHICH WAS early for my wife, but she did not want to fatigue Gabriella.

When we reached home, Gabriella went to bed, kissing me good-night and thanking us for a fine evening. Once she was in her chamber, Donata beckoned me to her boudoir.

Donata's maid Jacinthe unlaced and undressed her while I lounged in a chair with brandy Jacinthe had served me. I did not drink much of it, having no intention of rendering myself insensible again.

Once Jacinthe departed, taking Donata's evening dress away to be cleaned, Donata, clad in a peignoir, seated herself at her dressing table and spoke to me through the mirror.

"I heard delicious gossip about Colonel Isherwood tonight." She smoothed a concoction that was mostly lemon juice and milk on her cheeks then delicately wiped her face clean. "About him and his second wife, on the Peninsula. You must have met her there."

I knew full well what the delicious gossip about Isherwood during the Peninsular conflict was, and what had happened between himself and his wife at Salamanca.

I set aside the brandy and went to Donata. She gave me a startled look as I gently grasped her elbows and eased her from her chair.

"Gabriel, what …?"

I silenced her words by kissing her. She ceased speaking, her eyes holding welcome, her arms coming around me.

I took her to bed, my beautiful wife, and lay there with her all night. I could not say we were entirely silent, but my somewhat grueling day ended with satisfaction.

In the morning, I rose and stepped through the dressing room that connected Donata's chamber and mine to bathe and dress and have Bartholomew shave me. I'd lain in bed quite late, still exhausted, and Donata was again at her dressing table when I returned to her chamber, Jacinthe brushing out her hair.

"You did not let me tell you what I heard last night," Donata reminded me.

I hadn't. I did not want her to relate it now, but I knew I

would have to face it sooner or later. I sipped coffee Bartholomew had brought me, girding my loins for what was to come.

"Isherwood abandoned his wife," Donata said. "Left her high and dry while they were still on campaign and sent letters to London to begin the proceedings to divorce her."

"I know," I said. "Isherwood's commanders were not happy with him for his actions. But they'd never liked his wife and were relieved when she returned to England."

Donata gazed at me through the mirror as Jacinthe looped her hair into a knot. "The story related to *me* last night was that she ran off with a blackguard who used her shamelessly, before she fled to England in disgrace."

I fixed my eyes on my coffee and answered quietly. "I wouldn't say he was a blackguard."

CHAPTER 6

The room went very silent. When I at last looked up, Jacinthe was departing discreetly out the door.

Donata turned to me, regarding me with eyes so sharp they cut.

"Perhaps you should tell me the tale, Gabriel," she said, her voice too calm. "Before someone else gleefully informs me that you were Mrs. Isherwood's lover."

I rose and went to the door through which Jacinthe had departed, turning the key in the lock.

"I agree," I said. "I would prefer you hear my version of events first."

I did not resume my seat but remained standing, hand on my walking stick. Donata crossed her legs and rested her arm on the back of her chair, a nonchalant pose, but every line of her bore tension.

"If anyone used Marguerite Isherwood shamelessly, it was Isherwood himself," I began. "He was a brute of a man. Though Marguerite was no tame flower—she fought back and denounced him. In the end he wanted no more of her, but she was hardly heartbroken. He sent word to his solicitors in London and began the petitions in Doctor's Commons. I did not meet the Isherwoods until Salamanca, which is where he threw her out of his lodgings and told her to find her own way home."

Donata regarded me steadily. "And you, being gallant …"

"Isherwood had already annoyed me with his tactics, and his cruelty." I moved slowly back to my chair and sat. "He led a charge that did nothing but waste men, and he barely made it out alive himself. Sergeant Pomeroy saved his life, and Isherwood only shouted abuse at him, the ungrateful bastard."

A small gleam of interest entered Donata's eyes—very small. "I imagine Mr. Pomeroy was not cowed."

"I then had to save Pomeroy from arrest for striking an officer. I made out that it was an accident."

"Clever of you." Her words were cool.

"Not really, but it turned Isherwood against me, not that I'd hoped to make a friend of him. When I heard he'd stranded his wife, and had advised her to whore herself out—his very words—I stepped up to offer her a place to stay. I'd taken rooms in Salamanca itself, nothing luxurious, but dry and comfortable."

"Mm. I take it that you did not, like a gentleman, sleep all night in a hard chair."

I had to shake my head. "Mrs. Isherwood was in a towering fury at her husband, bent on making him pay. I did not try very hard to stop her."

"I see."

I knew she did see, exactly, and was trying to stop herself thinking of it.

"I have never been pillar of virtue," I said tightly. "My wife had run off with Major Auberge long before that, taking Gabriella with her. I was young and angry. Also lonely."

"It was seven years ago," Donata said. "You were not much younger than you are now."

"I feel so." I tapped my left knee. "*This* has made me an old man before my time."

"Hardly." The word was crisp. "I grant that you had no lady of your own, you were full of pride, and you wanted to rub Colonel Isherwood's nose in it."

"You are correct," I said. "It made us laugh that he was a cuckold."

Donata dropped her gaze at the word but only briefly. "Then it is no wonder he turned an interesting shade of red when he saw you at the Regent's dining table. And you a trusted friend of Mr. Grenville, no less."

Donata was no stranger to vengeance against a callous husband, but her face might have been carved of marble. I suspected she fought with herself—my affair with Mrs. Isherwood was long ago, but her first husband had paraded mistresses before her, which had hurt her deeply. She was not in a hurry for that sort of thing to happen again.

"What became of Marguerite?" she asked, her voice too casual. "Was she a permanent fixture in your rooms?"

"Indeed no. It was never a romance." Marguerite had been grateful to me, but I'd nursed no illusions she'd fallen in love. "I encouraged her to return to England. She'd had the mad idea of cuckolding her husband with as many officers as she could, but I pointed out the dangers of this step."

"Wise. The other officers might not be as kind as you."

I could not tell if her tone held irony. Donata could be cutting without the object of her wit aware of it.

"Quite," I said. "She had the chance to start a new life away from Isherwood, and I recommended she make use of it. I arranged for her journey to Lisbon and passage from there to Portsmouth."

"And that was that?" Donata unfolded herself but remained on the chair. "Or did you correspond with her?"

"Not at all. Marguerite wrote a friend, the wife of another officer, that she'd arrived safely in Portsmouth, and that she'd decided to settle near there. The officer's wife passed this information to me, but I have not heard of Marguerite since. My regiment moved on to Madrid; Isherwood's went elsewhere."

"Did the divorce go through? As you know, such a thing is no easy feat."

"I have no idea—I would assume so. With all the things that happened after Salamanca, I must say I forgot about the Isherwoods."

"Yes, you had plenty to occupy your thoughts, such as warring with Colonel Brandon, not to mention fighting the French army." Again the barest hint of irony. "Well, Gabriel, you have certainly given yourself motive for a duel with Isherwood. I imagine he was incensed by your presence last night. Even if he'd thrown away his wife, and the divorce did succeed, and he never saw the blasted woman again, you were a nice splinter to remind him of his humiliation."

"Perhaps."

"No *perhaps* about it. I wondered why he was so very cold to you, more than the coolness a man of higher rank might give to a captain. I ought to have guessed the reason why."

I looked at her in surprise. "How could you have?"

"Because I know you, Gabriel. If another man in enraged at you, it is most likely because of a woman."

I was not certain whether to be amused or indignant. "There are other reasons men fall out among themselves."

"Other gentlemen, yes. *You,* on the other hand, are courteous to the point of painfulness, you pay your debts, and you try to make it up to anyone you unintentionally anger. You are even polite to Mr. Denis, a known criminal. The only thing you do that engenders rage in other gentlemen is to be more attentive to their ladies than they are. Especially when the gentleman in question is a boor."

"In which case, he deserves it," I said feelingly. "I remember happily punching *your* husband in the nose."

At last, she favored me with a smile, though it was fleeting. "Precisely what I mean. Though I recall that when I first tried to share your rooms, as it were, you wanted nothing to do with me. I must say it rankles a bit that you chose Isherwood's wife long ago when you would not choose me."

So that was how she thought of it. I'd taken readily to Marguerite, when I had been decidedly rude to Donata.

"I mistook your character," I said, as gently as I could. "As I have told you before." I remembered the day when I'd met her in a room full of sunshine, where she'd given me her cutting look and dared me to a game of billiards. "But I noticed you were quite beautiful."

Her brows came together. "You disliked me and wouldn't touch me. Hence, I had to pursue you like a silly chit."

"I am very glad you pursued me," I said. "You made *me* look the fool, have no fear of that." I rose and went to her, taking her hand. "Of this, I have no regrets."

I lifted her fingers to my lips and kissed them. Donata looked a bit less angry when I lowered her hand, though I knew she would not soften to me for a time.

I'd been Marguerite Isherwood's lover years before I'd met

Donata, but Donata felt no warmth toward ladies to whom I'd given my affection, no matter how long ago it might have been. For my part, I wished every gentleman *she'd* bestowed affection on at the bottom of the sea.

More and more reason I could have killed Isherwood. Donata was correct. When trouble from my past came to call, there was usually a woman in the thick of it.

I WENT DOWN TO BREAKFAST AFTER THAT, LEAVING DONATA TO summon Jacinthe back to finish her toilette. I wasn't certain we'd resolved things between us, but Donata joined me an hour or so later in the dining room, after I'd finished my morning repast. As usual she'd taken a light meal in her chamber as she'd dressed, and now asked a footman for coffee.

"Dreadfully early," she said as she sipped. It was noon. "But when one is in the provinces ..."

"Gabriella was up and out promenading with Lady Aline at nine," I reminded her.

Donata shrugged. "She is young. When she is married, she will be more weary."

"I am sorry to hear marriage is so tiring," I said lightly.

She gave me a look. "I came down at this appalling hour to tell you the thoughts I had while I breakfasted. I would like to send for Mr. Quimby. He is the cleverest of the Runners, as you have told me. He can find out what happened."

I felt a qualm of disquiet. Lamont Quimby was indeed a clever man, methodical and patient. Where my former sergeant Pomeroy blustered about until he put his hands on a bad man, whether guilty of that particular crime or not,

Quimby investigated thoroughly and only brought his evidence to the magistrate when he was certain.

The trouble was, he was quite good, and if I had done this ...

"He might very well be arresting me," I said.

"I doubt it." Donata set down her cup. "Gabriel, you are sometimes rash and can be a fool about other men's wives, but you are an honest man, and not a murderer. Even if you were well inebriated at the time, it was at worst a ghastly accident." She waved a hand. "I don't even believe that. I think you stumbled upon Isherwood and picked up the sword. That is all."

I wished I shared her confidence.

"There is a witness," I said, thinking of Clement. "The footman I told you about. I need to speak to him."

"Do that. I will write to Mr. Quimby."

"As long as Spendlove doesn't get wind of it." Mr. Spendlove longed to arrest me on any charge, his idea being that I would give him all the information he needed to bring in James Denis in return for being let off. I knew full well that what Denis had let me learn about him would never convict him—Denis was far too careful. Spendlove, however, was persistent.

"Mr. Quimby does not work out of the Bow Street office, and he is wise enough not to speak loudly about his investigations," Donata declared. "He should clear this up in a trice."

I was not so sanguine. I finished my excellent coffee and rose to my feet.

"In that case, I will repair to the Pavilion and try to find young Clement. I will have to hunt up Grenville, or they'll never let me in the door."

"An excellent idea. Do remember we are taking the sea waters this afternoon."

Ah, yes. Donata would hire carriages to take us out into the Channel, where we would remove most of our clothing and have a dip in the sea.

"Of course," I said. "I like a good splash about. I enjoyed it as a lad, I remember. Swam mother-naked off the salt marshes in Norfolk, or down among the Broads."

"I'm certain you were a tear," Donata said calmly. "Please join us at four o'clock for more sedate bathing. The tide will be out then."

BREWSTER WAS WAITING FOR ME AS ALWAYS OUTSIDE THE FRONT door when I departed, and we walked together across the square to the house Grenville had hired.

"I had to tell His Nibs," Brewster said as we went. "If he'd heard it from someone else, he'd skin me. Always best to be straight with him."

I'd learned firsthand what happened to men who tried to dupe Mr. Denis. "I would be curious to hear what he thinks of the matter. If he has any interest at all."

"Oh, he does, guv," Brewster said darkly, but we'd reached Grenville's and could say no more.

I'd sent word ahead to Grenville, and he was waiting for us on his front step, settling his hat as we approached. "You know I cannot simply walk up and demand entrance to the Prince's residence, Lacey," he told me.

"Why not?" Brewster asked him. "You're in thick with His Royalness. Just tell him you want a chat."

Grenville shot him a weary look. "I doubt we'll see His Royalness, as you call him. I learned that he left for London in the middle of the night on Monday, sometime after supper."

I came alert. "Was this before or after Isherwood was killed?"

"Very suspicious," Brewster agreed. "Why'd he run from cool sea breezes to the hot stink of the Smoke?"

"I do not know exactly when he left," Grenville said. "But I believe his abrupt departure had to do with his estranged wife. He is convinced poor Caroline and her Italian servant are living as man and wife on the Continent. I heard his spies have turned up new evidence, or supposed evidence, and he rushed off to find out if it was true."

"Devil of a way to treat his wife," Brewster growled. "Why don't she beat him on the head? My Em would." Brewster, like most people, regarded Caroline of Brunswick more highly than he did the dissipated Regent.

"I agree," Grenville said. "Let us hope the princess can continue to enjoy herself. But you are not wrong, Lacey, that it would be good to discover whether the Regent left before or after the colonel died."

"I can find that out," Brewster said. "If I can get meself below stairs."

"Excellent," Grenville said. "Lacey and I will admire the new decor, while you interrogate the servants."

He sounded cheerful. Even Brewster wasn't morose. They, like Donata, did not believe I'd murdered Isherwood and thought we'd clear it up soon. It was good of them to trust me, but I with my head still aching a bit, would feel better when I had proof.

Again it was a glorious day, Brighton full of holiday-makers shopping, taking tea or coffee, enjoying life. Ladies with sketchbooks sat overlooking the water, while servants shaded them with large parasols.

Only a few days ago, I'd been one of the happy tourists,

strolling in the sun with my daughter on my arm, my stepson picking up stones on the shore. Now I was investigating a murder and trying to piece together missing hours of my life.

The three of us moved along the road skirting the Steine, until we faced the Pavilion, an exotic oddity in this town of clean-lined buildings.

Grenville gained admission by the simple ruse of telling the footman he longed to gaze upon some of the renovations he'd seen the night we'd been there. He knew the Regent had departed, he said, and we'd never bother the workmen...

The royal servants knew Grenville and respected him. Grenville had been skeptical of being allowed in today, but the majordomo welcomed us through the octagon-shaped hall into the main palace. We passed into what was called the Long Gallery, which would connect all the rooms, and to the music room, with its vast domed ceiling.

Young Colonel Isherwood had told us that the majordomo had broken the news of his father's murder to him. The major-domo today spoke to us serenely, never betraying with one word or twitch of mouth a hint that anything untoward had happened in his demesne.

Grenville and I thanked him, also not betraying our interest, and he left us to wander as we wished.

Brewster already knew the way to the servants' areas, and disappeared through a doorway set into the wall paneling. The door vanished when closed, looking like nothing more than the rest of the wall. I had found such a door when I'd made my hasty exit from the kitchen.

Grenville and I ambled through the music room and the gallery beyond it. We pretended to be intrigued by nothing more than the lavish architecture as we slowly but inexorably

made our way to the banqueting room where I'd found
Isherwood.

Today, that chamber buzzed with activity. Painters brushed
an undercoat on the walls, men on scaffolding worked on an
elaborate plaster palm that would cross the entire ceiling, and
two carpenters planed a doorjamb in long, even strokes.

The place where Isherwood had lain was bare, the floor-
boards clean. I dimly remembered he'd been sprawled across a
dust sheet, but that was gone, and no blood marked the wood. I
stooped to examine the spot, earning only a curious glance
from the workers.

"Here," I said to Grenville under my breath.

The workmen, sanding, scraping, and pounding, paid little
attention. Grenville leaned to study the bare floor then
straightened up when he saw nothing, expression unchanged.

"Show me where you went after you found him," he said.

I took Grenville through the narrow door that had been
hidden by draperies that night. The walls were bare today, and
the workmen watched us go without comment.

Once we reached the corridor, I stared blankly about,
trying to get my bearings, but my memories were still foggy. "I
ended up in the kitchen, I think."

Grenville stepped past me. "It is this way."

He led me along the hall and through another door. As we
stepped into a large busy room, I recalled the huge chamber,
dark and still, filled with tables, crates, and food.

Now, of course, the kitchen teemed with people. Men at
massive stoves stirred and basted, and women wielded knives
to chop produce or hack up fowl. Blood and melted fat
dripped to the floor. The heat was stifling, the odors cloying.

The man who must be in charge spied us, and roared, "'Ere!
You're not to be back 'ere!"

Grenville gave him a bow. "Just passing, my good fellow. Your roast on Monday night was a dream. I savored it well. Good morning."

The chef glared, though he looked somewhat mollified. Grenville beckoned me to follow as the cooks stared at us, and we ducked through another door to the servants' corridor.

"You know your way about," I remarked to Grenville.

"His Highness has taken me through the entire house—several times. He is very proud of every inch, or at least of what Mr. Nash has done with it. Clever man, is Nash. He'll make the place pleasing and not the monstrosity the Regent has dreamed up. Oh, I beg your pardon, good lady."

He tipped his hat to a maid who'd halted at the sight of us. She pushed herself against the wall so we could pass and did not meet our eyes. I bowed to her as I went by, but that made her cringe even more—she'd hoped I wouldn't notice her.

"Anything returning to your mind?" Grenville said after we'd gone a little farther.

"Not a bit. I needed my guide, who thankfully showed me the way out."

"Hmm." Grenville looked about then abruptly charged off down a passageway. I followed as closely as I could.

After taking us through several corridors and down a few short flights of stairs, he opened a door that led into a small courtyard. "Here?"

"Possibly." It had been dark, and I had been ill and disoriented.

"Let us pretend this is the correct door." Grenville stepped out and followed the passage to the gate at the end.

"This is very like it," I said. We walked through the gate and emerged onto a street. "I found myself in the maze of the market and bought a bud for my lapel from a flower seller there." I pointed my walking stick down a street, now humming with the day's activities, though no flower sellers were apparent at the moment.

"You saw no one else?" Grenville asked. "None but the footman?"

"No one," I said with certainty. I had been alone—that much I knew.

"Nor heard anyone running away, that sort of thing?"

I returned my walking stick to the pavement. "You want me to say I heard the murderer or saw another who might have been the culprit. I'm sorry, but no, I did not."

"The killer might have been long gone before you arrived," Grenville said. "Or might have been your lad, Clement."

"I recall looking him over for signs of blood or violence. I saw none. He was terrified—he obviously believed *I* was the killer."

"Well, either both of you are innocent, or one of you is guilty."

"Very helpful." I gave him a frown.

"I am attempting to be efficient, my friend. As you can be when you are not distraught. Your involvement in this is clouding your judgement."

"As is my lack of memory," I said grimly.

"*Oi!*"

I heard a familiar shout and swung around to see Brewster bolting out through another gate. He pointed a thick arm down the lane and charged after a retreating figure.

It was a tall lad with black hair and skin, his footman's livery awry, running as fast as he could. Clement, my conspirator from the night of Isherwood's murder, fled into the lanes, Brewster hard on his heels.

CHAPTER 7

*G*renville, after a startled look at the running Clement, sprinted down the road behind Brewster, never mind his pristine suit and polished boots. I had to let those more fleet of foot than I pursue the lad, while I hobbled in their wake as swiftly as I could.

Brewster, who could move rapidly for all his bulk, caught Clement in a lane that branched off North Street. When I reached them, Brewster had Clement against a wall with his arm across his throat, Clement struggling hard. The tall youth had fear in his eyes, but also resolve.

Grenville seemed none the worse for the chase, but I leaned against the wall to catch my breath. "Let him go, Brewster."

Brewster did not obey. "I introduced meself to him, so to speak, below stairs, and said you wanted a word. And off he went."

"Yes," I reasoned. "But he cannot answer me with you cutting off his air."

"He can. I know how to go about it."

I dragged in another breath and hauled myself upright. "Please don't be afraid, lad. In spite of appearances, I have no intention of hurting you. I wanted to talk, and you know what about."

Brewster did ease his hold, though he kept Clement trapped. "Why didn't he say so?" the young man asked angrily.

"Why'd ye run?" Brewster returned.

"I was off to see me mum." Clement scowled at him. "And this lout starts chasing me."

"In the Regent's livery?" I gestured to his satin knee breeches and coat, his silk stockings and well-made shoes. He'd left off the turban, his short hair glistening in the strong sunshine. "Why not change before you go?"

"I ain't a dandy with a dozen suits, am I? Not a different one for every hour, like Mr. Grenville."

"Touché," Grenville said, brows rising. "It is an apt question, lad. You'd have at least clothes to go home in. I doubt the majordomo will be pleased if you tear your finery."

"His Highness has got enough money to buy me dozens. I ain't doing nothing wrong, guv." He glared at me. "Call off your dog."

My "dog" growled at him.

"If you truly are visiting your mother, I hardly wish to keep you," I said. "We'll walk with you, shall we? I do need to speak with you, lad."

Clement sent me a belligerent look. "You'll fit me up for the magistrates. I never killed that bloke."

Brewster's grip tightened. "Do I look like a beak?" he demanded. "This is Captain Lacey. He's not in the habit of fitting people up. Even to save his own neck," he finished in disapproval.

"I promise you," I interrupted firmly. "No magistrates. I do not believe you murdered the colonel, but I am not prepared to tell you why on the street."

Clement looked me over with less fear than he should have being in the clutches of Brewster. Brewster was not a killer, but he didn't mind rendering a victim unconscious or breaking a limb or two.

At last, Clement gave me a nod. "All right then. But you don't say nothing about this to my mum."

"I would not dream of it," I assured him. I signaled to Brewster, but I knew Brewster only released the lad because he'd decided. Even in the days when Brewster had been briefly employed by me, he'd never done what I asked simply because I asked it.

CLEMENT AND HIS MOTHER LIVED ON THE NORTHEAST END OF Brighton, in a street of small, neat cottages. A well-kept garden lay before the house where Clement led us through a gate, the clumps of bright flowers and trained rose vines a testimony to a gardener of good taste and hard work.

Clement, followed closely by Brewster, strode up the path made of crushed stone to the front door. The lad gave us a warning glance before he walked inside, singing out, "It's me, Mum! I brought visitors."

A woman's voice floated from a room down the flagstoned hall, her tone filled with alarm. "It's not your day out. You'd better not be in trouble, my boy."

"Nah." Clement shot me a worried look. "Have some gentlemen with me."

Footsteps sounded and a woman emerged into the hall. She had dark skin, like her son, and resembled him greatly. She wore a frock of light brown trimmed with cream, her hair in a simple but elegant knot.

She did not look old enough to have a son Clement's age—I put him to be nearly twenty. Her smooth face was unlined and she had no gray in her hair, but from her expression, she was obviously his mother. The admonishing glare could have come from no other.

The lady addressed Grenville, guessing by his clothing and demeanor that he was the most highborn of us. "Clement is a good lad, sir. But not always. What has he done this time?"

Grenville gave her a gentlemanly bow. "Nothing at all, dear lady. Captain Lacey made your son's acquaintance when he dined at the Pavilion the other night, and today sought him out to give him a shilling for his service. Clement unfortunately got hold of the wrong idea and tried to flee. We thought we'd escort him home and assure him we have only kindness in mind."

A plausible tale, but Clement's mother regarded Grenville narrowly. She moved the skeptical gaze to me then Brewster, who hovered near the door, ready to prevent Clement from rushing out.

The lady was no fool. She nodded to Grenville but it was clear she was reserving her opinion. "In that case, gentlemen, let me offer you refreshment. I have a nice pot of tea brewed, and cook has made some of her excellent cakes. Take them into the parlor, Clement, and let them sit down. I won't be a moment."

She spoke clearly, with only a hint of the London cant Clement had. She bustled from us without a qualm, and Clement could do nothing but usher us into the sitting room.

I liked the house, clean and tidy, comfortable without ostentation. It was the sort of place I ought to be living in— I'd gone from faded, cheap rooms in Covent Garden to the opulence of Donata's Mayfair home in one day. I preferred the comfortable and informal to either penury or ostentation.

Grenville, who was at home anywhere, seated himself near the window and admired the view—across the garden and down a hill to the sea. Brewster declared he'd wait outside, meaning he'd station himself near the front door like a pillar.

"I have no intention of upsetting your mother," I told Clement, who hovered uncertainly as I sat down. "But I do need to ask you about the night Colonel Isherwood died. I want to know what you saw, and who, and when."

"I saw *you*." Clement rocked on his heels. "Standing over the colonel with a sword in your hand."

"I know that." I held on to my patience. "Yet you helped me leave the palace instead of sounding the alarm."

Clement hesitated. "Because I didn't think you done it."

"Why not?"

"Why do you think *I* hadn't done it?" he countered, folding his arms. He was a big lad, and strong.

"Lack of blood on your clothes," I said. "Your terror when you saw me with a sword. You had the fear of one thinking he would be killed next, not the guilt of a man caught."

Clement considered this then nodded. "Thought the same about you. A stab like that would have sprayed you all over. You had a little blood on you, but only what smeared from the sword. And you had the same fear, like."

I loosened in some relief. "Good. I'm pleased to find you are sensible. You do see, do you not, why both of us need to find out who really killed him?"

Clement regarded me in unhappy silence before nodding once more. "Please don't tell me mum."

"She will likely hear the tale sooner or later," I warned in a quiet voice. "Of Isherwood's death if nothing else, in a place you are employed. I assume you ran and fetched the major-domo that night, who gave you instructions to say nothing at all?"

Another nod. "I had to help him clear out the body." Clement shuddered. "We carried him out on the dust sheet and the majordomo gave the man to his son. Not nice work."

I didn't imagine it would have been. "I have not asked you why you happened to be traipsing around the Pavilion in time to catch me over Isherwood's body. What were you doing in the banqueting room at that time?"

If I expected him to stutter and stammer and try to come up with a lie, I was disappointed. Clement gave me a surprised look and said, "Quickest way to the kitchens, innit, cutting through that room. I was peckish."

Grenville chuckled. "How many nights in my youth did I wander my father's dark mansion in search of sustenance? And again when I was at school? There was never enough at meals to satisfy me."

I was not ready to take Clement's word without question, but I could not deny that I had done the same as a boy.

"I carried food and drink to the table all night," Clement went on. "Run off my feet, and didn't get much past a crust of bread for my trouble. I knew there'd be leftovers from the meal going begging." He glared as though daring me to tell him he'd been wrong.

Heels clicked in the hall, and Grenville sprang up to open the door. Clement's mother entered with a full tray, which Grenville took from her, setting it on the table.

"Thank you, sir." She gave him a curtsy. *"This* is how a gentleman behaves, Clement. Take note. A cup of tea, sir? I am afraid I cannot offer you other. I have no strong drink in my house."

"Tea is admirable, dear lady." Grenville took a seat as she sat down to pour out. "What do we call you, madam? We can hardly keep referring to you as Clement's mum."

She gave Grenville a quick smile but one that said she saw through his charm. "I am Mrs. Morgan. Cecilia is my Christian name. Mr. Morgan is deceased—I am a widow. We come from London, but we moved to Brighton when the Regent began hiring servants for his Pavilion. I sent Clement along to see if he could get a place, as the pay was decent. I would like to think the majordomo hired my Clement because he is clever and well-mannered, but I rather think it was because he's tall and looks fine in the livery."

"Mum …" Clement sank into the window seat, embarrassed.

Mrs. Morgan handed Grenville a cup and began filling another. "My husband was a merchant who sold goods from India as they came off the ships. A wholesaler. He did well in his business, if not brilliantly, and left me comfortable. I tell you this to save you the breath of asking questions about Clement's life. He was well brought up and mostly stays free of trouble."

I took the tea Mrs. Morgan handed me, noting the glint of amusement in her eyes. She was very curious about us in return but wasn't about to say so.

"Clement is a fine lad," I said. "And has caused no trouble that I know of. Before I drink your tea, I will introduce myself. I am Captain Gabriel Lacey, late of the Thirty-Fifth Light Dragoons. This gentleman is Mr. Lucius Grenville, a famous dandy and friend of the Regent. In spite of this, he too can keep himself from trouble."

"I have heard of Mr. Grenville, of course." Mrs. Morgan gave him a nod. "I thought it was you, sir. I read in the newspaper that you had arrived in Brighton with your new wife. My felicitations. I am honored by your visit."

"Not at all. Thank you." Grenville made a bow from his chair. "Captain Lacey enjoys teasing, you might have noted."

"I gathered that. The newspapers seem even more agog about your wife than yourself, Mr. Grenville. An actress, they say. A scandal, is it?" Her tone was curious, not condemning.

Grenville flushed. "A romance, in truth. Once I met my love, I could marry no other."

"A very good answer." Mrs. Morgan lifted her teacup. "If a bit affected. Well, gentlemen. Please tell me the true reason you've come, and what you want of my son."

"Never you mind," Clement blustered. "They wanted to give me shillings is all."

I exchanged a glance with Grenville. His uncertainty matched mine. This lady seemed intelligent, and the event concerned her son, but how discreet could she be?

"Bloke was killed at the Pavilion," Clement blurted out before I could decide. Under his mother's eye, he wilted, clutching the window seat's cushion. "A colonel what was at the supper party on Monday night."

"Colonel Isherwood from the Forty-Seventh Light Dragoons," I finished. "He was a regimental colonel at Preston Barracks."

Mrs. Morgan's teacup lowered slowly as she stared at first Clement, then Grenville and me. Her good humor drained away. "Colonel Isherwood?"

Grenville leaned forward. "Did you know him, madam?"

Mrs. Morgan regarded us sharply, animation returning to her face. "What is this? Why do you say he was killed, and at the Pavilion?"

"I found his body there," I said as calmly as I could. "As did your son."

"No!" Clement was on his feet. "I didn't find him. I found *you* finding him." He pointed a stiff finger at me.

Mrs. Morgan rose, anything genial in her vanishing. "Are you saying my son killed Colonel Isherwood, Captain Lacey? If you have come to accuse him, you will bring me evidence and allow me to send for my solicitor. Or did you, wealthy men about town, decide to badger a pathetic widow?"

There was nothing pathetic about this woman. She stood straight-backed and stared us down.

I set aside my tea and climbed to my feet. "Please. I am accusing no one. I want to get to the truth, because you can see the precarious position I might be in. I do not believe I killed Isherwood, but to prove this, I need to find out who did."

Mrs. Morgan's brow furrowed. "You don't *believe* you did? Do you not know?"

"Unfortunately, no. I remember little about the night."

She gave me another look, this one full of disapproval. "Strong drink is the very devil, sir."

Grenville broke in. "Captain Lacey believes he was given a substance that clouded his mind."

"Does he?" Mrs. Morgan's skepticism rang out. "Does he believe Clement did this—drugged him and set him over the body of a man my son killed? I'll thank you to consider your words, sir."

"I do not believe Clement murdered him, either," I said quickly. "I wish to clear his name as well as mine."

"Why?" Mrs. Morgan demanded, as though it were a

reasonable question. "Why should the likes of you stick your neck out for the likes of us?"

"Because I am interested in the truth." I grew stern. "I do not want to see an innocent lad hang for something he did not do. I do not care if the Regent himself murdered this man—I'd prosecute him with all my might."

Grenville had risen when Mrs. Morgan did, but remained a distance from us, trying to be the most unthreatening person in the room.

"You will find, madam, that Captain Lacey is a most honorable fellow," he said. "He is a champion of the downtrodden—not that the description belongs to you, Mrs. Morgan." Grenville bowed to her. "But he will work to make certain the correct person is punished for the crime, not the most convenient one."

The words were delivered in a smooth tone and one that slightly disparaged me. *He will always act honorably, even at detriment to himself*, Grenville was implying. *Drives his friends mad.*

Mrs. Morgan was not entirely reassured, but her anger wound down a bit.

"I wanted to ask Clement what he'd observed Monday evening during the supper and after," I explained. "He as footman would see all the guests, would know who went in and out and what servants were in the back stairs. He would know exactly when the Regent—and every other guest for that matter—left that night. I hope he can be my eyes and ears for what went on before Isherwood's demise."

Mrs. Morgan studied me, her indecision plain. Then she closed her eyes briefly and sat down once more.

"I don't trust many, Captain. That includes you and Mr.

Grenville. But I have also learned how to judge people quickly. You seem sincere—though in my experience, every confidence man does at first." She lifted her chin. "I will provide you some information, before you pry it of a busybody. I knew Colonel Isherwood. When we first moved here, he wished to court me ... not as a wife. I rebuffed him. I did not like him."

"I commend your taste," I said, resuming my seat. "I did not like him either."

"Mum?" Clement came forward, aghast. "What do you mean, not as a wife? You mean as his fancy piece?"

Mrs. Morgan scowled at him. "Is that difficult to believe? I am not in my dotage, and there has been more than one gentleman who wanted me on his arm. But I am neither desperate nor a fool. He tried to tell me how many gifts and riches he'd give me, as though I were an empty-headed ninny. I turned him away." She hesitated. "I am afraid I had to turn him away quite often. He was persistent ... and threatening."

"He was ever a blackguard," I said. "If he were still walking, I'd call him out for that."

Grenville stepped forward. "We can all agree the man was abominable. Pray keep that story to yourself, good lady, lest you be accused as well."

Mrs. Morgan's eyes flashed. "I imagine if every person Hamilton Isherwood angered or disgusted were accused, there were be a long parade before the magistrate. But I take your warning, sir. Clement could also be pointed at as a lad defending his mother."

Clement's eyes widened. "I didn't even know."

"If a magistrate wants a culprit, and quickly, he might not care," Grenville said. "Let me sum up—we have three suspects standing in this room. Captain Lacey, found over the body, sword in hand. Clement, on the spot and fond of his mother. Mrs. Morgan, who was bothered by the colonel and possibly frightened of him. I am beginning to be happy I went off to that soiree, as deadly dull as it turned out to be."

"Others were at the dinner," I said. "Lord Armitage and his wife, who have a fairly wild history. Bishop Craddock, who argued with Isherwood about the relevance of the army now that Bonaparte has been defeated. Quite strongly, I recall. I didn't know many of the others. Alvanley and a few of his friends I've met at Tattersalls." I frowned, trying to remember. "Alvanley introduced a French count."

"Comte Fernand Desjardins," Grenville said as he sat down and lifted his teacup. "He is an emigre—at least, that is his story. Came to England with his parents when he was a lad. They'd managed to get much of their money and belongings out of France before the Directorate came into power, and lived very well. Desjardins inherited the lot when his father passed away. He's a bit of a dandy—enjoys luxury and mixing in the highest circles. Even now that Louis has been restored to the crown, Desjardins seems in no hurry to move back to France."

"Ah," Mrs. Morgan said. "Did *he* quarrel with Colonel Isherwood?"

"They didn't speak together much," Grenville said. "I could see that Isherwood thought him a vacuous fop."

"I wonder why the Regent invited Isherwood at all," I broke in. "Isherwood had a talent for angering people, or being angry at them. He was quite self-righteous, I remember."

"There." Mrs. Morgan squared her shoulders. "All the more reason for the magistrates to look elsewhere and leave my son alone."

I glanced at Clement. "Isherwood lost his temper with you,

didn't he? When you didn't bring his wine quickly enough? Became violent, Mr. Grenville tells me."

Clement chewed his lip under his mother's sudden glower. "He did, yeah. But I didn't fight him or nothing. I walked away when he let me go. Sometimes the guests are a bit rude, or drunk."

Mrs. Morgan pinned him with her stare. "Does this happen often?"

"No." The answer was a bit too quick. "It's a good place, Mum. I'll not run away because a bloke thinks it's funny to knock me hat off."

"Clement, lad," Grenville said, his air of authority cutting through whatever protest his mother was about to make. "You are in a good position to discover things. What time did the Regent depart that night? Did Comte Desjardins, or any of the guests, have an argument with Colonel Isherwood ... or at the very least, plan to meet him later? You uncover what you can, and Lacey and I will do the same on our end." He sent us all a severe look. "I do not have to explain, do I, that discretion is called for?"

"You do not," Mrs. Morgan said. "I don't want anyone claiming my Clement did for a regimental colonel when Clement wouldn't hurt a fly." She turned on her son. "Do what Mr. Grenville says. I give you my leave to listen to the gossip and ask all sorts of questions of the other servants. Who knows? Maybe one of *them* did it."

"That is indeed a possibility," I said.

The Regent's lofty servants had pasts, and many had worked for aristocrats throughout their careers. Some might have served in the army, or worked for army officers—there were many opportunities for a man or woman to have crossed paths with Isherwood.

I rose. "I thank you for your assistance, madam. As well as for the excellent tea. And for lending us your son."

"You just make certain he's not banged up." Mrs. Morgan got to her feet. She was only half my height, but she stared up at me with a marvelous strength of will. "Promise me that, Captain, and I'll say nothing at all."

I assured her I would, hoping I could make good on the promise without heading to Newgate myself.

***

GRENVILLE AND I WALKED AWAY WITH BREWSTER, LEAVING Clement behind. His mother would send him back to work but wanted to speak more to him first, she said. Scold him up and down, I gathered, from Clement's chagrined expression as we departed.

Grenville set his hat firmly on his head, defying the breeze that wanted to tug it off. "The world is changing," he said. "Merchants are the new aristocrats. A lady from the East End can marry well, wear fashionable clothes, employ a cook, and host highborn gentlemen to tea without embarrassment."

"Why shouldn't she?" I asked. "Her husband likely worked hard to leave her and his son well off. Why should she hide her head in shame?"

"I merely observe it, Lacey. I don't condemn her," Grenville said, pained. "I am the most reforming of reforming men. Quite on the side of men being able to live a good life on their merits, not their birth."

I relaxed. "Never say so in front of my wife," I said in amusement. "She can trace every family in Britain back to Roman times."

"Then she'll know most families' originators are reprobates, scoundrels, and pirates. They gleefully slaughtered each other in a never-ending quest for power, right up to the present day."

Brewster, who'd walked behind us in silence now grunted. "You sound like them Quakers, the pair of you do. All of us the same? Give me strength."

"Do not worry, Mr. Brewster," Grenville said breezily. "I know you outrank us all. Even the Friends will acknowledge that."

Brewster only grunted again at Grenville's humor. He had a firm view of his place in the world and did not want anything to dislodge it.

"Did I hear you mention Quakers, Mr. Grenville?" a voice rumbled behind us. "Damned fools, the lot of them."

Grenville turned, ready to tip his hat to an acquaintance. The man who approached was Bishop Craddock, who had been present at the ill-fated supper and again at last evening's lecture.

Craddock was past sixty, but he had a firm body and few lines on his face. I'd thought him robust, and he was—the sort of gentleman who tramped miles across fields for the entertainment of it and took cold baths for his health.

He had argued long and loud with Isherwood about the relevance of the army before Alvanley had deftly turned the topic. Isherwood had never had any use for the clergy, especially bishops, considering the latter soft men who'd finagled livings out of wealthy parishes to climb to the top and make the rest of us miserable. Isherwood had especially hated bishops who sat in the House of Lords, of which Craddock was one.

"Your Grace," Grenville said politely. "A passing comment," he said in answer to the bishop's question. "The Quaker

Meeting House lies nearby." He gestured back along North Street.

"I know it does. Too blasted many of them in Brighton." His voice rang. "Cromwell has much to answer for. Did you know that more than a third of those who live in this town are Nonconformists? Methodists, Unitarians, Quakers, and other sorts of foul blights."

"Cromwell has been dead these hundred and fifty years," Grenville pointed out.

"That's as may be, but he's to blame. The Dissenters fled to Brighton when the crown was restored, the C of E back where it belonged. Do you know that if a Quaker does one small thing the others dislike, they boot him out? Shun him?"

"Do they?" Grenville asked, raising his brows. "I hadn't heard that. So unlike our dear C of E, which welcomes drunkards and sinners."

"Exactly." The bishop's voice rose. "God saves *sinners*, not sanctimonious, we-know-best, clergy-shunning, body-rocking, mouth frothers. Have you ever been to a Quaker Meeting? They say nothing, only sit there, eyes closed and swaying back and forth, until suddenly up jumps one and starts shouting. I ask you."

"I have not had that opportunity, no," Grenville said. "Sounds quite interesting."

"Then you have a different idea of interest than I, Mr. Grenville." The bishop bowed to us both, but not in anger. He'd said his piece, and didn't much care whether we agreed with him or not. "Good afternoon. I'm off to have a tramp down the coast to Eastbourne. Good weather for it."

He looked Grenville up and down, as though certain *he'd* never be up to such a long walk, glanced with disapproval at my walking stick, turned abruptly and left us.

Grenville waited until the man strode out of earshot before he spoke. "Such a pleasant gentleman. I hope *he* did not do away with the missing Quakers in his zeal."

"As do I," I agreed. "I have not made much of a start looking for them, I admit. I've been fixed on my own dilemma."

"I am at your service," Grenville answered at once. "It should not be too difficult to find what became of them, should it?"

"Huh," Brewster said. He'd faded back as the bishop railed but now joined us again. "You're a fool to think so, Mr. Grenville, if you don't mind me saying. Anything involving the captain is a right mess. If it didn't start that way, he will make it so."

WHEN I REACHED HOME, I FACED ANOTHER ORDEAL. DONATA had Peter and Anne downstairs, ready for us to make our way to the sea.

She regarded my tardiness with some impatience, but we set off in due course. Anne's nanny accompanied us, as did Gabriella in a pretty muslin frock and jacket.

For a certain sum, one could hire coaches that drove out through the shingle to a calm cove, stopping right in the water. There, using the coach as a shield from prying eyes, we uncovered to light clothing and plunged into the sea.

Donata was quite fetching in her thin muslin frock that clung to every curve. She swam sedately, but well, Gabriella happily paddling alongside her. Gabriella had often traveled to the coast with her family in France, and she enjoyed sea bathing.

Anne remained in the carriage, as both Donata and I had

great fear of her drowning if she so much as touched the water, but at least she could enjoy the air and a day out.

Peter was the most exultant of all. He swam and dove, played splashing games with Gabriella and me, and shouted and laughed at us both. Gabriella held her own against him in these games, with no intention of letting him best her.

Peter liked swimming out with me as far as we dared go, the cold water bracing. We stroked side by side, I slowing myself so I would not outpace him. In a few years, I suspected, he'd outpace me.

The sun headed westward but had a long way to go before nightfall. The sea glittered with light, a mist rising on its edge. It was beautiful, but the mist warned the evening would be cool.

"Papa!" Peter yelled. "Look!"

In spite of my thrill that he'd addressed me as *Papa*, I peered at what he excitedly pointed to. I shaded my eyes, and felt a pang of disquiet.

It was a boat, but upended, floating on the waves like a pile of boards, its hull black with water. I stopped Peter as he began to swim out to it.

"Stay here. Look after your mother." I left him behind me and started toward the boat.

When I reached the small vessel, I realized Peter had disobeyed and come after me. He was like a fish in the water, and easily caught up.

I put my hands under the gunwale of the boat. I realized I'd never shift it all the way over by myself but I could at least lift it enough to see if anyone had been trapped beneath.

Someone had, and he was dead. As I moved the edge of the boat upward, Peter's small hands helping to push, the bubble of air beneath the boat revealed the body of a young man.

He was dead with no doubt, his face blue and bloated. His body had been trapped under the plank seats across the bottom, which explained why he hadn't sunk into the sea, though he was quite wet.

His eyes were open, staring in terror, and the clear marks of strangling fingers were black across his throat.

CHAPTER 8

$\mathcal{P}$eter gasped at the sight of the dead man, but did not look as horrified as I'd feared he'd be. He gazed at the body in fascination but also sadness, genuine sorrow that such a thing had befallen another.

"We should fetch the magistrate," he said in a hushed whisper.

"That we should." I seized a rope that had also been trapped under the boards. It was wet, but the upended boat had kept it from becoming sodden. "We need to tow this to shore, to secure it so it doesn't drift."

Peter reached to help, and together, we lashed the rope to a hook in the gunwale. The young man inside was well stuck, so we would not need to turn the boat all the way over to get him to shore.

Peter and I shared the rope between us. We swam, and when we hit shallow water, we marched onward, hauling the boat with us.

We passed Donata, who was climbing into the coach that

had taken us into the sea. Donata's maid reached out with a cloak, hiding her clinging wet gown.

"Gabriel?" my wife called, startled.

Gabriella, already inside, peered out in concern. "Father, what has happened?"

I did not answer either of them, not wanting to shout the news across the water. I continued with the boat toward the shore, Peter assisting.

Halfway up the shingle, a stump of an old dock protruded from the rocks. I fastened the rope to it, looping it around and around and tying it as tightly as I could. I called out to a fisherman and asked him to please make certain the boat stayed put. I had to promise to pay him, but he nodded, settling down next to it without question and pulling out a flask.

I hoisted Peter, dripping, into the coach that had come alongside to meet us.

As we huddled, damp and shivering, blankets around us, I related what we'd found.

"Oh, the poor lad," Gabriella said. "Did his boat tip over?" The nanny cuddled Anne on her lap, the lady's eyes round. Anne, the only one oblivious to the drama, tugged at a ribbon on her dress.

"Difficult to tell," I answered.

I fixed to my mind the details of what I'd seen. Someone had strangled the man and set him off in the boat. Whether they'd tipped him over in hopes the sea would wash away the evidence of their crime, or the boat had caught in a bad wave, I could not say.

At home, Bartholomew dried me off and fetched me fresh clothes, and then I went out to seek the magistrate.

The magistrate's court was held in the Old Ship, a hotel that had stood on its site for many years. The Regent had taken rooms here before he'd purchased his Pavilion, and the hotel had been turned into a rather nice abode.

I went there in the hope that either the court was in session or I'd find someone who could direct me to the magistrate's house.

The court was in. The magistrate, a large man with red cheeks called Sir Reginald Pyne, presided over a hot room and a few offenders who looked ready to be anywhere but there. Pyne growled out his last sentence, threw down his gavel, and left the bench.

I intercepted him on his way to a large glass of port.

"Eh?" Pyne blurted when I quietly told him what I'd found. "What the devil are you talking about?"

"A man has lost his life," I repeated in a hard voice. "I tied up the boat and left a fisherman to look after it."

The magistrate looked longingly at the taproom, where his port would be waiting, then back at me. He heaved a long sigh.

"Then we'd best get to it before the fisherman steals everything including the pegs that hold the thing together."

THE BOAT HAD DRAWN A CROWD. THE FISHERMAN I'D RECRUITED to watch was still there, lounging on the shingle.

The crowd was a mix of fishermen in well-worn coats and men and women on holiday, the ladies with large bonnets and parasols. None moved back as the magistrate approached, the passersby too curious to make any deference.

"Get that turned over," the magistrate barked at the fisherman.

The fisherman stared at him balefully, then slowly rose and gestured to a man and boy further up the shingle.

Water had lapped halfway under the boat when I'd left it. Now it was three-quarters of the way, the tide coming in.

The fisherman's colleague and the lad caught the gunwale of the boat and began to haul it over. I stepped in to help—if I could brace myself, I was quite strong.

The boat rose, the cool of the wet wood cutting the afternoon's warmth. It teetered on edge a long moment, threatening to take me and the other fisherman back over with it. The body trapped inside slid downward as we heaved, the sound like a bag of wet sand.

At last, the boat rolled all the way over. I danced back as it fell, pebbles scattering over my boots. The body under the seat dislodged and fell into the inches of water in the boat's bottom.

The magistrate stepped forward and peered at the dead man, the crowd craning to see.

The young man's clothes were sodden, making it difficult to discern their color. The puffy blue face held few features, and those were twisted in fear. His body was slightly rotund, made even more so by his stay under the boat.

The magistrate studied the corpse for a few moments then raised his head to the crowd. "Anyone know him?"

No one answered. Most here were on holiday, not from Brighton itself. Perhaps the young man had been a traveler too.

"We'll take him to the coroner," Pyne concluded. "Circulate his description. Do *you* know him, Captain?"

"Not at all," I said. "You don't?"

The magistrate stroked his chin. "Hard to say, isn't it? Him all bloated like that. Coroner will go through his clothes, try to find a letter or paper that tells us. Poor sod."

He did indeed look pathetic, sprawled before us, too young to have died and in such a fashion. Not a rich man, I thought.

No gold chain on his waistcoat—although that could have been stolen.

I smoothed a fold of the young man's coat between my fingers—it was thick and coarse. A laborer perhaps, but his hands were fairly smooth, no signs of hard work on them.

I thought of where I'd seen such clothing before, and recently.

"Is he a Quaker?" I asked the magistrate.

Pyne started. He bent to peer at the young man again and sucked in a breath. "Lord help us," he said in a near whisper. "I think that's Josh Bickley."

I stared down at the corpse in renewed dismay. Bickley's son. This was the lad I'd been meant to find, to restore to his family. A bitter taste coated my mouth.

The magistrate adjusted his hat. "All I need. Walking into the nest of pious Quakers, telling them one of their own's been drowned."

"Or killed, perhaps," I suggested. "From the marks on his throat."

Pyne shot me a look of dislike. "Might have been ropes that tangled him. 'S for the coroner to say."

I straightened up, feeling stiff, and knowing I was right about how he'd died. "I can walk into the nest for you, sir. I am acquainted with the lad's father."

Pyne studied me as though I were a strange animal, but he gave me a curt nod. "I won't say that wouldn't relieve me of a burden." He pointed a thick finger at me. "But no suggestion of murder, mind. I don't need the whole lot of them raging around me."

I promised I'd be circumspect. I retrieved my hat, which had dropped to the sand, gave the magistrate a polite bow, and left the shingle.

No one noticed my passage. They remained huddled around the boat, gawping at the spectacle, and I moved off to perform my unpleasant errand.

———

As I passed the first pub on the street, Brewster emerged from it, pint in hand. He shoved the tankard at another patron and fell into step beside me.

"Now, where you going?"

I answered in a low voice, "To tell Bickley his son is dead."

Brewster's eyes widened. "Is that who was in the boat? And why're *you* off to break the sad news?"

I did not answer. Brewster never liked my answers anyway.

I was going because I had failed Mr. Bickley. He'd asked me to find his son. If I had begun the search immediately, I might have located the young man before he'd come to grief.

Bickley hadn't been too worried about his absence, I remembered, believing his son had gone off to visit friends after the meeting that Sunday. He also wasn't a youth—Miss Farrow had said Joshua was twenty, well old enough to take care of himself. Perhaps these reasons were why I hadn't rushed to search for him, and I'd also been distracted by my own bizarre situation.

I could only atone now by being the one to break the news, and resolve to find Josh's killer.

The Meeting House wasn't far. I did not know whether Mr. Bickley would be there, but perhaps someone there could tell me where he lived. I halted numbly when I reached the house, studying the tranquil garden behind the gate.

The garden, as I'd observed before, contained rows of greens—vegetables and herbs enough for a feast. Blossoms clung to the green and yellow squash waiting to be harvested and brightened a trumpet vine that climbed the cottage wall.

The house's door opened almost instantly, and Miss Farrow emerged. "Gabriel?" She arrived at the gate unhurriedly and unlatched it. "We have heard the terrible news. Wilt thou come in?"

"You have heard?" I repeated in surprise. I'd left the shore only ten minutes ago.

Miss Farrow regarded me with bleak eyes. "A lad ran here and told us. He recognized Joshua at once."

She opened the gate and ushered me into the garden. Brewster hung back, but she continued to hold it, as though expecting him to join us. Brewster shrugged and followed me in.

Miss Farrow closed the gate and led us into the Meeting House.

I removed my hat as Miss Farrow led us inside the Meeting House, and was struck by how blank the interior was. There was not a single picture anywhere, not even a cross. The walls were whitewashed, the floors dark boards. High windows let in light but no view, not even that of the pleasant garden.

The house reminded me of cloisters in Spain, barren but elegant in their simplicity. Yet even those had displayed crucifixes, or frescoes, if subdued ones, images of saints or the Virgin.

Miss Farrow took us through a large room empty except for wooden benches, into a smaller chamber in the back of the house. This too had white walls and empty benches, and I heard a clattering of dishes in a nearby kitchen.

Brewster stood gazing about at the white interior, as fascinated by it as I was, while Miss Farrow regarded us sadly.

"Now, Gabriel, please tell me what happened."

"Is Mr. Bickley about?" I asked her.

"Clive is at home. I will break the news to him."

I would have preferred to speak to him directly, but Miss Farrow pinned me with her stare, willing me to pour forth what I knew. I launched into the full tale, speaking quietly and gently, describing how Peter and I had found the overturned boat.

"I have also come to apologize," I said when I'd finished. "I had not yet begun the task to find Master Bickley. My lingering might have caused his death."

Miss Farrow's brows rose. "How canst thou presume to know the Lord's heart? Or even what a coroner knows? Perhaps Joshua was dead before we asked thee to search for him."

I blinked. "I hadn't thought of it that way, I admit."

"Do not take the Lord's will upon thyself. It is not becoming, Gabriel."

"Forgive me." I gave her a bow.

"And do not bow to me. I am no better, or worse, than thou art, friend Gabriel. We must put our sorrows aside and discover what befell Joshua."

"I agree," I said. "For that, I might have to intrude upon privacy and find out all I can about him. Was he fond of boating? Is that what he'd disappeared to do?"

"I doubt it," Miss Farrow said with certainty. "Joshua disliked boats. Would not go near one. If he was found inside a boat, he did not go into it on his own."

That fact coupled with the marks on his neck pointed straight to murder.

"You said he left on Sunday without a word," I went on. "Had he done such a thing before?"

"A few times. Josh had many friends and would often visit

them. He is a good lad." Miss Farrow looked sad. "*Was* a good lad. Did his duty by his father, attended every meeting. A cheerful fellow."

"These friends he would meet ..." I hesitated. "Was one a young lady, perhaps?"

Amusement flickered behind Miss Farrow's sorrow. "Nothing like that. Josh had friends among the Quakers who were women, of course, but he was too unworldly for an interest in anything beyond friendship." Miss Farrow cocked her head. "Or, perhaps I should say, the ladies had little interest in *him*."

She was painting the picture of a friendly young man who obeyed his father and went to church as often as he could. I'd only seen him in death, but he'd been plump and round-faced, like Bickley, not lithe and handsome. Even a saintly young Quaker woman might want someone a bit more dashing.

Even so, it did not mean that Joshua did not have a secret lady or any wild oats to sow. It only meant Miss Farrow and his father saw the dutiful side of him.

"Speaking to his friends could help," I said. "They might know why he ended up in a boat when he disliked them so."

Miss Farrow nodded. "I see the sense in that. But after we grieve, please, Friend Gabriel. We know Joshua is in a better place, of course, but selfishly, we will miss him."

That was the trouble with death. I too had been brought up to believe we should rejoice that the one we loved was with the Lord, but somehow I never could. I could feel only emptiness, the lessening of myself for the absence of that person. Miss Farrow might call it selfish, but I called it inevitable.

WHEN I ARRIVED HOME, I FOUND A SMALL MAN WITH DARK HAIR and blue eyes, his brown suit wrinkled from traveling, conversing with my wife in the sitting room. The man rose as I entered to hold out a neatly gloved hand.

"Captain Lacey. Well met. Well met, indeed." He beamed, very glad to see me.

"Mr. Quimby." I shook his hand, both pleased and trepidatious.

I'd first met Lamont Quimby, Runner from the Whitechapel house, earlier this year when he'd been sent to investigate a murder in St. Giles in London, one I'd feared Brewster had committed.

I'd gone to the Whitechapel magistrate, Sir Montague Harris, who'd become a friend, to ask for his help, fearing the zeal of Pomeroy and the vindictiveness of Spendlove. Sir Montague had provided Quimby.

Mr. Quimby was far quieter than Pomeroy and more careful. Runners worked for rewards they received upon conviction—the more wanted a man, the higher the reward. Quimby had struck me as being interested in truth rather than reward, though I suspected he gladly took the money when his man was convicted.

"I wish this could be a more cheerful reunion," Mr. Quimby said, releasing me. "Her ladyship has been explaining things."

"An even sadder mystery has just occurred." I waved Mr. Quimby to a seat and told him about Josh Bickley.

Donata looked stricken. "Oh, Gabriel, I didn't realize it was your Mr. Bickley's son. How awful. I am so sorry."

"Truly, a sad tale," Quimby said. "Do you know if the young man had any connection to Colonel Isherwood?"

I thought, but had to shake my head. "I do not see how. Mr. Bickley's son was a pious Quaker, having nothing to do with army men. The Friends are pacifists, and live simply. I doubt Josh would have gone near either the luxurious Pavilion or Preston Barracks."

"But he went missing before Colonel Isherwood died," Mr. Quimby said in his thoughtful way. "Perhaps young Master Bickley encountered the colonel's killer and was silenced. How long has the lad been dead?"

"From the look of things, a few days perhaps? I really could not say." In the army, I'd been able to judge how long a man had lain dead on the battlefield, but that had been on dry land. Water, especially salt water, changed things.

"I will inquire of the coroner," Quimby said. "He might, of course, have been a victim of an unfortunate accident."

"Not if he hated boats. Why should he have been in one?"

"Precisely," Quimby said. "I will have to find out." He turned to Donata. "I thank you for receiving me, your ladyship. I will have to speak to your husband and hear his rendition of the tale of Colonel Isherwood, but then I will leave you in peace."

"Of course." Donata sent him a gracious nod. "You will not be disturbed here. I am happy to leave everything in your hands, Mr. Quimby."

Quimby gave her a bow—I could see he was taken with Donata—and she glided from the room.

As Bartholomew, who'd sprung to open the door for her, closed it once more behind her, Quimby sobered.

"I will tell you plainly, Captain, that if I did not know you to be an honorable gentleman, I would, upon hearing your wife's story, immediately believe Colonel Isherwood's murderer had been you."

I acknowledged this, feeling bleak. "I wish I could explain exactly what I had done that night, and state with conviction that I did *not* kill him."

"I understand. Sir Montague Harris speaks highly of you. Very highly, and I agree. Sir Montague thinks so of very few. He was most pleased that I should journey down and discover what has happened. He promises discretion, but he is a man of justice." Quimby met my gaze. "As am I."

"I would not expect you to be otherwise," I said quickly. "Mrs. Lacey wrote to you because she trusts you." I cleared my throat. "But if you discover that the culprit is indeed me, I am willing to bear the consequences."

Quimby studied me with quiet eyes, as though wondering if my resolve was firm. "Take me through the evening, Captain." He seated himself at Donata's delicate writing table and drew from his pocket a worn notebook and small box that contained quills and ink.

Ignoring the rosewood and gold inlaid inkstand that adorned the desk, he dipped his pen into his plain bottle and scratched a few words into his notebook.

"Please begin," he said.

I paced as I spoke, too agitated to sit. "My wife and I received an invitation to dine at the Pavilion Monday night—Mrs. Lacey and the Regent are old friends, as are the Regent and Grenville. The majordomo took us and the other guests around the finished rooms so we could admire them. I avoided Colonel Isherwood, to be honest, and spoke mostly with Grenville and Alvanley—Lord Alvanley and I share an interest in horses.

"Eventually we went into supper. I enjoyed the food, though the conversation was not to my taste. When we weren't praising the Regent on the cleverness of the Pavilion, there was talk of farming and what sort of yields were expected this year, and the general state of the country. The Regent excused himself before the pudding was even served, but no one was surprised. He is easily bored, and his gout must make things uncomfortable. After supper ..." I paused.

"This is where things grow hazy. I know I spoke with Isherwood while we drank port, and it was not a congenial conversation. When I left the house, Isherwood was alive and well, growling he had to rise early and go to the barracks. I more or less remember walking with Grenville through the Steine, but not about what we said, or exactly when he left me." I ceased pacing and faced Quimby. "The next thing I knew, I was standing over Isherwood's body, his sword in my hand ..."

Quimby scribbled in his book, his pen loud in the stillness. "How did you feel?" he asked without looking up. "In body, I mean, when you came to yourself?"

"Horrible." I shuddered. "The room was cool, and I was shaking but blistering hot at the same time. My mouth was powerfully dry, and I had pain in every limb. When I finally reached home, I had unnerving nightmares and slept the day away without realizing it. My friends believe I was given some potion..."

Mr. Quimby lifted his head. "Indeed, such a sudden illness in so healthy a gentleman might indicate poison of some sort. You ate and drank the same things as everyone at the supper?"

"As far as I know. The footmen served us out of the same dishes, poured wine out of the same decanters or bottles."

"Hmm." Quimby carefully blotted his page with another piece of paper, and then leafed back through the book. "Your wife told me that you had pieced together a few more things. You spoke to the Quakers between leaving Mr. Grenville in the Steine and waking up to find Colonel Isherwood. When you saw Mr. Bickley yesterday, he asked you to help find the missing Joshua, who is now deceased."

I nodded regretfully. "Joshua and another woman—Miss

Purkis. Or perhaps Mrs. Purkis—I am not certain whether she is spinster, wife, or widow." I hoped very much that whoever she was, she had not come to the same end as Josh.

Another jot of the pen. "Have you remembered anything else since then?"

I closed my eyes to think, blotting out the fine sunshine streaming over the garden, the scent of sea in the air.

"No," I had to say. "I've had odd feelings and a few flashes, but when I try to grasp them, they are gone."

Quimby made another note before he laid down his pen. "I would like to speak to Colonel Isherwood's son. Can you arrange that for me, Captain?"

"I will." I hesitated. "I do not blame him trying to keep the murder quiet—journalists would make a meal of it, especially since it happened at the Pavilion. Will you follow his wishes?"

"As I assured you, I am a man of discretion." Mr. Quimby shut his notebook and rose. "Even so, a man has been killed, violently. I will not announce my intentions regarding Colonel Isherwood, but I *will* find who killed him and make an arrest. What the colonel's son wishes to do after that is up to him, of course."

"Of course," was all I could say in response.

"And now it seems we might have to find out who killed young Mr. Bickley. That death can obviously *not* be kept quiet, but will provide a plausible reason for me to be here, if an unfortunate one." He let out a breath. "Well, I certainly will have much to do."

Quimby gave me his affable smile as he shook my hand and took his leave. I accompanied him to the front door, which a footman opened for him, and I watched him walk steadily down the lane.

I reflected that the small Runner who took quick, firm

steps, moving aside for and tipping his hat to a passing lady and gentleman, might be the most dangerous man in England. Mr. Quimby was quiet and unremarkable, yet he worked with an efficient ruthlessness that could topple the most violent of criminals.

I hoped he would not have cause to topple me.

I SENT A MESSAGE TO GRENVILLE AFTER THAT, ASKING HIM TO set up a time when I could speak to Lord Armitage. I wanted to know what had jarred me so much upon seeing him and his wife at the lecture. I ought also to meet with others who had been at the meal. Grenville should be able to arrange things so that the encounters wouldn't seem unusual.

While waiting for his response, I continued to be doting husband and father, suggesting a promenade before our evening activities. We had all been distressed about the death of Josh Bickley, and a walk in the fresh air would do us good.

It was fine to stroll arm in arm with Donata, she staving off the bright sunshine with a parasol, Gabriella carrying a matching one. Peter ran about on the shingle, playing games only he knew the rules to. At one point, Donata and Gabriella walked out to meet Peter, but I preferred to remain on the road, not as easy on the shingle with my bad leg.

I reflected as I watched them that our dog, Oro, would have enjoyed running on the beach and into the water. However, we'd had to leave the fellow at Donata's father's estate in Oxfordshire, Donata rightly pointing out that our very small house in Brighton, which had no stables, had nowhere to put up a large dog.

As I waited for my family to return, a woman emerged

from a nearby house and headed in my direction. Behind her came a gentleman in a well-made if not fashionable suit.

The woman had grown somewhat plumper than I remembered but there was no mistaking her. I stared in surprise as she halted before me, but she seemed not surprised at all.

"Captain Lacey, well met." She held out a hand. "You recall me, surely? Marguerite Gibbons. At least, I have added the *Gibbons* since Spain."

I should not be amazed, and yet I was. She'd written her friend that she'd settled in the south of England, and her former husband had just been murdered.

The woman who stood before me was Marguerite Isherwood, Colonel Isherwood's rejected wife.

CHAPTER 9

*M*arguerite regarded me with a twinkle of amusement, relishing that she'd rendered me mute.

Seven years had not aged her much. Her dark hair held no gray, her face no lines. Gone was the bitter self-deprecation that had once marked her, but otherwise, her cheeks were as pink, her stance as upright, her smile as broad.

Her hand, covered in thin leather, remained outstretched. Awkwardly, I took it.

The man who'd followed her stepped to her side, extending his hand when Marguerite withdrew hers. "William Gibbons, sir, at your service."

I made myself follow formalities. "Captain Gabriel Lacey."

"An old friend from army days." Marguerite's voice held merriment. "When I followed the drum on the Peninsula."

Her gaze dropped to my walking stick and the leg it supported, but she refrained from comment. I'd been a whole man when she'd last seen me.

Mr. Gibbons, like his suit, was plain, no handsomeness in

his face. But it was a comfortable face, with brown eyes that were pleasantly crinkled, his hair brushed with gray. A man one would enjoy chatting with down the pub.

"Pleased to hear he is a friend," Mr. Gibbons said to his wife. "Those were unhappy times."

"They were indeed trying," Marguerite replied. "Captain Lacey was ever courteous."

I swallowed a cough. "Thank you," was all I could manage.

Marguerite's smile deepened. "I find myself in much more agreeable circumstances now." She took her husband's arm.

Mr. Gibbons gave me a nod, his pride obvious. "Yes, I am the most fortunate of men."

Divorce, I well knew, carried a stigma for both the divorced wife and the husband, as well as anyone who married either. Scandal followed them, whispers continued. Yet Gibbons had been happy to marry Marguerite, scandal be damned.

Isherwood was dead now, making Marguerite a true widow.

Mr. Gibbons glanced at someone behind me and made an abrupt and deep bow. Marguerite released his arm and dropped into a respectful curtsy.

"Your ladyship," she murmured.

I was aware of Donata coming to rest beside me, her warmth cutting the sudden chill of the summer breeze. She smelled of wind and the sun, dust from the shingle beach.

"Good evening," she said politely.

Marguerite and Mr. Gibbons returned the greeting deferentially and then said nothing more. One did not converse freely with a daughter of the peerage unless they had been introduced. The fact that they knew she was an earl's daughter and viscount's widow did not surprise me. Our marriage had been announced and speculated about in every newspaper.

"Mr. and Mrs. Gibbons," I explained awkwardly to Donata. "Visitors to Brighton." I turned to them. "My wife, Lady Breckenridge."

"*Mrs. Lacey,*" Donata corrected me as she gave the Gibbonses a neutral smile. "The sunshine is lovely, is it not? Such a change from London's dreariness."

A safe and expected thing to say. We all agreed the weather in Brighton was far superior to London's smoky gloom.

Donata ended the conversation. "Enjoy your evening. Forgive me—I must ask the captain to drag our son from the water before he becomes a fish."

After polite chuckles, another "Your Ladyship," and a curtsy and bow, Donata nodded regally and led me off.

I remained silent as I trudged clumsily across the shingle and a few paces into the sea to lift Peter from it. He was not happy to leave his impromptu swum, but he clung to me as I hoisted him to my shoulder and carried him out.

When I glanced to the promenade once more, Marguerite and her husband had gone.

Donata did not mention the encounter on the walk home. Though Gabriella was clearly curious, she said nothing, perhaps sensing my tension. When we reached the house, Donata admonished Peter for submerging his shoes and getting his trousers wet to the knees, then adjourned to her rooms to ready herself for supper.

I returned to my own to change myself, but Donata soon entered my chamber through the dressing room between.

"Gabriel?" she said as she threaded a diamond earring through her earlobe. "Are you quite well? When you were speaking to those people, you became an interesting shade of green. I thought you'd be ill. Are you still weak from whatever concoction you were given?"

I wanted suddenly to sit, but it would be discourteous while my wife stood. I leaned one arm on the mantelpiece, wishing the cold hearth contained a fire.

"She was Isherwood's wife," I said.

Donata froze, her fingers at her ear. She stared at me for several ticks of the clock before she slid the earring all the way in and did up the delicate clasp.

"I see." Her voice was wintery.

"I could hardly point this out while we stood on the promenade," I said. "Nor did I wish to say anything in front of Gabriella and Peter."

"Quite."

"I had no idea she was in Brighton."

"Obviously not," Donata said. "Your color indicated her presence was a blow. Mr. Gibbons is her second husband, I take it. Does he know you were her lover?"

Donata enjoyed being blunt. She'd once explained that it was much easier to voice unpleasant truths and be done than to dance around them for days.

"From his manner, I would say no, he does not," I answered. "I did not enlighten him."

"No reason you should. Interesting she has turned up now that Isherwood is dead."

"Perhaps her stepson sent for her. He would naturally write her of the incident."

"True," Donata said.

She remained composed, but I saw the anger deep in her eyes. I considered apologizing, but I wasn't certain how to word things or what I was apologizing for. I had no intention of taking up with Marguerite again, and likewise, Marguerite seemed happy with Mr. Gibbons. She obviously no longer had interest in me.

I'd never been an eloquent man, and as I struggled to wrap these thoughts into phrases that would not anger Donata further, Jacinthe glided in from the dressing room.

Only Jacinthe could interrupt a tête-à-tête between Donata and me, no matter how heated our argument. Donata turned away, her mouth a thin line.

"Message for you, sir." Jacinthe held out a sealed piece of paper. She hovered as I opened the letter, no doubt waiting for a response.

"It is from Grenville," I announced. "He wishes to meet. Or rather, he summons me to him."

Donata's voice was cool. "You ought to go then. He'd not write if it weren't important."

"True." I nodded to Jacinthe, who curtsied and departed, answer received.

"Give him my best wishes," Donata said stiffly.

Donata prided herself on pretending extreme indifference as to my comings and goings—a wife should not live in her husband's pocket, she said—but I could see she was not pleased.

I would not mind at all having her next to me most of the time, but it apparently was not the done thing in our world. I took her hands, leaning to kiss her cheek. "I will return forthwith."

I thought I saw a slight softening in her eyes, but I could not be certain. I kissed her again, and departed.

GRENVILLE DID NOT NOTICE MY AGITATION WHEN I ARRIVED AT his house a quarter of an hour later. He waved a paper at me.

"I have set an appointment with a few of our companions

from the Regent's supper table," he announced. "Comte Desjardins is home and will welcome our visit."

Brewster, as usual, accompanied us as we set off on foot to Desjardins' lodgings. Grenville rarely walked anywhere in London, using his carriage or phaeton to keep his pristine boots from the mud, but during this sojourn he was delighting in tramping everywhere.

Comte Desjardins had taken a residence not far from our square, in a new house on the west end of town. Brewster made his stolid way down the outside stairs to the kitchen while a footman admitted Grenville and me through the front door.

We followed the footman up a flight of stairs to a sitting room filled with light. The room faced the sea, and the late evening sunshine flooded it.

That sunlight touched the long barrel of a gun, which was pointed straight at us.

CHAPTER 10

$\mathcal{I}$ instinctively stepped sideways to my right, out of
the line of fire. Grenville ducked aside as well. I
noticed that the footman had quickly vanished down the stairs.

"Steady on," Grenville said sternly.

Comte Desjardins, his round face flushed under a shock of
pale hair, did not move the shotgun. "It is no matter," he
answered in French. "It is not loaded."

He pulled the trigger to demonstrate.

An explosion sounded, gunpowder bursting from the
firing pan. A scattering of shot whizzed between me and
Grenville and out the open doorway, pockmarking the hall's
paneling.

The comte, a tall, well-muscled man, tanned from the
outdoors, blinked blue eyes at the gun. "Ah. I am so very sorry."
He'd switched to English, his accent heavy, and now returned
to French. "It is a Purdey. A gift for me from the Regent. I hear
they are very fine guns for hunting."

He lowered the piece, and I breathed out, lingering
gunpowder stinging my eyes and throat. How the devil the

man hadn't realized the gun was loaded was beyond my under-
standing. He was either a liar or a fool.

Pounding footsteps sounded on the stairs and seconds later,
Brewster tumbled into the room. "Guv!"

Before I could stop him, Brewster lunged forward and
wrested the gun from the startled comte's hands, pointing the
barrel to the floor.

"What daftie would shoot off a birding gun inside a parlor?"
Brewster demanded.

Desjardins began snarling at him in French, and Brewster
backed away, still holding the gun.

"Can't understand a word he says," Brewster said. "Same
below stairs."

Grenville came forward to interpose. "Forgive our servant,"
he said to Desjardins in French. "He feared we'd been killed.
He'll take the gun away and clean it for you. As you say, it is a
fine piece." Grenville touched a gloved finger to the barrel in
Brewster's arms.

Even I'd heard of James Purdey, a manufacturer of fowling
pieces and guns in a shop in Princes Street near Hanover
Square. His weaponry was highly praised and widely sought
after by the *haut ton*.

Desjardins relaxed. "It was a mistake. I said I was very
sorry. The man who delivered it from the Regent never told
me it was loaded and primed. A joke, I think."

"One in poor taste," Grenville said tightly.

I translated to Brewster what Grenville had said and
advised him to take the gun to the stable yard behind the house
for the task. Brewster gave me a sour look.

"Not leaving you alone with a bloke what aimed a gun at
you. He wants the thing cleaned, I'll sit here in this room and
do it. He might pull out a knife next."

Ordering Brewster to do a thing he did not want to was useless, I knew. Grenville, always the diplomat, asked leave to ring for a servant, whom he bade bring tools so Brewster could begin, as well as a sheet to protect the carpet.

The bemused footman, the same who'd showed us upstairs, complied, and Brewster fell to it, taking apart the gun with the dexterity of a professional.

The comte sent him a worried look. "That shooter is quite fine. Will the oaf ruin it?"

The "oaf" did not understand French, and continued with his task. "I trust Mr. Brewster," I answered.

Brewster glanced up as I said his name and scowled, not trusting *me*.

"A splendid gift," Grenville said. "The Regent was generous."

"He was." Desjardins lifted his chin, his pride apparent.

I was not certain what to make of the man. At supper, Desjardins had sat several seats down from me and had devoted most of his conversation to Lady Armitage. When he had joined in with the rest of us, he was loud about keeping the lower classes in their places and mourning that he'd had to leave a large estate in France because of said lower classes.

He regarded us both affably now, chagrined about his mistake in firing the gun, but with a gleam of amusement in his eyes. Grenville watched him coolly.

"You've lived in England many years," I remarked to Desjardins. His suit resembled Grenville's and must have been made by a Bond Street tailor. He also wore scent, a dark spice that spoke of the best perfumery in London.

Desjardins flushed, his amusement dying. "A bit rude of you to point out my exile, sir. I feel it keenly."

"Your pardon. I only meant you would have had time to cultivate the Regent's friendship."

"Ah. Yes, that is so." Desjardins brightened. "The prince has been good to me and my family." He glanced out the window. "I have never grown fond England, if you must know. There is much rain, and I am not used to the dreary flatness of the land. In the south of France, we have high mountains and deep valleys, so dramatic."

He could not have traveled much in Britain, then, which had plenty of mountains and valleys in the north and the west. I'd grown up in Norfolk, very flat country, which I'd too found dreary as a youth, though I appreciated its beauty these days.

"Life is easier in France now for aristocrats, is it not?" I asked pretending to be ingenuous. "As the monarchy has been restored."

"But for how long?" Desjardins shook his head. "Already the king's cousin, d'Orleans, makes noises that he ought to be on the throne, where he will create an assembly like Britain's Parliament. Bah." He skirted Brewster and made for a full decanter on the sideboard. "Such an assembly will only tear power from him and begin evicting us once again. Our time is over."

His despondency was genuine as he filled glasses with brandy and carried them to us.

"Thank you," Grenville said, accepting his. "At least you can have *this* again." He raised his glass.

"Yes, yes." Desjardins nodded. "Now that the long war is over, we can have brandy once more."

"Without resorting to smuggling." Grenville laughed, took a sip, and made a satisfied noise. "Quite fine.

"Indeed, indeed." Desjardins drank, face flushing.

I wondered at his sudden nervousness. *Had* Desjardins been

a brandy smuggler? Grenville had indicated he'd lived well in spite of having to flee France. Brandy could bring a high price from Englishmen who'd not wanted to do without it.

"May I speak with you about our supper the other night?" I asked after we'd drunk. "At the Pavilion?"

Desjardins gave me a blank stare. "Yes, why not? The Pavilion is a garish monstrosity, is it not?"

"It is unfinished, yet," Grenville said generously. "And Mr. Nash is a gifted architect."

"Perhaps." Desjardins waved Mr. Nash away. "What is the question? I barely remember what I ate—it was so bland."

"Colonel Isherwood," I cut in, unable to wait for Grenville to work his way around to the important points. "He died that night."

Did I see a flicker of worry in Desjardins' expression? Or did I simply wish to?

"Yes, I heard. Took ill. He was a boorish fellow—I'm not surprised if he had an attack of bile." Desjardins paused, his eyes widening. "You don't mean that something was wrong with the food? Good Lord, I ate plenty, even if it was vile stuff."

"No." I needed to shut down that train of thought. "Nothing to do with the food or drink."

"Well, that is a mercy." Desjardins took a long gulp of brandy. "I didn't like him, but poor fellow."

"Yes." I hardly knew how to ask my questions without violating Isherwood's son's wish that the murder stay quiet, but Desjardins' rather vacuous expression gave me hope he'd not tumble to what had truly happened. "Did Isherwood speak to you of anything in particular?" I ventured. "Or indicate he'd meet anyone after supper?"

I trailed off as Desjardins sent me a peculiar look. As I hesitated, he turned from me and carried his empty glass to the sideboard. "Do you not remember, Captain? Or are you testing *my* memory?"

"I'm afraid I was a bit inebriated myself. If the colonel shared his plans, I missed it."

Another stare, and Desjardins' voice hardened. "I do not know how you could have. You and he had a fierce altercation. Not in front of company, but I saw."

"Saw what?" Grenville asked. "I admit I do not remember this myself."

Desjardins pointed a sturdy finger at Grenville. "*You* were parading your lady wife about and fending off questions about her origins. I thought the company uncivil—why should you not marry a backstreet actress if you wish? The captain and Isherwood stepped into an anteroom. I followed, hoping to find more port there. You did not see me, and when I heard your argument, I kept to the shadows to not embarrass you."

"As I said, I had taken too much drink," I said, keeping my voice steady. "The events of the evening are a blur."

"Mmm." Desjardins clearly did not believe me. "He threatened to kill you over an old slight—something to do with the Peninsula." He fluttered his hand as though uninterested in what the slight was. "You clearly stated that if he tried, you'd defend yourself, even if it meant his death. You were quite adamant. Lost your temper, I'd say. The violence in your words made me shiver. I withdrew and heard nothing more. Rather lucky for you he dropped dead of an illness that night, or you might have been charged with his murder."

"THE FRENCHIE TELLS THAT STORY TO A MAGISTRATE, YER DONE

for," Brewster declared as we walked from Desjardins' house. "Everyone knows you're good at threatening people."

Grenville had related the conversation to Brewster at his demand once we'd taken our leave. Desjardins hadn't had much to add after he'd told me of my threat to Isherwood, which I did not remember, try as I might.

He'd started back in on the gaudiness of the Pavilion, the dull food, and the generosity of the Regent in giving him the gun, which Brewster had cleaned and reassembled for him. Brewster had laid the gun aside, unloaded, rather than hand it back to Desjardins.

"I'd prefer another witness to the encounter," Grenville said. "Several, in fact. Isherwood is dead, and Desjardins says you threatened the man, but it is only his word. He could be inventing the tale for his own amusement. He seems to enjoy stirring things up."

"It is plausible, unfortunately," I said. I closed my mouth, knowing full well what I had begun to argue with Isherwood about.

"He tried to kill *you*," Brewster growled. "The Frenchie, I mean. Shot that fowler right at you."

"An accident," Grenville said, but he did not sound convinced.

"Not possible he didn't ken it were loaded," Brewster said. "Thing was full of powder and wadding, the pan nicely primed. Weighs more when loaded too. He's lying, or he knows sod-all about guns."

I had thought the same. "Why would he shoot me—or Grenville—in so obvious a fashion? Why would he wish to? No, he must simply be a fool, or entertaining himself with us."

And yet, I'd seen the cunning in Desjardins, a cunning that

must have kept him alive and made him wealthy when his family's compatriots had gone, bankrupt, to the guillotine.

We parted ways at my door, but tonight we'd meet again at the Steine for a fete and fireworks which all the town would attend.

I dined by myself, as Donata was out at calls, Gabriella with her. Peter had already gone to bed. I reflected upon what I had learned from Desjardins, which was little except that I had argued with Isherwood.

I drew my fork across the thick sauce that coated my beef. We had also learned that Desjardins was rude and spat his opinions while pretending to be naive. He'd insulted Marianne and Grenville with his comment about her being a "backstreet actress," referred to Brewster as an oaf, and stated that I had a harsh and brutal temper.

This last was true, and made my appetite fade. While I could not trust my memory about all the events of Monday night, I had attacked men before. I had killed them in battle, instinct making me shoot and stab until I lived and my enemy died.

A year ago, I'd had no qualm about aiming my pistol at a lout called Stubbins who'd beaten a young woman of my acquaintance. The fact that I'd shot him in the arm instead of through the heart was because of my contempt for him, not because I'd feared the noose.

I was perfectly capable of committing murder, and I knew it.

In this mood, I dressed myself, with Bartholomew's assistance, for the night's outing.

"Mr. Grenville wants to return to London, so Matthias says," Bartholomew informed me as he tied my cravat.

"Does he?" I regarded Bartholomew in surprise. "He never said so."

"He don't like to. But he told Matthias we should let the magistrates here decide a wandering madman killed Colonel Isherwood. Nothing to do with us."

Grenville had to have known that Matthias would tell his brother this tale, and Bartholomew, the brother in question, would relate it to me.

"London is devilish hot and miserable at the moment," I said. "Are you certain he said he wants to be there?"

"Well, his estate, then," Bartholomew amended. "Inviting you and her ladyship, of course."

"Tempting." I made myself stand still while Bartholomew ran a brush over my already immaculate suit. "But I'd rather remain and discover what truly happened. Withdrawing my head like a tortoise will not change matters."

Bartholomew shrugged. "Won't help her ladyship if you're arrested."

"It will be hell for all of us. But if I did this deed ..." I shook my head. "I cannot push it off onto another."

"Mr. Grenville has a nice residence in the Italian states, sir. Two, in fact. One near Venice and one south of Rome."

I looked straight at him. "You suggest I retreat to one of these places?"

Bartholomew flushed. "If you must, sir. Be a better place for her ladyship and the youngsters than watching you be dragged to Newgate."

I could not say he was wrong. "I am hoping it is a monstrous mistake." I glanced into the mirror to see that my hair was already escaping the careful combings Bartholomew had spent the last half hour on. "But I will keep it in mind. A house south of Rome would be handy for the ruins of Herculaneum and Pompeii."

"As you say, Captain." He was humoring me. I finished dressing without bothering to continue the discussion.

Donata had returned home as I'd dressed, and Gabriella and I waited downstairs for her to change for the evening. I did not mind the wait, as I welcomed the time to speak with my daughter. We did not talk of important things, but the little pleasantries of the day and her interest in the people Lady Aline took her to meet. Another father might grow listless at his daughter's chatter, but I treasured every moment of it.

Donata spoke little as we rode in the carriage to the Steine gardens, and not at all to me. Her coolness unnerved me, but I chose to say nothing for the moment.

I tried to admire the gardens lit with lanterns and the walks lined with bright summer flowers, pale now in the darkness, but I could find little joy in them. The fact that all of Brighton laughed and played under the stars when Joshua Bickley had died rather horribly made me unhappy. But he'd been an ordinary lad, and a Quaker, nothing to do with the wealthy gentry who'd come to Brighton for the sea air and company. They'd already forgotten him.

I saw no sign of any of the Friends, though I had not expected to. To my relief, I saw no sign of Marguerite Gibbons either.

As usual on our nightly outings, Donata was greeted by her friends, who were eager to sweep her away. Gabriella glanced longingly back at me as she dutifully put her hand on Donata's arm and strolled off with her.

Grenville met me on one of the long paths, he too alone. Marianne had her own acquaintances in Brighton and had fallen in with them, so Grenville and I wandered by ourselves, though not for long. Grenville, ever popular, was quickly hailed.

One of the gentlemen who caught up to us was Lord Armitage. This time upon seeing him, I did not feel the strange dizziness that had come over me when I'd spied him at the lecture.

I recalled what Lady Aline had told me about his history, and wondered how easily he rested knowing his lady had married him only because his brother had died. They'd seemed companionable enough at the supper and lecture, but who knew what truly went on in a marriage?

Lord Armitage had a large voice and the booming confidence of a man few contradicted. He had dark hair and light green eyes, and though he was not very tall, he had the muscular physique of a man who kept his daily port and beefsteak from settling on his body.

"Grenville." He engulfed Grenville's hand. "And Captain Lacey." He gripped me with excessive power. "I heard Desjardins nearly potted you today, the ass."

"Indeed." Grenville touched the side of his head. "I had to confirm that my ear was still attached."

"He's a blunderer with a blunderbuss." Armitage bellowed laughter at his joke. "He means no harm, the dullard. Never has adjusted to English ways."

"If he left France during the Terror he's been here nearly thirty years," I said.

"Indeed. And yet ..." Armitage threw out his arms. "I spent plenty of time on the Continent and Peninsula, as you know. Never could understand the Portuguese. Their language sounds like Spanish but isn't, and those black cloaks they wear —like medieval monks. Very strange."

"Those were students," I said. The universities at Oporto

and Coimbra had swarmed with young men in swirling black, much like what young gentlemen wore in the Inns of Court in London. "They dress in the cloaks."

"Can't think why," Armitage said with good humor.

Grenville lifted his quizzing glass but did not gaze through it. "A strange attitude for a diplomat," he said. "Are you not supposed to be ... diplomatic?"

Armitage found this hilarious. "When I'm at the negotiating table, I know how to push through a treaty, never fear. But I mean the habits of the common folk of these countries were a mystery to me. Couldn't ever make them out, whether in Spain, the Austrian Empire, or Venice. Glad to return home, my plenipotentiary days behind me."

Several young men in the latest stare of fashion—coats bright yellow, pantaloons billowing—dashed past us, laughing and swearing in high-pitched voices. Grenville regarded them with raised brows.

Armitage, not noticing them, turned his gaze on me. "You landed well when you reached home after Spain, did you not, Captain? Rich widow, eh? La Breckenridge is quite a catch."

Something hot pinched between my eyes. "I will thank you to speak civilly of my wife, sir."

Another laugh. "To be certain, to be certain. No offense, Lacey. Desjardins tells me you asked him about Isherwood. You and he were at odds all night. I remember the colonel from my brief time on the Peninsula. You once had a tendresse for *his* wife, I recall hearing."

My voice chilled further, even as I made note that he and Isherwood had been acquainted in the past. "Nothing I intend to discuss," I said.

"A gentleman doesn't talk about his affairs, and all that rot, eh?" Armitage said. "*She* wasn't much of a lady, in fact. Isherwood was well rid of her."

Grenville sent him a cool look. "I say, have a care, Armitage."

"You mean the Captain might defend her honor? Why should he? It was all in the past. Mrs. Isherwood is likely rollicking through France by now with every comte in the place—or she's long dead."

"She is happily married," I told him. "To a respectable gentleman. Grenville is correct—you should have a care."

"Marguerite Isherwood is married?" Armitage's mouth gaped open. "Are you certain?"

"I have met the man. Today, in fact. Mrs. Gibbons, as she is called now, seems quite content with him."

Armitage's mouth went even more slack. "Good Lord. You mean the wretched creature is *here?*"

"Yes," I answered, my anger rising. "I must ask you to please cease speaking of her altogether."

Armitage continued to stare at me, then an expression of peculiar glee came over him. "Oh, but you don't know, my dear fellow, do you?"

He was longing for me to say *Know what?* so I remained silent.

His expression turned to one of pity. "You truly do *not* know, I see. Mrs. Isherwood—or Mrs. Gibbons, if the marriage is true—was a damned spy. Indeed, Captain, though you are amazed. She was never caught at it, but yes, she was a spy for the bloody Corsican."

CHAPTER 11

*T*he breeze that slid between the trees had a sudden icy bite.

"You are claiming Mrs. Gibbons worked for Bonaparte?" Grenville said as my mouth refused to move. "Again, I say, have a care Armitage. Slander can be costly."

"Ha," Armitage barked. "Why do you suppose Isherwood put her aside? Nothing could be proved, but he could not afford to have her near. Rumors about her would ruin his career, wouldn't it?"

I at last found my voice. "I find this highly unlikely."

"She had many an officer in her snare, both English and French," Armitage said in enjoyment. "She passed information right under Wellington's nose."

His declaration gave me pause. I admitted I hadn't known much about Marguerite, but she hadn't seemed the sort to betray her country to Napoleon.

I remembered her as a vivacious woman but one devastated by the failure of her marriage. She'd been defiant but also hurt and dazed. Our conversations, what there had been of them, had been on any topic *but* cavalry maneuvers or plans to push the French army out of Spain. Not that I would have been privy to such plans, in any case.

"She could hardly have pried important information from me," I said. "I was a junior captain in Salamanca, never called in to discuss strategy. I never knew where I'd be going until the day of the battle. Even then it wasn't always clear."

Armitage's eyes twinkled in the darkness. "Even so, Captain. She might have mistaken your importance—or perhaps she was simply taking her leisure with you. Her machinations no doubt wearied her after a time, and she sought amusement."

He had the same irritating habit of tossing off insults as did Desjardins.

"You knew the Isherwoods well, did you?" I asked, drumming my fingers on the head of my walking stick.

"Barely at all. I encountered them socially from time to time, as Isherwood comes from an old and highly regarded family. But I heard quite a lot about them. Everyone did." *Except you, apparently*, his amused look implied.

"In other words, you impugn her character without evidence," I said.

Armitage gave me a mocking bow. "I have heard you are quite the gentleman with the ladies. The war is over now, but do not relax your guard. Women like Marguerite never cease. And you say she is here in Brighton?" This seemed to bother him, though he kept up the bonhomie.

"With her husband."

"Whom you say is an ordinary chap. Ha. Probably a bloody spy as well."

"I say, Armitage," Grenville said in a pained voice. "You will find yourself on one end of a dueling green if you continue to fling such accusations about."

Armitage let out a laugh. "I am joking, my friends. Speculation and amusement about a nobody. I trust none of our words tonight will be repeated?"

He cast a warning gaze at us both, the aristocrat commanding his inferiors.

Grenville's quizzing glass was now at his eye. "Of course they will not be." The iciness in his tone chilled the air. "It is never a question."

Armitage had the grace to look embarrassed. "Forgive me, Grenville, but you have not met the gentlemen I have in my life. Diplomats are the least trustworthy people in existence. And upon them hang the fate of nations."

I wondered if he included himself in that number.

Armitage liked to dominate, I could see. He wanted control of a place, a conversation, and what was said when his friends left him. I wondered if that control had extended to his brother, to the point of deciding that the woman who was to marry that brother would be better off with Armitage himself.

To give him the benefit of doubt, war played arbitrary tricks on people's lives, altering them forever, as it had altered mine. There was nothing to say his brother had simply not stood in the wrong place at the wrong time.

Armitage took his leave of us and breezily walked away, heading toward the lighted part of the green from which the fireworks would be viewed.

Grenville dropped his quizzing glass into its pocket then removed a handkerchief and dabbed his mouth as though he'd tasted something foul.

"His is an old title," he said, tucking the handkerchief away. "Which makes him believe himself untouchable. My family is far more lofty than his, but as I am a distant twig, he dismisses me. You, of course, are a dust mote in his very small mind."

"So I gathered." I leaned on my stick, my energy giving way. "His accusation of Mrs. Isherwood is unlikely, in my opinion. She was an unhappy woman, ill-used. She does not deserve more dishonor piled upon her."

Grenville was looking me up and down, his famous brows high.

"Is something amiss?" I asked tersely.

"You are a man of great reserve, Lacey. You know my entire history, while bits and pieces of yours turn up at the oddest times."

"Not quite. You had a daughter you kept to yourself."

"*I* never knew I had a daughter until the fact was slapped in my face." He took on a fond look. "She is doing well, by the way. Gained much applause for her portrayal of Portia at Drury Lane this spring."

"So I have heard." Grenville's obvious pride in Claire Bennington would divert me any other time. "Forgive me if I have not provided you a list of my paramours from the time I was able to understand what one did with a woman until my present marriage. It would hardly be kind to the ladies."

"That is not what I mean, which you know very well," Grenville returned. "But I would have thought *this* information relevant, as the woman's husband has been murdered." He let out a sigh. "Unfortunately your affair with Mrs. Isherwood makes you still more of a suspect. Gentlemen have battled over ladies before. Do regularly, in fact."

"It was a long time ago." I heard the weakness of the statement even as I said it. "She was far better off without the blackguard Isherwood. Why should I fight him about her now?"

Grenville rubbed a finger under his lip. "I'd love for your memory of the night to come flooding back."

"As would I." I tamped down despair as the emptiness of those hours rose up to mock me. "But I've lost time before when inebriated. I may never recall what happened."

"I doubt you went temporarily mad." Grenville must have read my unhappiness, because he put a kind hand on my shoulder. "Never fear, my friend. We will discover what occurred and why you were dosed and by who. We will pull together and not let you down." He removed his comforting touch. "However, you must oblige me by telling me the tale of you and Mrs. Isherwood. Then we will decide whether Armitage is correct about her, or if he is simply being a fathead."

My uncertainty about the question bothered me. I believed my assessment of Marguerite the true one, but Armitage had sowed doubt.

I noted the crowd gathering on the green. "The fireworks are about to begin."

"Indeed. Let us return to our happy families and enjoy ourselves."

Grenville gave me an encouraging nod and led the way back to civilization.

GRENVILLE REJOINED MARIANNE, AND WAS SOON SURROUNDED by her friends—actors and actresses who were quite taken with him. I broke from them after a few moments to seek my wife and daughter.

The Steine was very dark beyond the lantern-lit main path. While the park had a simple layout, there were patches under trees that were inky black, a perfect trysting spot for lovers or a hiding place for robbers.

I fancied I spied Lady Aline Carrington, or at least her outlandish headdress, feathers waving above a large turban. Donata and Gabriella would be near her, or Aline would know where I could find them.

A loud *bang* announced the first of the fireworks. It rose in a red nimbus, bursting over the towers of the Pavilion to rapturous applause.

More explosions followed the first, white, orange, and green spangling the night. The crowd surged in front of me, cutting off my view of Lady Aline. I skirted them, moving along a path overhung with trees, plunged into darkness as I sought the light.

I felt a rush of air to my right. Assuming I was about to be assailed, I sidestepped, bringing up my walking stick to fend off the villain.

Another explosion of fireworks sounded behind me. In front of me came a second bang, nearly lost in the blasts in the sky. I saw a bright flare of gunpowder and then I was on the ground, my face in the mud, instinct preserving my life.

Desjardins' gun had been a long-barreled shooter. This was a pistol, I could tell from the sound and a chance gleam from the fireworks.

I roared as I surged to my feet, anger propelling me upward. I ran forward, recklessly assuming that the shooter had only one pistol, which would now be spent.

Empty air answered my assault. I struck out with my cane but encountered no one.

The boom of the fireworks smothered any sound of retreating footsteps. I plunged along in the direction I imagined the shooter would have run, until I was rewarded by the outline of a man against the sky.

I snarled and launched myself at him. A large pair of hands caught me, wrested away my stick, and shoved me several feet backward.

"It's me, guv." Brewster held my walking stick protectively in front of him. "What the devil you attacking *me* for?"

"Brewster. Bloody hell." I sucked in a breath, my heart banging behind aching ribs. "A blackguard shot a pistol at me."

"'*Struth*." Brewster thrust my walking stick back at me. "That's twice in one day. Was it the Frenchie?"

I took the cane and rested it at my side, my knee now hurting powerfully. "I do not believe so. The comte wore a distinctive scent, and I did not smell it."

"A man can wash," Brewster pointed out.

"True, and I couldn't smell much over the gunpowder and the fireworks." My rage dissolved into stark worry. "Where are my daughter and Donata? If there are madmen with pistols about, you need to be watching over *them*, not me."

"Don't fuss yourself—they're with Mr. Grenville and a whole host of ladies and gents."

"Where?" I began striding toward the pack watching the fireworks, forcing Brewster to catch up with me. He did so with a grunt of irritation.

"Certain ye want to join them? You look like you've been kissing the ground."

I glanced down at myself. A bright wave of fireworks showed my suit plastered with mud, my cravat and waistcoat black with it.

"Bartholomew will not be pleased," I observed.

"Naw, he'll be chuffed. He likes looking after your clothes."

I ignored him. If I hurried to Donata and Gabriella, there

would be questions and alarm, and I might serve them better by finding and stopping the fellow instead.

"As I am not fit to be seen, let us hunt for the shooter," I said.

Brewster glared at me. "No, ye should take yourself inside in case he tries again."

"Exactly, and we should find him before he does. He must have run that way."

I pointed with my stick to the road beyond the Steine. It was the darkest path, and I'd seen no one running on the lighted ones. The strongest possibility was that he'd fled across the street and into the labyrinthine back lanes of Brighton.

"You expect to find him in there?" Brewster demanded. "Brighton has paid night constables. Let them do their job."

"He shot at *me*, Brewster," I said in a hard voice. "This was not arbitrary, but personal. He waited until I was in the shadows to strike."

"I know that, and I'll scour the town for him, but right now, ye need to get inside where he can't shoot at you anymore. That is, if you'll stay away from the windows."

Part of me reasoned that Brewster had the right of it, but being a target boiled rage through my blood.

"Someone is going to much trouble to make my life hell," I snapped as I headed for the road. "Making me believe I killed a man and then trying to kill *me* in return. I have had enough of it."

"Go back to London," Brewster advised as he caught up to me. "Much safer."

His sarcasm was sharp, and I did not bother to answer.

"Captain Lacey?" A woman's voice stopped me before I reached the other side of the street. "Are you fleeing the fireworks? You never liked them much, I remember."

CHAPTER 12

I turned to see Marguerite Gibbons ambling from the Steine across the empty street. She was alone, no husband or servant to guard her.

I met her in the middle of the road to escort her safely to the other side. "Have a care, madam," I said. "A man has just shot at me."

"Good heavens." Marguerite looked me up and down, taking in my ruined clothing. "I thought the wars were over."

"I've found England to be as dangerous as a battlefield. You should not wander about on your own, Mrs. Gibbons."

"I often do." Marguerite glanced at Brewster, concluding he was my servant, to his obvious annoyance. "Perhaps following the drum made me fearless. But do not worry. I am not an ingenue but an aging woman who has potted more than one would-be pickpocket with my umbrella."

Her eyes sparkled with warmth, bright under the shadow of her feathered hat.

"Even so, I should return you to your husband."

"*This* husband, yes. I would have fought you if you'd suggested such a thing on our last acquaintance."

In another circumstance, I might have enjoyed reminiscing with her. Marguerite and I had been friends, if only briefly. But I was furious at the attempt on my life, still shaken by the death of Joshua Bickley, and sickened by the entire course of events.

"Isherwood is dead," I said bluntly. "Murdered. I have been shot at twice today, and there is nothing to say a third time will not come. It is unsafe to stand next to me. I will take you back to the park and retire."

Marguerite gaped at me. "Twice?" I noted that she showed no reaction to my declaration that Isherwood had been killed, but I assumed her stepson had told her the truth of his murder.

"My husband is home, not at the Steine," Marguerite went on. "He does not like crushes and said he could see the fireworks as well from our rooms, which is true. I wanted air and to discover who was in Brighton for the summer."

"Lord Armitage for one," I said. "You recall him from Salamanca?"

Her eyes widened. "I do. Goodness. I had no idea he was in Brighton …" She looked thoughtful.

I took her arm and firmly led her along the street, making for the promenade where I'd seen her emerge from a house. "Armitage claims you were a spy for Napoleon." I saw no reason not to reveal this to her. "I told him he was an idiot."

"He said that?" She was more amused than alarmed. "I am hardly surprised. Lord Armitage violently disliked me and encouraged Isherwood to be rid of me. I have no idea why except that I am outspoken, and Armitage prefers women to be obedient. I am glad of the divorce now. It left me free when I met Mr. Gibbons, a far, far better man than Isherwood ever was."

I noted that she did not deny being a spy, and had neatly turned away the question.

"Did your stepson send for you?" I asked.

"Giles? No, actually. We were never close—Isherwood made certain of that—and he has corresponded little with me since the divorce. I was summoned by Major Forbes."

I slowed in surprise. "Forbes?"

"Indeed. He also violently dislikes me, but he felt it his duty to inform me of Isherwood's passing. Major Forbes thought I deserved to know he had been murdered. Or possibly he was warning me he thought I'd done it."

"And you rushed here to discover what had happened?"

Another laugh. "You are correct to be skeptical, Captain. I suppose I came to reassure myself Isherwood was truly dead. Mr. Gibbons feared there might be some legal tangle with inheritance and decided we'd better make the journey. Isherwood was well off, and I am named in his will—at least, I was once upon a time. If so, the money would be welcome."

A practical man, was Gibbons, encouraging his wife to seek an inheritance from a man who'd abandoned her.

We'd gone deep into the narrow lanes of the old town, Brewster keeping a sharp eye out.

"Where are you lodging?" I asked Marguerite.

"Worry not, Captain. I will not hang on you and prevent you going home to your lovely wife. She is quite fond of you, I can see. Mr. Gibbons and I have taken rooms in Ship Street."

I turned my steps that way. The Old Ship, where I'd sought the magistrate, sat on the corner overlooking the sea, but Marguerite directed me to a plain house in the middle of the lane.

Mr. Gibbons exited the house as we approached by means of a door next to the ground-floor shop. "Captain Lacey, well met again."

"I found him rushing from the park," Marguerite said, withdrawing her hand from my arm. "Someone shot at him, it seems."

"Truly?" Gibbons raised his brows. "Perhaps you heard a firework and mistook it?"

"Not when the pistol discharged five feet from me," I explained. "I thought it best I see your wife safely home—even quiet Brighton has dangers."

Gibbons tucked Marguerite's hand in the crook of his elbow, looking not at all worried that I had walked closely with her in the dark. "We've lived on the coast for years, Captain, and know its perils."

He dismissed the threat, as she did. I wished the pair of them well.

"Good night," I said, tipping my hat.

"Good night, Captain," Marguerite said. "Thank you for your courtesy."

Gibbons echoed her farewell, and I bowed and left them.

"Odd folk." Brewster shoved his hands into his coat pockets and slouched next to me along Bedford Row. "Want me to find out what they're really here for?"

"The reading of the will presumably. But it would be wise to keep an eye out. Discreetly, of course."

Brewster returned an irritated look. "I'm always discreet, guv. They'll never know I'm there."

Brewster was a large man with a loud voice, but I believed him. Mr. Denis employed only the best.

I WENT HOME AT BREWSTER'S CONTINUED PRODDING, BUT ONLY after he promised to return to the Steine and make certain Donata and Gabriella were looked after. He seemed aggrieved I'd think he wouldn't go, and disappeared into the night.

Bartholomew was surprised and appalled at my ruined suit but quickly had me out of my clothes and into a banyan and slippers. After he left me, I sat at my writing table with pen in hand, trying to make sense out of all that had happened thus far. My lists were disjointed, my handwriting shaky.

Finally I threw down my pen and gave up.

Noise below announced the arrival of my family. I went to meet them, relieved to see both Grenville and Brewster escorting Donata and Gabriella, Grenville having taken them under his wing. Brewster departed at last, but Grenville lingered.

I kissed my daughter good night, and she held fast to me. "Did you grow ill, Father? You ought to have told us—we'd have come home together."

Brewster had apparently kept the story of the shooting to himself. "I am well," I assured her. "I decided to have an early night and did not wish to spoil your enjoyment."

"Spending an evening with you is always enjoyable, Father." My daughter gave me a winsome smile, making me wonder if she teased or was serious. "Good night, sir." She touched another kiss to my cheek and then went upstairs.

Donata sent me a steely glance, but she said not a word as Jacinthe relieved her of her light wraps and escorted her up. I called a good-night to Donata, but she never turned, never answered.

Grenville cleared his throat. He beckoned me into the front sitting room and closed the door against the servants, who were shutting down the small house for the night.

"Donata learned early in her first marriage not to twit her husband about his indiscretions," Grenville said in a quiet voice. "So she will not mention she saw you hurry away from the park with Mrs. Gibbons."

I groaned in dismay. "Oh, good Lord. Mrs. Gibbons followed *me*. I haven't put it out of my head that *she* shot at me."

Grenville's eyes widened. "Shot ..."

I quickly told him what had happened. "Brewster insisted I take myself indoors at once. Mrs. Gibbons caught up to me, and I took the opportunity to quiz her on why she'd come to Brighton."

Grenville went very still as he listened to my tale. "I must learn never to turn my back on you, old friend," he said when I'd finished. "You fall into adventures faster than any man I know."

"Someone is trying to make my life very difficult," I agreed. "I am grateful you remained with Donata and Gabriella, though I believe I rendered them safer by leaving them. I seem to be hunted only when I am alone."

"You should not be left alone then." Grenville eyed me steadily. "But I'd go down on my knees and beg Donata's pardon, or she might show you the door. No—to be honest, I believe she would simply retreat from you and pretend to the world that all was well."

"All *is* well. Damnation. I thought married life would bring me peace."

Grenville laughed at me, blast the man. " Marriage is hardly the definition of *peace*. With a beautiful, accomplished, lively woman, still less so. Guard what you have. Believe me, I take my own advice. Marianne may do with me as she pleases."

I sensed a new lightness in Grenville, yet tension also. He was happy, but the price of his happiness was fear of losing it.

"I will explain things to Donata," I promised him. "Thank you, once again. Good night."

Grenville gave me an encouraging nod and took his leave. I squared my shoulders and walked upstairs, making for Donata's chamber.

The door was locked. I tapped on it, and after a time, Jacinthe opened the door a crack. "My lady is abed," she told me.

I did not believe her, but now was not the time to force my way in. "Please tell her ladyship to sleep well, and that I look forward to speaking with her tomorrow."

Jacinthe could summon a blank expression to rival any empty-eyed statue. "Yes, sir. Good-night, sir."

That seemed to be that.

I sought my own room only to be stopped by Bartholomew. "Mr. Brewster has returned, Captain." His young face held disapproval. "He wishes to see you on the moment."

I wanted my bed, exhausted by the day's events, but Brewster would not disturb me were it not important. Retaining my dressing gown and slippers, I went downstairs.

Brewster, as usual, had refused to enter the sitting room, so I met him in the foyer. "His Nibs wants to see you," he said.

I studied him in perplexity. "Mr. Denis is in London. He can't mean for me to travel there tonight."

Brewster was already shaking his head. "No, guv. He's here, in Brighton. At my digs, in fact. Wants to see you—*now*."

CHAPTER 13

I saw that Brewster expected me to rush off immediately, perhaps without even bothering to dress.

"It is late," I said. "Make an appointment for me to speak to Mr. Denis in the morning. He can call here for breakfast if he wishes."

Brewster scowled. "Now you're joking with me. He's come a long way and is not in the best temper. It's only gone midnight."

"We retire early in the provinces. Tell him you could not move me."

"He won't believe that, guv. You know I can wrestle you there or strike you down and carry you, so do me a favor and walk yourself. I'm not in the mood to strain me back."

"Oh, very well." I'd already known I'd give in. "My wife is furious with me, so remaining home tonight will not be comfortable. But you will wait until I dress myself. If Donata decides to bolt the doors permanently once I'm out, I prefer to have something more to wear than a banyan."

Brewster did not find me amusing, but he conceded to give me ten minutes to shovel myself into clothing with Bartholomew's assistance.

Brewster's lodgings lay around the corner from Donata's, in a narrow but pleasant lane with cozy houses, each with a patch of garden in front. The garden before Brewster's cottage held clumps of geraniums and sweet-smelling stocks, with vines of climbing yellow roses pale in the moonlight.

Several men as large and hard-eyed as Brewster lingered near the house, and one leaned on the railings that separated the garden from the road. A dark carriage waited on the street.

Lamps lit the house inside, and the landlady and Mrs. Brewster were hastening through the tiny foyer, bearing trays of coffee and food. Mrs. Brewster looked relieved as we entered.

"There you are, Tommy." She shoved her tray at him. "Make yourself useful. Mr. Denis brought an entire troop of his men, Captain, and they all want feeding."

Mrs. Brewster took another tray from the landlady, sent the woman off to the back stairs, and led me and her husband into a small dining room.

A table nearly filled this chamber, with little space left for the narrow sideboard. The fireplace was cold and dark, but candles filled sconces and pewter candlesticks on the table, brushing warm light over all.

James Denis had commandeered one end of the dining table, where he sat quietly, writing on a sheet of paper. I reflected that almost every time I responded to the man's summons, he contrived to be scribbling something when I entered.

Two large men had fit themselves awkwardly on the far

side of the table, against the shuttered windows. Denis never went anywhere without bodyguards.

Denis glanced up at me then returned to his missive, writing in swift, neat strokes. Brewster noisily unloaded from his tray a platter of meat, hunks of bread, and slices of meat pie. Mrs. Brewster followed with a coffee pot and cups.

"There now, Captain," she said. "I've brewed you coffee, as I know you prefer it. Tea for you, Tommy." She stared pointedly at Denis's men, both of whom had begun to reach fingers toward the pile of meat. "There's plates on the sideboard and forks and knives, and cloths to wipe away any mess."

The two men exchanged a glance, and one made his way to the sideboard to retrieve plates.

Denis, who'd not looked up during this exchange, at last laid down his pen and fixed me with his gaze. "Thank you for attending so late, Captain."

Brewster had made it clear I'd had no choice. "Urgent matters?" I asked, not bothering to hide my irritation.

Mrs. Brewster handed me a steaming cup of coffee then proceeded to serve the tea.

"Please sit." Denis waved a hand at a chair. "We have traveled all evening and have not dined."

It sounded like an apology, of sorts, which surprised me. His men unashamedly took up large portions of meat and bread and backed away to eat them.

A sip of Mrs. Brewster's well-brewed coffee calmed me somewhat. "You'd have had time to dine *and* sleep if you'd waited until morning to speak to me," I said.

Denis gave me a hard look from his cold blue eyes. "I understand from all Mr. Brewster has reported to me that you do not regard this situation as dire. I assure you, I believe it is most dangerous. Someone is trying very hard both to ruin you and end your life."

I'd raised the cup again but set down the coffee instead of drinking. "I grant that I have been the subject of unfortunate circumstances."

"Not the subject. The *object*. The most obvious was the shot taken at you tonight during the fireworks. Mr. Brewster told me of this when I arrived, but I had already been sufficiently concerned to make the journey down."

"I have evoked someone's ire, yes." I could hardly deny it. "But I cannot fathom who. My cousin Marcus was the last person who wanted to kill me, but we have reconciled ... I believe."

"I can think of any number of people who would not mind if you no longer existed."

Brewster, behind me, snorted. "Aye, that's the truth."

Denis touched his fingers as he counted off. "Your wife's in-laws. You and she recently thwarted them from gaining control of her son. Then there are men you have given up to the law, plus the families of such men. Enemies of mine who wish to provoke me. Or someone from your past you have angered or injured. I am certain there are many of those, given your uneven temper and your insistence on righting what you perceive are wrongs."

I nodded as he lowered his hand. "I admit I have clashed with many, and they have not fared well from it—I am too interfering for my own good. But why wait until I am on holiday in Brighton to attack? London would be an easier place to get at me."

"That is the significant point you have missed." Denis's eyes held a grim light. "Why indeed choose now? You arriving here must have triggered the need to target you."

I wrapped my fingers around my cup on the table, the coffee pleasantly warm. "Are you saying you believe I did not kill Isherwood? That this was a trap to destroy me?"

"You might have killed him—I do not know. You could have been forced to do it. Or, as you hope, another set the stage for you to be found over the body. But something went wrong, and you were not found."

I had been, by Clement, who I'd turned to aid me.

"Not long after the colonel's murder, a young man you were asked to search for turned up dead," Denis went on. "I doubt it is coincidental. Then, a man holds a loaded weapon and happens to discharge it when you enter a room. Finally, a person follows you tonight until you are alone and shoots at you. Too many things to be random incidents."

I could hardly argue—he laid it out in too neat a pattern. "I will have to make a list of my enemies," I said lightly. "You realize *you* would be on such a list?"

"I assure you, Captain, that when I wish you gone, you will be." Denis's directness was chilling. "However, these present occurrences are not my doing. I will find out who this malefactor is and stop him."

I lifted my coffee once more. "You are going to much trouble. I had no idea I was so useful to you."

"I would do so for any of my men. Besides, I believe I will have another mission for you and would prefer you whole so you can achieve it."

"I see." The words were nonchalant but stirred my disquiet. Denis's missions always turned out to be dangerous, but he made it impossible to refuse them.

"I would like that list you offer," Denis continued. "Begin with people you have seen in Brighton, anyone connected with your past."

"Major Forbes," I said at once. "He was never fond of me. But I cannot believe he'd kill Isherwood, or allow him to be killed. He worshiped the man."

"Time can alter feelings," Denis said. "Write the list and send it to me. Add details—where are these people now? Are they likely to make elaborate plans against you? And how will your ruin or death benefit them?"

I looked at him in annoyance. "I am supposed to be having a holiday."

"You will have no holidays if you are dead. Send your wife and family home and run this person to earth."

I recalled the burning anger in Donata's eyes as she'd passed me on the stairs a half hour ago. "My wife," I said with ironic humor. "She will likely be at the top of the list of those who wish me harm."

Denis rested his hands on the table. "Not at all. As in my case, if that lady wished you out of her life, it would happen quickly and permanently. Reconcile with her and help me solve this problem. I need your services."

He made clear that keeping myself from harm did *him* a favor. I did not know whether to laugh or grow enraged.

Denis closed his mouth and simply gazed at me, which I knew indicated the interview was over. Instead of hurrying obediently away, I deliberately lingered to finish my coffee.

Brewster shot me a warning look as we walked back to the square. "One day he'll have enough of your cheek. When he decides to teach you a lesson, he'll probably use me to do it. To teach me a lesson too."

He sounded so morose that I turned to him in surprise. "I'd have thought you be glad to land your fists in my face."

"I've grown too fond of you, and he knows it. We're not meant to be friends."

I was touched by his words. Brewster had done much for me over the past year or so, and I'd given him much trouble in return.

To cover the awkward moment, I said heartily, "I'll make certain I irritate you until you're ready to plant your boot in my arse."

"Oh, you already do that," Brewster said darkly. "Now let's get you home so I can take to me bed."

I DID NOT WANT TO LEAVE THINGS WHERE THEY WERE WITH Donata. A conversation should clear up the matter, I was confident. But when I returned, her door was shut fast, and I did not have the heart to bang on it and wake her.

Bartholomew, who was clearly curious about where I'd been, took my clothes as I shed them and dropped my night-shirt over my head. I told him the bare outline of what Denis and I had discussed, and asked him to get word of it to Grenville if I did not see the man sooner.

At last I went to bed, but I could not sleep. The spike of fear that had pumped through me when the pistol had gleamed in the darkness now spread its way past my defenses, making me shiver and sweat.

Such reactions had crept upon me during my soldiering days, when I'd realized hours after a furious battle that I was still alive. The line between life and death had been thin, and finding myself on the living side had sometimes shaken me.

In those days, I'd been young, reckless, and selfish and hadn't much cared whether I survived, and I'd shaken off my qualms. Now I had a wife, I'd found my daughter, I had a son in Peter, and a new baby daughter I longed to watch grow up. I had no wish to be the goal of another man's vendetta.

What Denis speculated made sense. I had gone through my life imposing my will on many—I'd commanded men in the army who'd died, I'd helped send murderers to the noose, and I'd become known as James Denis's man. Any of *his* enemies, or mine, or families or friends of those I'd harmed could have decided it was time for me to pay.

The thought that Donata, Gabriella, Peter, or Anne might pay for my sins filled me with horror. A madman might well decide to harm them to hurt me.

When I at last slept, I dreamt, oddly, of gliding over the sea in a small boat. Donata and my family were with me, seemingly enjoying themselves. I held the sides of the boat, waiting for terrible things to happen, but nothing did.

I rose in the morning after the fitful sleep to find Bartholomew waiting to bathe and shave me for the day.

It was early, and Donata would be asleep. Her closed door and the silence behind it confirmed that.

I looked in on Anne in the nursery, making her laugh as I bounced her in my arms. I held her close, remembering my fears of the previous night, then returned her to the hovering nanny and breakfasted with Peter and Gabriella.

It was a fine morning, and I needed a walk to clear my head. Gabriella was to visit Lady Aline—the lady's carriage would call for her at ten. I was reluctant for her to go, but I knew Lady Aline and her retinue of servants would keep Gabriella safe. I waited until the carriage arrived and saw her into it myself, and ordered one of our strongest footmen to accompany her. Gabriella glanced at me in curiosity as we said our farewells, but did not argue.

Peter, on the other hand, insisted he join me on my walk. I did not want to let him, but I also knew if I ordered him to stay home, he'd simply slip out and follow me. Better that I had him next to me where I could watch over him.

Brewster, who uncannily knew whenever I stepped out of my door, met us at the end of the square. I kept to the broad promenade along the sea as we strolled. No tiny lanes or shadowy passageways today.

Peter, as usual, wanted to play on the shore. He liked to pick up rocks and skim them across the water, as I had done as a boy. I accompanied him, and we looked for flat specimens and practiced pitching them.

I turned back from one go to see Mr. Bickley picking his way across the shingle to us. He was dressed all in black, his coat billowing with the wind, a broad hat firmly on his head.

I went forward to meet him, Brewster staying next to Peter but keeping an eye on me.

"Mr. Bickley," I said in a kind tone. "I have not had the opportunity to tell you how sorry I am for your loss."

The man raised his head and regarded me bleakly. "It is God's will."

His words were flat, uninflected, but I saw the grief deep in his eyes.

"I know," I answered. "But we who are left behind do not always find comfort in that."

"I lost my wife some years ago," Bickley went on, as though I had not spoken. "And my brother after that, in the war—he was not a Quaker. I thought saying good-bye to them the hardest tasks I had undertaken. I was wrong."

Losing a child was something none of us should endure. For too long a time I'd been uncertain whether Gabriella lived or died. When I'd found her alive, my entire world had glowed with new light, a curtain of darkness dissolving.

"If I can help in any way," I began. "I am devastated that I did not find Joshua before the worst happened."

"No." Bickley's word was sharp as he focused on me. "Thou art not to blame, Gabriel. *I* am."

CHAPTER 14

I stared at Bickley, wondering if he were confessing to murdering his own son.

The man drew a breath and continued as wind brought us the sharp smell of the sea. "The fault is mine for my wickedness. Joshua died for my sins."

I was relieved he spoke metaphorically. "The guilt is *not* with you, sir. An evil man has done this, and I intend to discover who."

Bickley studied me with empty eyes. "How will that matter? Then another will lose his life, *his* family will be ruined, and none of that will return my boy to me."

His words gave me a pang of uneasiness. Murderers were hanged, but that never stopped more innocents from being killed. What did we achieve?

Then again, I would not let whoever murdered that poor lad get away with it.

I thought Bickley would say more, but he only gazed at me and then beyond at Peter. A profound sadness came over him, the stiff breeze tugging his coat.

I had no idea how to comfort him. Any words that came to me sounded inadequate in my head, so I kept them confined there.

Bickley's focus drifted back to me. "After the inquest, I will leave Brighton and go to Chichester. My half-sister has agreed that I will dwell with her."

I gave him a nod. "I hope you find peace there."

"I was supposed to find peace *here*," Bickley said. "Good afternoon, Gabriel. And good-bye."

He held out his hand, and I shook it. Bickley's eyes welled with tears as he clung to me for a few seconds.

Then he released me, turned abruptly, and marched across the shingle, making for the main part of town.

"Poor bugger," Brewster said, watching him go. "A strange cove, but I feel that sorry for him. Can't be easy, having his son murdered like that."

"No." I glanced at Peter who had returned to skimming rocks into the ocean. He was not the son of my body, but I was growing to care for him as though he were my own.

"He never mentioned Miss Purkis," I said. "The Quaker woman who has also gone missing."

Brewster nodded. "Noticed. You think she's dead too?"

"I sincerely hope not." I called to Peter. "Come, lad, let us go back. Your mother should be awake by now."

This aspect did not excite Peter, but for my part, I was anxious to speak to Donata.

Jacinthe did not wish to allow me into Donata's chamber. I planted myself solidly in the doorway and stared her down. As I was now head of the household, I could bodily move her aside if I chose and be considered justified doing so.

None of this disturbed Jacinthe, who'd been looking after Donata since Donata had been a girl. Donata's own mother was not as fierce.

"Let him in," my wife said wearily. "He will only stand there if you do not, and he is creating a draft."

Jacinthe's expression told me she considered me the loser of the battle, but she opened the door deferentially. As I entered, Jacinthe fetched a mending basket and walked sedately out.

Donata said absolutely nothing. She sat at her dressing table, peering into the mirror as she arranged curls of her hair with her fingers.

The windows giving to the sea were open and I moved to them. I gazed out at the beauty of the gray ocean, breathing in the clean air.

After the silence had stretched between us, I turned to her. "Grenville told me I ought to go down on my knees before you. But this one doesn't bend well." I tapped my leg with my walking stick. "So I will have to remain standing."

Donata kept her eyes on the mirror, lifting a strand of gold to test against her throat. "Absolute nonsense," she said in a quiet voice.

"The truth of it is, no lady can hold a candle to you."

Donata at last glanced at me, but the spark in her eyes showed she was not appeased. "I did rather coerce you into marrying me, I admit. I remember not giving you much choice."

I regarded her in amazement then returned to my contemplation of the sea.

"It astonishes me every day," I said softly, "that you condescended to notice me at all. A most beautiful lady with a swift and intelligent mind, and you chose to favor *me*. I have been, all this time, humbled, and grateful."

Another silence. When I turned again, she gazed at me, her mask of studied sangfroid gone. We regarded each other—anger and remorse, frustration and regret wafting through the space between us.

"Well, you *are* rather handsome," Donata said lightly.

I went to her and peered around her into the mirror. I saw my hard face, too weathered by the sun, a long nose, unruly dark hair, and wide dark eyes.

"I will never believe you on that score," I told her. "I married you before you could come to your senses and pass me over."

Donata flushed, but instead of answering, she waved her hand at a folded paper on the dressing table. "Grenville sent me a note this morning. He told me what happened to you last night and why you fled."

I would have to thank Grenville profusely for his intervention. "Then you know what a fool I was acting, confused and going off in all directions."

Donata's coolness vanished. "Good Lord, Gabriel, someone tried to shoot you. I have no doubt they were aiming for *you*, as you were alone at the time."

"True," I said. "Mrs. Gibbons only hailed me as Brewster and I chased after the scoundrel into the streets."

"That was not what I meant." Donata squarely met my gaze. "You need to have a care. Mr. Denis should assign three or four men to guard you—obviously Mr. Brewster cannot do it alone."

"Mr. Denis is here in Brighton. He commandeered Brewster's lodgings and sent for me last night, at midnight, if you please."

"I know," she said. "Bartholomew told me—that is, he told Jacinthe. What is Mr. Denis's opinion of all this?"

"That a person from my past plans to end me." I pulled a delicate chair next to her and sat down, rested my arms on my knees, and related my conversation with him. I ended with a weak smile. "Denis also ordered me to reconcile with you."

"Ah." Donata's expression shuttered. "So that is why you were so eloquent."

"I meant every word of it." I lifted her hand and pressed a kiss to her palm. "I hate that I distress you because I can be a dolt. I hate that my past is rising to plague us. I hate that you believe my affection for you could ever wane."

Her fingers tightened on mine the slightest bit. "I was raised to never show what I felt, no matter the circumstance," she said softly. "*You* are happy to let the world know your true feelings."

I tried a laugh. "I was raised badly, as you know."

"I wish I could convey what you do so easily." Donata's mouth turned down. "I can only express myself in barbs and witticisms."

"In public, yes." I took up her other hand and laid both against my chest. "In private, you may pour out your heart. I will treasure every word and repeat them to no one."

Donata bowed her head. When she looked up again, her eyes were wet.

She did not, however, unleash her soul and shower me with expressions of love and devotion. She only sighed and moved closer to me.

Soon we occupied the same chair, but I feared it collapsing, so I lifted her and moved with her to a sofa. There we ceased speaking, finishing the conversation without words. By the time Donata sent for Jacinthe again, I considered us well reconciled.

When I went downstairs, Donata still dressing, I spied Mr. Quimby approaching the house across the empty square. I bade Bartholomew show him in.

"What news, Mr. Quimby?"

The man somberly removed his hat and gave it over to Bartholomew. "I've come from the coroner. May we speak?" He glanced into the sitting room.

I gestured him inside and shut the door behind us. "Joshua Bickley?"

"Indeed." Both of us remained standing, uneasy, in the middle of the carpet. "The lad did not drown in the boat. You were correct that he was killed, strangled from all appearances, and then placed there. That is the coroner's opinion."

I balled my fists. "You mean they tried to make it look like a boating accident? Josh didn't like boats, according to Miss Farrow."

"The coroner believes the man who strangled him was quite strong, with large hands." Quimby glanced at the one resting on my walking stick. "Like yours, Captain."

I took a step back. "I did not kill the lad, Quimby. I promise you that."

Mr. Quimby did not seem to hear my declaration. "The inquest will be later today. You will be called to give evidence."

"I assumed as much." I calmed myself. "I will answer any questions put to me, but I do not have much more information."

Quimby sighed. "Death by violence is a great horror for the Friends, but I know they do not believe in hanging murderers either. It is why they have invented such frightening jails. They believe they are being kind, but those places result in the death of souls instead of bodies, in my opinion."

One of Mr. Denis's men had described these reforming places to me—stark buildings built in a circle, monotonous exercise, men always watched, and menial and unrelenting tasks. The man had not told me whether he'd been in such a place himself, but he'd spoken of it with horror.

"Then we are looking for a strong man with large hands," I concluded. "Unfortunately, I imagine we'll find any number of candidates."

"It could have been a hired murder," Quimby pointed out. "A ruffian brought in to do the deed, who will be miles away by now."

"True, but why would anyone wish to kill Josh Bickley? From what I have heard of him, he was a harmless young man, a friend to many."

Quimby shrugged. "One never knows. He was a Quaker, but could have become discontented with that way of life, perhaps left them to fall in with a bad lot. Or he simply met a villain who killed him for whatever coins he had in his pockets."

"Or he might have been trying to do a good deed and came to misfortune," I said. "A Quaker woman, older than he, has also vanished, and I wondered if Josh had gone to discover what became of her. I fear harm has come to her as well."

"Indeed." Quimby looked unhappy.

"There is an opinion that these things are happening as part of an attempt to ruin me or take my life," I said, carefully not mentioning Denis's name.

"An interesting theory." Quimby looked thoughtful. "Sir Montague has mentioned that you are quick to anger people."

"Only those who are brutal to others. Though I suppose I put my nose into much business that doesn't concern me." I touched the offending appendage.

Mr. Quimby gave me a tolerant smile. "I will see you at the inquest, Captain. It will begin at two of the clock."

"I will be there," I promised.

Mr. Quimby took his leave. I saw him to the door, and we parted cordially. Brewster turned up as soon as Quimby was gone—he'd likely been waiting until the Runner departed.

"His Nibs wants that list of your old enemies," Brewster said. "He sent me to remind you."

I made a noise of exasperation "I haven't had a moment to do it. He can wait an hour, can he not?"

"I'll not be delivering *that* message." Brewster sat down on a chair in the hall. "Only the list. I'll wait."

$\mathcal{I}$ gave up, retreated to the dining room, and rang for pen, ink, and paper along with my noonday repast.

Writing the list as I sipped coffee and ate bread and butter was disheartening. I started with those from my past who were now in Brighton—Major Forbes and Marguerite Gibbons. Forbes had disliked me intensely, certain I had helped destroy Isherwood's marriage. It was highly unlikely he'd murder Isherwood himself to hurt me, but Forbes had always been a bit mad, in my opinion.

It was possible Marguerite nursed resentment with me for telling her to go back to England instead of taking care of her for the remainder of the war. Her new husband, though he seemed a genial fellow, might not be happy that I'd been his wife's lover, plus he wouldn't have any warm feelings toward Isherwood for divorcing her in the first place.

There were other men in the army I'd angered. I'd counter-manded bad orders, shouting at colonels who were ready to take my men straight into slaughter. Colonel Brandon, my mentor, had been often been furious with me, for many reasons, enough so that he'd once tried to send me to my death.

I wished I could discount Brandon, but I slowly wrote his name. He and I had reconciled somewhat after I'd cleared him of murder, and still more after I'd married Donata, but Brandon knew how to nurse a grudge.

Then there were Donata's cousins, as Denis had mentioned, who'd wished to marry her and keep her son's money and estates in the family. Peter's guardian would have great influence over him and control much of the funds until the lad's majority.

Donata's most odious cousin, Stanton St. John, had fled to the Continent after his last attempt to rule Peter, but he might have secretly returned. Stanton certainly hated me enough to cause my utter ruin.

I'd also helped bring murderers to trial in the past few years. If any had survived their conviction—perhaps returning after being transported—I could picture them taking their revenge. Or, if they had not survived, their families doing so.

It was a depressingly long list. I finished writing, sanded the sheet, folded and sealed it, and took it to Brewster.

"This is all I could think of." I held out the paper to him. "Mr. Denis might be able to add more, including himself."

Brewster rose, his bulk filling the small hallway. "You heard 'im. If His Nibs wanted you dead, you'd be gone before you knew it."

"How cheering," I said. "Tell him I said good morning."

Brewster had the gall to grin. "Right you are, guv. Don't stray a step without me."

"I can't obey that command. I must attend the inquest, which begins in a few minutes."

Brewster heaved a sigh. "Go on, then. I'll deliver this and run after you."

He departed. I left word with Bartholomew to tell Donata where I'd gone, then fetched my hat and walked swiftly to the magistrate's court at the Old Ship.

A room had been cleared in the back for the proceedings. Gentlemen filled the chamber, including Quimby and Sir Reginald Pyne, the magistrate I'd fetched when I'd found Josh's body. A number of Quakers were present as well, both men and women, their plain, dark clothes blending with the everyday suits of fishermen and tradesmen.

Clive Bickley was there, supported on one side by Miss Farrow and on the other by a young woman in Quaker garb. The other Friends stood around him, holding themselves apart but in no way drawing curiosity. Dissenters had been in Brighton long enough to be an ordinary part of the scenery. None of the Quakers looked at me.

A stooped gentleman with an air of authority—the coroner, I gathered—took a seat behind a table and gave the room a stern look.

The room was full, with not enough seats. The jury, a group of gentlemen in the corner, jammed against each other on benches. I ended up standing along the back wall with others who'd crowded in. Brighton saw its share of death by drowning, but by now I imagined the word had leaked that Joshua had been murdered, an altogether different prospect.

The coroner cleared his throat, and the muttered conversation in the room ceased. The coroner rumbled through a preamble, naming the court, the date, and the case.

The coroner called a surgeon to give his evidence first. This surgeon, a portly man with pince-nez on his nose, consulted his notes. "I examined the body and found that death was caused by strangulation. Two bones in the neck were broken and the trachea crushed. There was no water in the lungs."

The gatherers murmured and shuffled until the coroner glared them to silence.

"Thank you, sir. You may step down." The coroner made a note on one of the papers in front of him. "I call Sir Reginald Pyne."

The magistrate rose and made his slow way to the front of the room. He swore his oath to speak the truth and drew himself up to his full height.

"Yesterday afternoon, a gentleman came to me and said he'd found a body in a boat. I went along with him to the shore near Charles Street and saw that he'd pulled the boat up on the shingle. Inside was the body of a young man, pinned to the gunwale on the bottom by the seat and a few boards. That young man turned out to be Joshua Bickley, one of the Society of Friends."

All eyes turned to Mr. Bickley, who dropped his gaze. The young woman at his side held tighter to his arm, and Miss Farrow patted his shoulder.

The coroner nodded his dismissal to the magistrate. "Call Captain …" He lifted a paper to examine it in better light. "… Lacey."

I limped to the front amid stares. An officer in a cavalry uniform frowned at me, and I looked him over, trying to place him. He was familiar, but the association did not come to me at the moment.

The coroner eyed me sharply. "Full name?" he barked.

He had it on his sheet, but I said, "Captain Gabriel Lacey, of the Thirty-Fifth Light Dragoons. On half pay," I added for explanation as to why I was not in uniform and on duty.

The coroner barely nodded. "On the seventh of July you

went sea bathing with your family. Please describe what you saw."

I leaned on my walking stick and told him how Peter and I had spied the boat and towed it to shore before I sent him home and went for the magistrate.

"And the magistrate identified the young man as Joshua Bickley." The coroner made notes then pinned me with his hard stare. "Were you acquainted with Master Bickley?"

I shook my head. "I had no idea who the young man was until the magistrate announced his name."

"But you are acquainted with his father."

"Briefly acquainted. We have spoken a few times."

The coroner tapped a paper. "You spoke to him on Monday night and again on Tuesday afternoon."

The man was well informed, but I imagined Mr. Bickley himself had mentioned this when initially questioned.

"Yes ..." I said hesitantly.

The coroner gave me an impatient look. "Did you speak to him, or did you not?"

"The trouble is—I *believe* I spoke to him Monday evening but I have no memory of doing so."

The coroner's thin white brows went up. "What do you mean you have no memory of doing so? You very clearly remember finding the boat with young Joshua's body inside it. Or was Monday too long ago for you? You do not seem to be in your dotage, young man."

Amid titters around me, I swallowed, uncomfortable. "I might have been inebriated."

A general laugh filled the room. I glimpsed Clement's mother in a blue striped shawl and large bonnet on the edge of the crowd. She did not smile.

The coroner scowled. "I see. Well, Mr. Bickley tells me you

did speak to him, and I must take him at his word. He also told me he asked you to help him find out what had become of Joshua, as he was growing concerned. Do you remember *that?*"

"Not from Monday night," I said, my face heating. "Mr. Bickley repeated the request on Tuesday, when I spoke to him again."

"And did you try to discover what had become of Master Bickley?"

I grew still more warm. "Not right away. I had other duties to see to." I hardly wanted to confess I'd been busy trying to clear myself of the murder of Colonel Isherwood.

"Including sea bathing," the coroner said. "Frolicking in the waves while a young man was dead and a father worried."

I could only flush again. "I am afraid so."

"That is hardly fair of thee." Mr. Bickley had taken a step forward, the ladies on either side losing their hold of him.

The coroner gave him a sharp look. "Never mind, Mr. Bickley. You will have your chance to speak in a moment."

Murmurs of sympathy rippled for Bickley, but I received only scowls.

"Captain Lacey," the coroner continued. "What person do you suppose caused Master Bickley's death?"

I opened my hand. "I have no idea. Perhaps Joshua came across men moving contraband. I hear smuggling is rife in this area."

"Spoken like an ignorant Londoner," the coroner snapped. "That is our affair. But I understand your reasoning. Your proposal is that Master Bickley stumbled upon some villains committing a crime, and they strangled him and put him into the boat and then overturned it to make his death look like an accident."

"I can think of no other explanation. I have been told

Joshua did not like boats and so likely would not be in one intentionally."

"Thank you." The coroner spoke firmly. "One speculation at a time, please."

More laughter. Mrs. Morgan, Clement's mother, remained stiff-lipped and disapproving.

"You are a rather strong man, Captain." The coroner gave me a pointed look.

"But not nimble." I tapped my leg with my walking stick. "If Joshua had run from me, I could not have given chase."

The coroner did not look convinced. "If he trusted you, and if you came from his father, he might not run."

I squared my shoulders. "I give you my word, sir, upon my honor, that I did young Master Bickley no harm. I never met the lad, and did not know it was he in the boat until told by the magistrate."

"That you remember." The coroner's gaze was severe. "The wounds put his death late Monday night or very early on Tuesday morning. Do you remember anything else about that night through your inebriation?"

"I dined with my wife at the Pavilion, upon invitation. After that, I apparently spoke to Mr. Bickley but then was in bed asleep until late Tuesday afternoon."

I spoke in a ringing voice, but my mouth was dry. I skirted the truth, but I could not very well blurt out in court that I'd wandered about Brighton and come to myself over Isherwood's body. I'd find myself quickly locked away to wait for the Assizes. I doubted I'd have had time to kill Josh and put him into a boat, meet with the Quakers, and go on to kill Isherwood, but I wished I could *remember*.

The coroner sifted through his papers again and at last gave me a nod that I could go.

"Call Mr. Clive Bickley."

I hated to see the poor man in his grief forced in front of all eyes, but Mr. Bickley moved forward without hesitation.

The coroner, ignoring me as I returned to my place against the wall, addressed Bickley in a gentle voice. "I know that you, as a Quaker, Mr. Bickley, will not swear an oath, so I will not ask it. You can sign an affirmation later to satisfy the lawyers, but I will take what you say as truth."

"Thank you," Bickley said in a near whisper.

"Now then. Please tell me what happened with your son—when did he go missing?"

Bickley cleared his throat. "Sunday last, after Meeting."

"Did he give any indication where he was going? Something like, 'I'm going out for a walk, Father?' or 'I'll be with my mates at the seaside?'"

"No. Nothing like that." Bickley swallowed, his cheeks staining red. "My son and I had quarreled. He was very angry with me."

"About what?" The coroner's pen hovered, ink arrested in the act of dripping from its tip.

"I'd prefer not to say. A private quarrel between father and son."

The coroner's eyes narrowed. "You understand that the quarrel might have led to his disappearance, Mr. Bickley? Perhaps even his death?"

Bickley acknowledged this with a nod. "I do know. But as it might have nothing to do with it, I will not speak."

Another murmur from the collected crowd, this one of surprise. The coroner tried to glare Bickley into obedience, but the man proved stubborn.

The coroner heaved a sigh. "Very well, but be warned that the magistrate or I will have it out of you if it proves relevant."

I too very much wanted to know what Bickley and his son had quarreled about, and why he'd not mentioned this to me.

Perhaps Joshua had tired of the constraints of the Friends, or fancied a young woman of whom Mr. Bickley disapproved. Or had Josh simply shown the rage against his father that many young men experience in their lives? Even if Bickley and Josh had maintained a pleasant friendship, at some point a youth wants to break free and live his own life, as I knew from bitter experience.

I pictured the young man storming out, his father sadly watching him go. Bickley would have reasoned Josh would return after he cooled down, and they'd discuss things more calmly. But Joshua hadn't returned.

The coroner continued. "When did you become alarmed at your son's absence?"

"I wasn't." Bickley's voice wavered. "He has friends in Hove he visits from time to time. I assumed him there. But when I sent a message to those friends, they said they hadn't seen him. He'd never been there."

Bickley's face crumpled into misery. The sympathy in the room was rife. The young woman—niece? cousin?—went to Bickley and caught him before he could collapse.

The coroner did not look happy that his witness could obviously answer no more questions, but he waved Bickley back to the cluster of Friends.

The coroner scanned the room. "Are there any more who can attest to the whereabouts of Joshua Bickley in the days before his death, or who can shed light on his demise?"

The whispering died down. Men and women glanced about, but none came forward to volunteer information.

"Very well." The coroner gathered his papers with a heavy hand. "The jury will adjourn to conclude their verdict. Keep in mind I have more cases to go through today, gentlemen," he said to the men in the corner.

The gentlemen of the jury looked put-upon, but huddled into a tight knot to discuss things.

As much as I wanted to go say a word of comfort to Bickley, I remained where I was. Miss Farrow was next to him now, speaking rapidly to him. The young woman, her eyes as full of tears as Bickley's, held his hand.

Mrs. Morgan, after a long look at me, slipped out. I'd have followed her, but I wanted to hear the jury's conclusion—though there was not much doubt what it would be.

The jury did not take long to deliberate. They approached the table, and the coroner asked for their verdict.

"Willful murder by person or persons unknown," one of the men intoned.

Whatever the coroner said to that was drowned by the voices of the excited crowd. I left the room, putting on my hat as I walked out of the inn.

Brewster, who'd entered as the jury finished, fell into step beside me. "Looks like she wants a word." He nodded at Mrs. Morgan, who waited at the end of the street. Clement, in his footman's livery, had appeared out of nowhere to stand next to her.

I moved to them and tipped my hat to Mrs. Morgan. "The verdict was willful murder," I said.

"I guessed that. What else could it have been?" Mrs. Morgan, her colorful shawl a bright note in that gray space of town, beckoned me to follow as she walked across the road to the promenade.

Clement hurried after her, looking uncomfortable, and Brewster and I followed.

"Well, tell them." Mrs. Morgan gave her son a mother's impatient glare. "Exactly what you told me."

Clement was not happy, but he drew a breath and looked me in the eye. "You asked me to poke about and find out when His Royal Highness left the Pavilion Monday night. He had his things packed up earlier that evening, but he'd departed by three in the morning."

My eyes became fixed on his, pools of deep brown framed by thick lashes. "And you and I found Isherwood's body at ..."

"Two in the morning, sir."

My heart beat faster. "Then we have a new suspect."

CHAPTER 16

*C*aptain Lacey, you cannot run to the magistrate and accuse the Prince Regent of murder," Mrs. Morgan said crisply.

Around us men and women drifted down the promenade, ignoring the clump of us blocking the way as they determinedly enjoyed the sunshine.

"I realize that." I made myself say the words, because of course I wanted to hurry back to the court and tell Pyne and the coroner this very thing.

I could easily envision the Regent, spoiled and hedonistic, running Isherwood through in a crazed duel, and then making certain another was caught as his murderer.

I liked the idea, because it would mean I hadn't killed Isherwood. But Mrs. Morgan was wise, and caution stilled me. First, I'd have difficulty explaining why anyone should not believe me a madman; second, I'd have to confess how much I knew about Isherwood's death; and third, if I *had* been given a mind-blotting concoction beforehand, that spoke of careful planning. I could not imagine the impetuous Regent coolly coming up with such a scheme.

Mrs. Morgan watched me. "It would be your word and my son's to the Regent's."

I saw her worry about repercussions against Clement. I let out a breath. "Do not fear, Mrs. Morgan. I will hold my tongue —at least until I am very certain. Clement—can you find out why the Regent departed so late? And what he did in those hours between rising from the supper table until he left the Pavilion?"

"I already have." Clement looked annoyed I wouldn't think he'd done so. "He went to visit a lady right after supper. It's why he was in such a hurry to excuse himself."

"A lady." Of course. "What lady?"

"Lady Hollingsworth. She has a house in Brighton—or at least, her husband does. She arrived here alone, and off he went to meet her."

The Regent, despite his bulk and his gout, still indulged himself ardently with the fairer sex. While physically he might not be as active as he had been in the past, he still preferred the company of the ladies. I hardly blamed him on that score.

"Did he return to the Pavilion after visiting her?"

"Oh yes. Around one, it was. No one can tell me exactly where he was at *that* time." Clement beamed in triumph. "And then he was off at three, heading for London. So he might have gutted the officer, sir."

Mrs. Morgan remained skeptical. "No one knows exactly where the pair of *you* were either. Find out what His Highness was up to in those hours, Clement. Once you know *everything*, Captain Lacey, *then* make your report. The Regent's not the best of men, we know, but he is the sovereign these days and could make life very difficult for you if he chose."

I knew I would have to tread carefully. But at least it gave me a direction.

"Thank you, Clement," I said in sincerity. "You have done me a great service."

Clement continued to be pleased with himself, but his mother was more practical. "That remains to be seen. And Clement is only doing his duty—which he should get back to." She gave her son a pointed look. "I'm certain you don't have leave to be away."

"I do," Clement said, aggrieved. "They let me out for air once in a while, Mum."

"Be that as it may, it's time you were back inside, before you get that livery dirty. I imagine I'd be expected to pay for it."

Clement gave a long-suffering sigh, kissed his mother resignedly on the cheek, and ran off across the road, heading for the Pavilion.

"He's a good lad," I said.

"You do not have to humor me, Captain. I know he is." Mrs. Morgan's dark eyes sparkled. "I would not be one bit surprised if His Highness committed this deed and then fit you up for it, but it is a sticky situation. I too will ask questions of my most gossipy friends about Lady Hollingsworth and the prince's comings and goings that night." She gave me an approving look. "I like you, Captain. You have been kind to Clement, and I will not let you down."

I bowed. "Thank you, dear lady."

She fixed me with a steely gaze. "But if I find you *have* done bad things, and are using Clement to cover up for you, may God have mercy on your soul."

Her words rang with the certainty of a high court judge's.

I gave her another bow. "I'd deserve your wrath, madam. I would require God's mercy, indeed."

BREWSTER HAD REMAINED SILENT DURING THE EXCHANGE, BUT he made his feelings known as we turned toward home.

"You going to step up to His Highness and accuse him of stabbing the colonel? If so, I'm asking His Nibs to give you a different nanny."

"Do not worry," I said to soothe him. "I realize the futility of trying to question the Regent. However, Grenville might be able to find out exactly what happened that night." I pondered. "I also ought to write Colonel Brandon about this business."

"This is the colonel what got your knee broken?"

I nodded. "Brandon remembers Isherwood and all that happened in Salamanca. He was not best pleased with me about my part in it, but he might have ideas regarding who would want to kill Isherwood—besides me, I mean."

Brewster looked skeptical. "Surprised you're still alive, guv."

"So am I, believe me."

We hadn't progressed far down Bedford Row when a man stepped out of a side lane to confront us.

He was the cavalry officer who'd stared at me at the inquest. I remembered, with sudden clarity, that I'd seen him the afternoon I'd begun inquiries about Isherwood's murder. After I'd conversed with Bickley and Miss Farrow, I'd spied this man in the street. He'd studied me as though he'd speak to me but then had not.

The officer was a few years younger than I, and tall, his bearing straight. He wore the same regimental colors as young Isherwood and Major Forbes—blue coat with gold facings and gold braid. The jacket was trim, the trousers neat over his boots.

Brewster positioned himself watchfully next to the officer

as the man gave me a perfunctory bow. "Captain Christopher Wilks, at your service."

I held out my hand. "Captain Gabriel Lacey, at yours. Thirty-Fifth Light. You are in the Forty-Seventh?"

"Indeed." Captain Wilks shook my hand. "I saw you at the inquest today."

"And I you."

Brewster looked back and forth between us, frowning at our politeness.

"A bad business," Wilks went on. "Perhaps we can speak?"

Brewster and I had come as far as West Street, near the Customs House. In a lane beyond this was a small tavern. I noted that a few gentlemen walking along this street wore small black caps on the crowns of their heads—the Jewish synagogue was near.

Captain Wilks and I agreed to enter the tavern. The regulars lifted their heads and regarded us with suspicion when we walked in, but soon went back to their ale and quiet muttered conversation.

Wilks raised his brows at Brewster, who took a stool against the wall near the table where we seated ourselves.

"He is trusted," I told Wilks. "Whatever you say to me will not be repeated." That is, to anyone but Denis, should Brewster believe Denis needed to know it.

Not until we had full tankards in front of us did Wilks come around to what he wished to say.

"I heard the coroner ask you to account for your whereabouts the night—the early morning rather—when Joshua Bickley was killed."

I nodded. "I was at supper at the Royal Pavilion. With my wife, several friends, many acquaintances, and the Regent himself."

"Including men of my regiment," Wilks acknowledged. "Colonel Isherwood and Lord Armitage. Colonel Isherwood is now dead, from a sudden fever, his son says."

"Lord Armitage is one of the Forty-Seventh?" I asked in surprise.

"Nominally." Wilks looked disapproving. "He was at Austerlitz, as he no doubt will have told you. After Armitage returned to London with his wife, he bought himself a commission and joined our regiment on the Peninsula just before Ciudad Roderigo."

Ciudad Roderigo had been a very bad business, and the fact that Armitage had been there startled me. "I was at Salamanca," I said. "The Forty-Seventh combined forces with my regiment there, but I never met Lord Armitage."

"Because he stayed in the rear, dining with other aristocrats in Spanish noble houses." Wilks's disgust was plain.

"You mean he wanted the credit for fighting Napoleon without actually having to soil his gloves."

"Indeed," Wilks said. "Lord Armitage and Colonel Isherwood were friends, I believe, or at least acquaintances. They were often in each other's company. However, I do not like to gossip about the colonel, especially now that he is deceased."

"I understand." I took a sip of ale to indicate I would not press him. I wanted to, very much, but I understood the sort of man Wilks was—one who obeyed the rules of honor. I had quarreled with Colonel Brandon for years, but I would never disparage him in front of a man from another regiment.

"Is this what you wished to ask me about—the supper at the Pavilion?" I inquired.

"No, you misunderstand. You told the coroner that you dined at the Pavilion and then went home and slept after you spoke Mr. Bickley. But you did not. I saw you."

My heartbeat quickened, and my hand tightened on my tankard. "Did you? Where?"

"In a public house. One very near the Quaker Meeting. It's a friendly place and I take an ale there on nights I am off duty. You came in alone, sat down in a corner and asked for coffee. I could see you were in a bad way, which is no doubt why you wanted the coffee. You told the coroner you were inebriated."

"I was," I said cautiously. "I must have imbibed too well at supper."

"You were befuddled, yes, but in a strange way. I've seen many a drunken man in my time, but you seemed more alert and aware, your speech not slurred."

I had absolutely no memory of walking into this pub, let alone drinking coffee. "Is that all I did?" I asked, my tone sharp.

Wilks watched me carefully. "You truly do not remember?"

"Of course not. If I had, I'd have told the coroner."

He held up a hand. "Peace, Captain. I came to you about this because you seem a decent fellow and genuinely puzzled about that night. You sipped your coffee and appeared to calm yourself. Then the publican handed you a paper. You read it and shoved yourself up and away very quickly. I watched you go, wondering, but you disappeared quickly. I assumed you'd received dire news."

A message? But from whom and about what? "What did I do with the paper?" I demanded.

"Crumpled it in your hand, as far as I can remember."

"I didn't throw it into the fire?" I asked in agitation.

"There was no fire. It was a warm night. You had the paper when you rushed out, I believe. You might have thrown it away after that, of course."

"Which public house?" I rose, unable to sit still. "Can you direct me?"

"The Fox and Hen, in a lane near the Quaker Meeting."

Which I must have entered after speaking to Mr. Bickley. Bickley had not mentioned I'd been reeling drunk when I spoke to him, and neither had Miss Farrow. Therefore I possibly had drunk something in that tavern—something in the coffee—that rendered me senseless. Hadn't Marianne told me that coffee could disguise the taste of opium?

And what on earth had been in the message that took me away?

"Forgive me, Captain," I said. "I must go there at once."

"Quite understandable. I will accompany you."

The captain generously left coin for the ale we'd barely touched and led the way out. Brewster dumped as much ale down his throat as he could before wiping his mouth and hurrying after us.

Brighton was as cheerful as ever despite the sadness of the inquest—holiday-goers shopping and dining, locals haggling at the markets, vendors desperate to sell wares to tourists who might depart tomorrow and never return.

The Fox and Hen, sporting a lively painted sign of a large hen chasing a frightened-looking fox, was steps away from the Quaker Meeting House. One of the Quakers, working in the garden, glanced up in curiosity as we raced past.

While I wanted to charge inside and shake the publican until he told me what I wanted to know, I made myself calmly order ale for us all—I'd pay this time—before I addressed the man behind the bar.

"Do you remember me from Monday night?" I asked.

The publican, busy trying a broach a new keg, glanced up and grunted. "Can't say I do."

"I sat ..." I looked to Captain Wilks for guidance.

"In the inglenook." He pointed. "Near the fireplace."

The publican remained at his task. "Many men do. My taproom's a busy place."

"I ordered a coffee, and then you brought me a note or letter," I said. "I grew alarmed when I read it and ran out."

The publican shook his head, then he paused and turned his head to study me. "Oh, aye, I remember now. You gave me a crown for my trouble. Thank ye kindly."

"Excellent." At least he recalled a good tip. "Do you know what the message said?"

The publican straightened, resting his hands on the bar. "No. I don't read, meself. Have me son do that for me. Why don't *you* know what it said?"

I warmed. "I cannot explain."

The publican's face creased in a smile. "Far gone in drink, were ye? You were swaying a bit as you sat, I remember. Probably didn't mean to hand me so much for nothing, did ye? Well, ye can't have it back. It's mine fair and square."

"I'd be obliged for your help." I dipped into my pocket and brought out another crown. "Did anyone else read this message? Or did I drop it on my way out?"

"How should I know? We sweep up all kinds of bits every night when we shut the doors. You wouldn't believe the things we find. If you dropped it on the floor, it's long gone to the rag and bone man."

I stifled my disappointment with effort. "Did anyone besides yourself see the message?"

"That important, is it?" The publican frowned at me. "Sit yourself down, sir. I'll ask me son."

I took the nearest chair, barely containing my restlessness. Brewster and the captain joined me, Brewster slurping this ale determinedly.

The publican finished setting up his keg before he wiped his hands and disappeared through a door.

"Is the place familiar to you?" Captain Wilks asked me. "Anything you remember?"

"Not at all," I said in disappointment as I looked around. "If I'd wanted coffee, why did I not step into the coffee house?" There was one nearby, which I'd passed when I'd tried to retrace my steps from Monday night.

"You were muddled," Brewster said. "Happens."

"Possibly." I scanned the room, noting the fireplace with its bench built into the wall—the inglenook. My eye went to a cartoon pinned above the bench, of a popular actress of the stage, her curvy proportions exaggerated, her large cap balanced on an abundance of golden curls.

One of my dreams returned from Tuesday morning, when I lay in a stupor—of my wife in such a cap, her hair changing from dark to pale, and then her face becoming Marianne's. I'd heard Marianne's voice telling me I was a lazy lie-abed.

I stared at the cartoon, rising from my seat to study it. The image of the blond actress must have stuck in my brain and then transformed into my inebriated dreams.

If I could remember that, could I remember other things?

I scrutinized the taproom again, but nothing leapt at me. I slid onto the bench in the inglenook, where I could see the picture as I had then.

"I remember that." I pointed to it as Brewster and the captain followed me. "I must have stared quite hard at it."

"Course you did." Brewster still held his tankard. "You're ever one for the ladies, and she's a fair specimen."

Or did the picture mean something else to me? I could not think what.

"This must be the lad," Captain Wilks said.

The publican approached us, followed by a tall young man in his twenties, his lankiness just turning to harder muscle.

"Do you know anything about the message delivered to me here this past Monday night?" I asked him without preliminary.

The young man gave me a slow nod. "I do, sir. Dad tells me you don't remember it."

"Did you happen to see what was in this message?" I tried to curb my impatience.

"I did. Sorry, sir, but it were only a bit of paper. Couldn't help but see what were written on it."

"Don't drag it out, lad," Brewster growled. "What did the bloody thing say?"

The young man flushed. "I don't recall exactly. But it said for you to go outside. To meet someone." His color deepened. "I assumed a lady."

My throat tightened, making speech difficult. "Why did you assume that?"

"'Cause I saw you with her. You ran out, and a lady with a large cloak and hat took your arm. You disappeared with her in the dark, and that's the last I saw of ye."

CHAPTER 17

I gazed at the publican's son in astonishment, and the drawings on the paneling in the inglenook seemed to spin. "Did you see this lady? Who the devil was she?"

The young man shrugged. "It were dark and she was all shrouded in the cloak."

I jumped to my feet. "How tall, how broad, or how thin?"

The lad shook his head, bewildered. "Ordinary, I'd say. Not as tall as you. Not a rotund lady, but not small either. But then, I really only saw her cloak."

His description helped not at all. I stood taller than most men I knew, and I towered above women, which potentially made the wearer of the cloak anyone in Brighton.

"Sorry, sir."

I sat back down, letting out a long breath. "Well. Thank you, in any case. It's more than I knew before." I drew a half crown from my pocket. "I appreciate your candor, lad."

The coin disappeared. "Thank you, sir."

The publican's son turned away as though dismissed, but I said, "Before you go, will you think about the note? Was it written neatly, in a fine hand, on good paper? Scribbled on a scrap? Anything is helpful."

The young man rubbed his stubbled face. "Paper was heavy and new, but not a whole sheet. Only one line, in printed letters, not written. That's how I could read it. I can't read handwriting so well."

He was a sharp observer, at least of things he saw close to. I couldn't blame him for knowing no more details of a woman shrouded in a cloak on a dark night.

"Thank you," I said sincerely. "If you recall anything else, please send word." I gave him the address of our hired house, and he nodded before he turned away with his father and ambled back to pulling pints.

"Printed," I said to Brewster and Captain Wilks. "To not give away who wrote it?"

"How would you know who wrote the bloody thing?" Brewster demanded. "Would ye run around Brighton comparing everyone's handwriting to it?"

"Perhaps I knew that person well, or had seen their hand-writing before."

Brewster shrugged and sipped his ale, skeptical.

Captain Wilks broke in, "The greater question is, who was the lady? Not your wife, I take it."

Chills settled over me as I realized who the lady, if it had been a woman, might very well be.

Marguerite had had every reason to hate Isherwood and want him dead. He'd cruelly abandoned her at Salamanca, leaving her to her fate.

I remembered the Spanish sunshine on the walls of the old city, the wide space of the Plaza Mayor, its sandstone a warm, golden hue. I'd loved the town when we'd ridden in after the battle in the hills, soldiers seeking comfort and drink. Bells of the cathedral had silvered the air, and heat shimmered on the stones, the sky arching high and blue.

Isherwood and Marguerite had performed their final quarrel in the square, he turning his back on her and striding away. She'd never wilted, only glared after him as he'd marched off with a sneering Forbes.

Then Marguerite had turned, flung out her arms, and declared at the top of her voice that she was free.

The plaza had teemed with life, the people of the ancient city relieved that the French army, who'd used the town as a garrison, had been chased away, but mistrusting of the English who'd taken their place. They'd been disapproving of Marguerite spinning in the middle of the square, laughing. A group of nuns had eyed her severely, but I'd seen Marguerite's bitterness, her near despair.

Marguerite had been left alone, without protection, in a country strange to her, in the middle of an army.

As Donata had said, I'd had to be gallant. Marguerite and I had taken up residence in a hostel down a sloping back street near the cathedral, with a cheerful landlord and his wife to look after us. Our room had overlooked the Tormes that flowed languidly past the city, and the many-arched bridge the ancient Romans had left in their wake.

Forbes had found out about our liaison and taken me to task. It had nearly come to a duel, but Colonel Brandon had intervened and sent Forbes off. Brandon had then given me a scathing dressing down, but I'd laughed at him. Marguerite had been a warm, giving, charming woman, and the brief time I'd spent with her had become a happy memory.

Isherwood, of course, had made certain her reputation was blackened. I never discovered why the devil the man had put her aside in the first place, except that he was a selfish bastard

—possibly his commanding officer disapproved of her, which would mean Isherwood might not be promoted.

The man had been made a colonel, so obviously the divorce had not ruined his career.

Lord Armitage had posited another reason Isherwood had shunned her, his claim that Marguerite had been a spy for the French.

For any of these reasons, Marguerite could very well have wanted Isherwood murdered. Had she decided I should be the man to kill him for her?

Or had she sent the note to ask for my help? Perhaps I'd become angry at Isherwood for threatening her, and we'd tracked him to the Pavilion. Or perhaps Marguerite had killed Isherwood before I could stop her, and I'd taken the sword from her.

She'd fled, and I'd been left standing with the sword, swimming out of my stupor.

"Damnation," I whispered.

"The machinations of a lady do not mean you killed the Quaker lad in a drunken rage," Captain Wilks said. "I would find the lady—she can tell the magistrate you were with her instead of Josh Bickley. Embarrassing for your wife, no doubt, but it would save you from the noose."

"Pardon?" I blinked. I'd been a long distance from thoughts of Bickley's son—how could the note and Marguerite have anything to do with him?

Brewster took a noisy sip of ale. "Could have been a bloke waiting for you. Bundled up in a cloak in the dark—might have been a man, pretending to be a lady to draw you out. Once you were with him, he could have taken you anywhere. Be best if you remembered all what happened, guv."

"Thank you, Brewster. An excellent suggestion." I gave him

an ironic look, pulling myself out of my thoughts. "Thank you in truth, Captain Wilks. This has been helpful. I believe that once I track down this lady, all will become clear."

Wilks firmly shook my hand. "If I discover anything more, I will send word." His grip tightened. "I feel it only fair to warn you that if I discover you *did* murder young Master Bickley, I will go straight to the magistrate."

"I would expect no less." I gave Wilks a nod as he released me. "I would do the same."

<hr />

"GENTRY IS DIFFERENT FROM ORDINARY FOLK, AIN'T THEY?" Brewster made this observation as we walked through the lane toward Ship Street, my stick ringing on the cobblestones. "All polite and cool, shaking hands while promising to have you arrested. If I said that to a mate, I'd be fighting for me life. Or laughed at."

"He will not find evidence that I had anything to do with Josh's death," I said, then I sucked in a breath. "At least, I damn well hope not."

"Then where are we off to in such a hurry?"

I hesitated. If I told Brewster my thoughts, he'd report all to Denis. Denis might decide to interrogate Marguerite himself, and his methods were not always gentle.

"Someone I need to speak to," I said. "I will be perfectly safe —no need to come with me."

"Huh. Not bloody likely."

Brewster hunkered into his coat, though it was a warm afternoon, and prepared to follow me.

I gave up and let him, knowing I'd never shake him if he wanted to stick with me. Not long later, I knocked on the door of the house where I'd left Marguerite with her husband the night before.

"They're out, dear," the landlady said to my inquiries. She had a pleasant pink face and a kindly smile. "Enjoying the weather, no doubt. Shall I tell them you inquired?"

"Please do." I handed her a card, which she held close to her face to peer at. "Ask them to call on me at their earliest convenience."

"I will, dear. Good day to you."

She was inside, shutting the door before I could so much as respond to her polite farewell.

"See what I mean?" Brewster continued his observations as we turned for Bedford Row. "This is who you think lured you to the Pavilion that night, yes? You leave a card and ask them to call, instead of pushing in and tearing up the place until you find your evidence."

"They may have nothing to do with it," I said severely.

"That's not what your face tells me. You're convinced. Want His Nibs to find them for you?"

"No." I made the word hard. "I said I don't want Denis involved at all. That is why I will ask you to say nothing until I'm certain."

We were almost to the square. Brewster put a heavy hand on my shoulder and pulled me to a halt.

"Understand summat, guv," he said, his face grave. "His Nibs wants you cleared of all this murder business, whether you did it or not. He's not having one of his best men strung up for murder or transported to Van Diemen's Land—if *that* got about, it would weaken him in the eyes of some, and that could spell disaster for him. He's got friends in high places, and he's prepared to use them to keep you from the muck. But you have to trust him to do his bit."

I did not back down. "I know all about the corrupt magistrates who bow to James Denis. It is a reason I have fought all this time to stay away from him. Likewise, I do not want to be known as one of his best men. I am not a criminal."

"It's a bit late for that. He's done you far too many favors for you to spit on him now."

"I know he has."

Denis had done me the greatest favor of all—saved my beloved wife from death. Under the hands of any physician or surgeon but the one Denis had sent, Donata would have been lost, possibly Anne with her, and I knew it.

"Then don't keep things from him," Brewster said. "Let him help. He's good at it."

I growled in my throat, ducked away from his hand, and strode on. "At least let me speak to the woman before he does."

"Unless she's fled town," Brewster said behind me. "Her deeds done."

With Isherwood dead, would Marguerite consider she'd achieved her end? She could return to her blissful existence as the wife of an ordinary gentleman in an ordinary town and forget the past.

I wondered if her husband, Gibbons, was in on the plot. They seemed close, so he might very well be.

"If I fail to lay my hands on her, then I will ask Denis to run her to ground," I said, turning. "Only if he promises that *I* can speak to her. I will know what questions to ask."

"We'll see." Brewster's words were final. "Where to now? Discover if the woman is sea bathing?"

"First I must speak to another lady," I said. "The most important one."

Brewster understood, and gave me a nod. "Ah. Wise of you, guv."

UPON OUR RETURN, I WAS PLEASED TO FIND THAT DONATA HAD not gone out on calls but sat in her boudoir, writing letters.

She looked up from the writing table when I entered, hesitant but no longer unwelcoming. I kissed her cheek then drew a chair next to hers and told her about the inquest and what Mrs. Morgan and then Captain Wilks had revealed.

"Are you certain Mrs. Gibbons was the woman in the cloak?" Donata asked once I'd finished. She toyed with the end of her pen. "Why would she lure *you* to commit the deed for her? That would be most ungrateful of her, after you helped her in Spain. You paid her passage home, did you not?"

"Yes, but perhaps Marguerite did not mean for Isherwood to be killed. Perhaps she only wanted to hurt him or scare him, but killed him accidentally and fled. Or maybe I took Isherwood's sword from him and ran him through in a rage." I let out a sigh. "I simply don't know."

Donata regarded me with a keen eye. "You are a strong man, Gabriel, but Colonel Isherwood was hardly in a decline. Quite a robust gentleman. I am surprised anyone in his regiment believes that he took ill in the night and simply died. He was in the pink of health."

"He lived in a private house on the Royal Crescent, not the barracks. How could the regiment know what truly happens there?"

"Major Forbes knows," she reminded me. "It is only a matter of time before a man like that shouts the information from the rooftops. If he realized you were discovered by Isherwood's body, you'd even now be in some filthy jail."

"I quite agree," I said, despondent. "The man loathes me.

Isherwood was a god to him. Could do no wrong, in spite of all evidence to the contrary."

"But perhaps the two had a falling out, and Major Forbes *did* kill Isherwood, or at least arranged for you to be found over his body."

"I've considered that. I doubt Forbes would be satisfied to have me found as the murderer—Forbes would kill me himself and claim he had been defending Isherwood. He'd be glad of the excuse to rid himself of me." I shook my head. "Everything at the moment points to Marguerite."

My wife sent me an impatient look. "I know you are determined that Mrs. Gibbons was the woman in the cloak, and she somehow convinced you to help kill her former husband. But consider how well acquainted I am with you. Mrs. Gibbons cannot be the only woman in all of England who would seek you out and ask for your aid on a dark night. I can name any number."

I flushed. "Who happen to be in Brighton? Connected with Isherwood, who was stabbed to death that very night?"

"The cloaked woman might have absolutely nothing to do with Isherwood. The woman might not have sent the note at all, but you chanced to encounter her when you charged out of the pub, and the publican's boy only assumed she'd summoned you."

"Now you are introducing too many possibilities," I said in exasperation.

"Because there *are* many possibilities. The message said you should go outside and meet someone. No indication who, not even whether it was a man or woman. Printed, not written, so you could not judge whether it was a woman's writing or a man's, or whether you'd seen the writing before. A cloaked woman appears, or as Brewster pointed out, perhaps a man hiding in a large cloak. The publican's son didn't see this person well in the dark. Or he or she might have simply been asking you for the time or the direction to the Old Ship."

"Unlikely ..."

"I am only listing alternative explanations, so you will cease fixing on one. We will discover whether it was Marguerite Gibbons and why she wished to see you, if so, when we ask her."

"I called at their lodgings on my way home," I said. "She and her husband were not there."

Donata widened her eyes. "Fancy that. In Brighton, by the sea, on a fair day. How very strange that they went out. If they'd packed their bags and fled, the landlady would have told you."

"Unless they left their bags behind."

"You do enjoy making difficulties. You left word that they should call, and if they have nothing to hide, they will."

I regarded her a moment. "I would have thought you'd have leapt at the chance to pin all these troubles on Mrs. Gibbons."

"Like a jealous harridan?" Donata gave me a pitying smile. "I admit, I *am* jealous of her, but only because she had you at a time when I was so miserable. While you celebrated your victory at Salamanca, Breckenridge returned to London. To see his son, he told me, but he spent his entire month of leave trying to make me admit Peter was not his. Bloody man. He certainly would not take me at my word, and I grew terrified of being in the same room with him. Do you know what it is like to hope your husband never returns from battle?" Donata dropped her pen onto the desk and shivered. "But you once told me that Breckenridge had ways of making certain he was nowhere near the bullets, so that hope was in vain."

I reached to her and cupped her cheek, trying to still her

agitation. I wanted to apologize for some reason, to tell her I'd have shot Breckenridge myself if I could have.

Donata's voice quieted. "You did not know me then, nor did I know you existed. Had I known about you, and what would happen between us … it might have been easier to bear. Even if you were with another at the time."

"I hate the man every time I hear about him," I said, my dark anger stirring.

"I hated living with him. Poor naive girl that I was, I could not discern a good man from a bad before it was too late." Donata put her hand on mine. "*You* are one of the good ones."

"Am I?" I withdrew from her touch. "Then why would I have been so glad to murder Breckenridge for you? It makes me believe I could have killed Isherwood for Marguerite."

"And if I believed *that*, I'd even now be in Oxford with my son and daughter, and bar the door to you, because it would mean you still loved the dratted woman." She drew in a breath. "I have to be confident that you do not."

"Love?" I said in astonishment. "I never *loved* Marguerite. It was a brief affair, the aftermath of battle, me scorning convention and gloating about it. Love never entered into it, on either of our parts."

Donata's smile was savage. "And I am jealous enough to be terribly pleased by that."

"My dearest Donata, do you believe that my tenderness can be aroused by any lady but yourself?" I pressed my hand to my breast, wanting to make her laugh.

"Do not overstate things, Gabriel. You *have* loved other women—your first wife, Gabriella, your mother. You also must have had many youthful infatuations."

I waved away the callow passions of my young years, all gone in dust. "Believe what you will. Marguerite never loved me, or I her. She seems to be very fond of Gibbons, I am happy to report."

"There you are, then. Why on earth should Mrs. Gibbons summon you to help her slay Isherwood and then leave you to be arrested? You helped her in Salamanca, she liked you, and from what you've told me, you parted amicably. By all evidence, she married happily instead of living all these years nursing resentment—so why would she exact this sort of vengeance on you?"

I rose, unable to keep still. "I have no bloody idea. Marguerite was never the most prim and proper of women, which is likely why Isherwood wanted her gone. Her vivaciousness and lack of respect for idiot senior officers had caused Isherwood to be called on the carpet more than once. I suppose he finally decided he cared for his career more than his wife—always did, I suspect."

"She was well rid of him then," Donata said calmly. "Once she realized that, she'd hardly wish to kill him, would she?"

I made myself resume my seat, my knee chiding me for my energetic pacing.

"Lord Armitage tried to tell me she was a spy for the French." I massaged the offended knee as I spoke. "That would give her another motive for getting rid of Isherwood. If Isherwood found out, or suspected ... He'd not only put her aside but threaten to reveal her duplicity, and she'd be executed as a traitor. He could hold that over her for years. Perhaps Marguerite decided to end the threat."

"Armitage is not the most reliable of informants," Donata said. "He loves to spread gossip about others, presumably to keep them from repeating the stories about him and his own wife. Did Mrs. Gibbons seem a likely spy? What sort of information could she have obtained from you?"

"Nothing." I had argued this with Armitage. "I was not high enough in the chain of command to know anything of importance."

"Therefore, she did not throw herself at you to discover secrets to pass to the French marshals." Donata drummed her fingers on the desk. "It is likely Isherwood himself whispered that rumor to justify his leaving her. When a woman knows her own mind, and says so, gentlemen will spread all sorts of falsehoods about her."

She spoke from experience. Few women knew their own mind better than Donata.

"I can discover whether the rumors began with Isherwood," I said. "I will buttonhole Forbes, who was Isherwood's friend longer than anyone."

"Buttonhole him, but do not bloody his nose," Donata advised. "Let us not forget about the Regent. Isherwood's death might have nothing to do with Mrs. Gibbons, her husband, and what happened in Spain. Your lad Clement reported that the prince was at the Pavilion at the requisite time."

"Yes." I returned to that with some hope. "Why the Regent would kill Isherwood, I cannot fathom, but the two might have quarreled. I do not know why Isherwood was even invited that night."

"Grenville could find this out. I can have a chat with Lady Hollingsworth—I've known her for years. His Highness might have confessed all to her."

"If it wasn't simply a horrible accident," I said. "The Regent, showing off his prowess with a sword, runs the man through. I can envision such a thing."

"Unlikely. Colonel Isherwood wouldn't have let him. As I said before, Isherwood was a strong man, and the Regent can barely stand with his gout."

"True. But Isherwood should have been able to fight off *any* attack," I finished glumly. "Which is why I return to Marguerite once more. Isherwood might not have believed his danger, either from her or from me, and so did not defend himself."

Donata fixed me with her stubborn look. "I do not believe you killed this man, Gabriel, no matter what. And I will prove it, whether you wish me to or not."

I'D LEARNED WHEN TO CEASE ARGUING WITH DONATA. SHE SET her mind on a course, and she would not be dissuaded. I'd leave her to ferret out any details from Lady Hollingsworth, welcoming whatever help she could give me.

I descended to the sitting room to write my letter to Colonel Brandon, asking him to tell me what he remembered about events in Salamanca. I gave the missive to Bartholomew, who would send it off by quickest post.

Brewster arrived after that, having gone home once he'd seen me safely inside. He looked gloomy. "His Nibs wants to see you."

"Again? Is he not satisfied with my lists?"

"How should I know? He asks to see you, and I fetch you."

I did not fight him, knowing the futility of it. Brewster led me out, not to his own lodgings, but to another row of new houses that faced the sea.

Denis had hired it this morning, Brewster told me, as things were too cramped in Brewster's rooms. Denis had decided to remain in Brighton until he was satisfied I would not be accused of Isherwood's murder and so had let an entire house. I knew Denis didn't care much about who really had killed Isherwood, as long as I wasn't arrested for it.

That was a large difference between Denis and myself, I reflected as Brewster knocked on the door of a white-painted house with large windows. I was never satisfied until I discovered the truth, even if the truth proved to be ugly or inconvenient. Denis was happy to let the truth go hang unless it interfered with his life or his business.

The house was pleasant inside, its white-paneled rooms made cozy with plenty of sunlight. Simple elegance. Denis received me on the first floor, in a chamber at the back of the house which he'd converted to a study.

One of Denis's men ushered me in, Brewster following with a heavy tread. Denis did not always like Brewster accompanying me into his presence, but I knew Brewster had come to make sure I didn't do anything foolish.

Denis was not alone. Along with his usual bodyguards stood another man, silent and unobtrusive. I halted in surprise.

He was thin-boned with a shaved head, his intelligent eyes containing no expression whatsoever. The man was a criminal, a killer, who'd been transported to the other side of the world and had illegally made his way back. He was also the brilliant surgeon who'd earlier this year saved Donata's life and that of my daughter Anne.

"I have called him to consult with us," Denis said from where he sat at his desk, his blue eyes almost, but not quite, as cold as the surgeon's. "To see if he can tell us what sort of concoction you were fed, and what it could make you do."

CHAPTER 18

The surgeon had positioned himself near the fireplace, which lay between two windows. I realized that anyone who looked in from below would not be able to see him.

He studied me now without changing expression. Even Denis's guards appeared more interested in the problem than he did.

"Describe what happened," he commanded.

No greeting, no waiting until I'd been offered a seat or refreshment. Denis said nothing at all, expecting my response.

"I'll do my best." I launched into my tale. "Even the memory of coming to myself in the Pavilion is fuzzy," I concluded. "I managed to get out of the building and make my way home. When I woke, I remembered nothing at all—I've been trying to discover exactly what I did that night and who truly killed Colonel Isherwood, but there are still large gaps."

The surgeon watched me stolidly. "No, what *exactly* do you remember? What was your last memory before the absence of them? Were you disoriented when you came to, or clear of mind? When you slept, did you have odd dreams—could you sleep at all? Did you seem to experience things that could not possibly have happened?" He ceased the rapid-fire questions and pinned me with a hard stare. "I will need all details."

I told myself that a physician must be much like a general— a commander could only know how to meet the enemy if he knew precisely where they were, how many soldiers they had at the ready, and what weaponry they possessed. The more details, the more prepared he could be.

"I remember talking with the other guests at supper," I said. "Mostly about common concerns, such as the weather, farming, and events in the newspapers. Desjardins regaled us with a tale of a chamber pot Bonaparte supposedly left behind in Madrid, and how it was auctioned off for a very high price once he was deposed." I paused, recalling how Desjardins had laughed very hard, and Isherwood had upbraided him for telling such an anecdote in front of the ladies.

The surgeon took it all in, again without changing expression. "Go on."

"I recall enjoying a glass of port afterward. A fine vintage from the Douro Valley in Portugal, near Régua. I had gone into an antechamber and Isherwood joined me there. Isherwood took me aside and sneered something about his former wife. Bad taste to bring that up, I thought, and told him so. He even threatened to speak to *my* wife, but apparently he did not."

Denis cleared his throat. "I'd have a care whom you reported *that* detail to."

"In case they believe I murdered a blackmailer?" I grimaced. "There is nothing to say I did not."

Denis only gave me his bland stare. "Continue."

"After that, I walked with Grenville in the park. I haven't the faintest notion what we said to each other. I smoked a cheroot. He said good night, and …" I spread my hands. "The rest is a blank until I found Isherwood dead in the Pavilion."

The surgeon listened to all this dispassionately. "Have you had any flashes of memory? Even vague feelings you don't understand?"

I hesitated. "When I saw Lord and Lady Armitage at the lecture on Tuesday night, something tickled in my brain. But I have no idea what."

"That is all?"

"Earlier today, when Captain Wilks took me to the tavern he said I'd been in, I remembered a picture on the wall, one of an actress. But that likely only means I truly had entered that tavern."

"You slept after you went home," the surgeon stated.

"Indeed, I went to bed. I tossed and turned a bit before sleeping—had dreams first of Isherwood, then of faces coming at me, changing and merging. I woke late in the afternoon with no idea I'd slept away much of the day." I let out a breath. "That is all I can truly tell you."

"No, there is much more." The surgeon rested one elbow on the mantelpiece. "When you woke in your bed, was your mouth dry? Did you have a headache? Any other aches in your body? Were you flaccid or rigid? Did you twitch or were you completely relaxed? Were your feet and hands cold or warm?"

His hard look said he expected me to answer the litany, no matter how embarrassing.

I swallowed. "I was sick in a basin before I went to bed, and I woke with a dry throat and headache. My back was sore, I recall, and my knee ached—though it usually does in the morning. Flaccid, I think." My face warmed. "I was restless, my hands tingling, my feet rather numb. The warm water with my shave felt good. I was much better after I dressed, and able to walk through town, though I was a bit fatigued. Later that evening, Grenville's wife told me my eyes were slow to focus."

The surgeon listened in silence. No nodding as I listed my symptoms, no flick of eyes or thoughtful movement of brows. I might have been speaking to a statue.

The clock ticked. Outside, people walked by the house, their voices loud through the windows open at the top for air. A woman's voice: "... Spending so much time in a carriage, bumping over roads for hours, and there was nothing *there*." A man; "I thought the church quite fine ..." The woman again, "No different from the parish church in ..."

They faded, disgruntled travelers irritated the world hadn't arranged itself to please them.

"There are several possibilities." The surgeon's clear words were startling after the quiet. "It is a question of what would be available to the person or persons who gave you the dose."

Denis took up his pen and dipped it in ink. "The possibilities are?"

"From the ordinary to the extraordinary: Laudanum. Opium, ingested, not smoked. Either of these mixed with a large quantity of alcohol. There are purer forms of opium being distilled as medicines; one in particular relieves all pain but might render you immobile at the same time."

"I walked from place to place without trouble, it seems," I said. "Spoke to people, in fact."

The surgeon went on as though I hadn't interrupted. "There are oils from the Dutch East Indies that render a person quite inebriated and cause memory loss. An extract from a plant from the Americas can make a man see things that do not exist, and he does not remember his trance when he awakes. The natives of certain regions use it in religious ceremonies."

Dubious, I asked, "How likely are such substances to be in England? In Brighton?"

"I possess some of each I have mentioned," the surgeon said. "The very distilled opium I use only rarely, but I keep a small quantity about in case it's needed. However, all my medicines are locked away in London."

He'd given Donata a medicine when she'd borne Anne to help heal her, and I'd never learned what. I hadn't cared, so long as Donata recovered.

I thought about what Marianne had told me the night of the lecture. "Mrs. Grenville suggested that sailors bring such things into the country all the time. Actors apparently make use of dangerous substances to enhance their looks or give them the courage to enter the stage."

Denis was making plenty of notes, his pen lightly scratching in the stillness. "Laudanum would be the easiest thing to give you." He wrote a few more words and laid down his pen. "But you are familiar with it and would recognize the taste. Also, as you have used laudanum often to quell pain, it would take a very large dose to render you insensible. You would have noticed drinking such a quantity."

"The purer distillation of opium is more likely, in this case," the surgeon told him. "The oil from the East Indies is less likely, though some apothecaries sell it ... discreetly. I have not seen in England the American juice that causes delirium but that does not mean no one else has obtained it."

I gazed at the surgeon in disbelief. "So I am looking for a person who has visited an apothecary not adverse to selling exotic potions."

"That is a possibility," the surgeon said. "You could also search for an avid gardener who knows a thing or two about extracting and distilling substances from plants. The opium poppy is cultivated not only for medicine but for its bright colors and edible seeds."

"In other words, anyone in England could have given me this substance," I said despairingly.

"Not anyone," Denis pointed out in his cool voice. "Only those close to you Monday night. You drank any number of substances—wine at supper, port afterward, coffee at the public house."

I thought of Captain Wilks. He himself could have doctored my coffee—a bitter enough drink that I might not have tasted any addition. Or the publican could have, paid by my enemy to do so.

"Would I not have noticed someone emptying a vial into my port or coffee?" I asked testily.

"Not if you were distracted," Denis said. "Arguing or debating, speaking to another while your glass remained behind you … It is a simple matter to slip a dose to a person without their knowledge."

I did not like contemplating how he knew this. "Which puts me no closer to the truth."

"On the contrary." Denis looked over his notes. "How long do the effects of this distilled opium last?" he asked the surgeon.

"Two or three hours if a small dose but it can also obscure memories from before the dose is taken. As it wears off, the patient sleeps, has nightmares, headaches, and wakes with numbness and very little interest in copulation. He remains slightly inebriated by it for as much as an entire day."

He described my condition so exactly that I shivered.

Denis switched his focus to me. "Then the concoction could only have been given to you in a narrow window of time, by any person you met Monday evening. I suggest you look at each one very carefully. Also consider that the person who gave you the substance might not have known it would make you forget taking it. This was fortunate for them. But they might worry that one day, those memories will return."

"Am I likely to regain the memories?" I asked the surgeon.

"Not very," he answered without hesitation. "Events wiped away by substances such as these are usually gone forever."

I didn't like the despondency his answer gave me. The blank in my mind was unnerving, and he'd just told me I'd have to live with it the rest of my life.

"I wonder if Isherwood himself gave me the dose," I said, mostly to distract myself from my disquiet.

"Possibly, but I'd wonder at his purpose." Denis neatly pushed his notes aside, his tone suggesting he was finished with the conversation. "Determining who had such an opium solution and the opportunity to feed it to you will no doubt reveal the killer and why they wished you to be accused of the crime."

"Must be driving them spare that you ran off," Brewster put in. "And that the dead colonel's son won't tell anyone he was murdered."

"Indeed." Thoughts began to turn in my head—I was a slow thinker but my advantage was that I never let my thoughts cease. "I wonder what would happen if the murderer believed I *had* regained the memories?"

"Disaster," Brewster said, full of gloom. "That's what. And me having to come behind to pick up the pieces."

THE SKY WAS DARKENING TO EVENING BY THE TIME I RETURNED home. Gabriella had returned from her day out with Lady

Aline, but she intercepted me before I could enter the drawing room for a much needed coffee.

"Stepmamma is in there," she whispered. "She said she needed to compose herself."

I raised my brows, foreboding chilling my blood. "Compose herself for what?"

"She had callers while you were out, and she sent me away so she could speak to them alone." Her brown eyes held worry. "I did not know them. Mr. and Mrs. Gibbons?"

I turned abruptly on my heel, thanking Gabriella, who was too polite to ask more questions. I quickly entered the drawing room and shut its door behind me.

Donata reposed on a sofa, her feet on an ottoman she'd drawn to it, her legs crossed at the ankle. A lit cigarillo wafted smoke from a bowl on a nearby table, and Donata held a glass of brandy she was in the act of finishing.

"You could have put them off," I said before she could speak. "The Gibbonses. I'd have interviewed them. There was no need for you to."

"There *was* need." Donata spoke calmly, but I saw the brandy glass trembler. "It is not often a lady can interrogate her husband's former mistress."

I made for the brandy decanter and poured myself a measure. I drank it in one go, the smooth liquid burning to my stomach. "At least you could see that she is happy, living with her husband, her old life behind her."

"Happy in her marriage, yes," Donata said. "Unnerved of course by Isherwood's murder, but not unduly so, I think. Do sit down, Gabriel. You make me nervous when you hover."

I poured more brandy and folded myself onto the sofa next to her.

"That's better," she said. "I wished Mrs. Gibbons had come

alone so I could quiz her more pointedly, but that would hardly do, would it? They expected to find *you* here, not me, and Mrs. Gibbons would never embarrass her husband by calling on you on her own." Donata plucked her cigarillo from the bowl, thin smoke rising. "By the way—I was correct. Marguerite Gibbons was *not* the woman who accosted you outside the public house on Monday night."

I sipped my second glass of brandy more slowly. "You believe her?"

"It is not a question of believing her. Mrs. Gibbons and her husband were still in Portsmouth at the time you were in the public house—she has many witnesses who will swear the Gibbonses did not leave home until Tuesday afternoon. They arrived in Brighton late Tuesday night."

I deflated. "I suppose that is easily checked."

"I do not intend to take her at her word, of course, and I have sent a note to Mr. Quimby that he should find out. But it is highly unlikely the woman outside the public house was Mrs. Gibbons. She could not be in two places at once."

"Then who was the woman?" I said half to myself.

"What does Mr. Denis say about it? He has many resources —he needs to use them."

"Mmm. He has hinted that he intends to help me out of this dilemma only so he can use my services for something else. He has not told me what."

Donata took a pull of her cigarillo, her eyes narrowing. "Well, we will have to take care of that problem when we come to it. What did he want today?"

My injured knee was unhappy so I lifted my foot to join hers on the large ottoman. "To have his pet surgeon ask me about my inebriation."

Donata listened with interest as I related the surgeon's

speculations. I ended with my plan to put it about that I was beginning to clearly remember events of the night.

"That will be exceedingly dangerous," Donata said, worry entering her eyes. "If the murderer believes you know his identity..."

"He will confront me, and then we will have him," I said firmly. "I do not intend to meet him alone in a dark lane, unarmed. I will have Brewster, Quimby, and other stout fellows with me to arrest him." I quieted. "It may be that there will be no murderer to find but me."

"We have discussed this." Donata tossed her spent cigarillo into the bowl. "I do not believe you killed Isherwood, no matter how angry you were with him. He was horrid to his wife, yes, and angry at you for helping her, but that was seven years ago, and he had not seen you since. It is unlikely you were still incensed enough about that to run him through—and even then, you'd challenge him to meet with seconds."

"I hope you are right," I said. "Then again, who knows what would set me off if I'd drunk a strong concoction of opium?"

"I suppose it is true we can't know that, but I still do not believe you'd lose your sense of honor, even then. And how do you plan to let it be known that you've regained your memory of the night? Invite all those we supped with at the Pavilion to dine? There were twenty people there—we haven't the room."

I laid my arm across the back of the sofa, letting it touch her shoulders. "I will ask Isherwood's son if he'll allow Mr. Quimby to announce that Isherwood was murdered. Mr. Quimby can imply that I know something about it and am helping to find the killer. Which is true."

"Young Isherwood might not agree," Donata warned. "He was adamant, you said, not to put the stain of murder onto his family, and not to embarrass the Regent." She took a breath.

"Oh, Lord, what if the Regent truly *did* kill Colonel Isherwood? You'll cause a terrible scandal if you reveal it."

"The Regent causes enough scandal on his own—will anyone notice?" I spoke lightly then sobered. "I understand your fears. A man who accuses his monarch of a capital crime will not be well received, even when that monarch is unpopular already. I hope it will not come to that."

"I had planned to call on Lady Hollingsworth today, but the Gibbonses arrived. I will go tomorrow and persuade her to tell me all the Regent said to her that night, including any intention to run back to the Pavilion and stab Isherwood."

"Would she tell you?" I asked doubtfully.

"She would." Donata gave me an arch glance. "My dear Gabriel, I know many things about many people. Most will take great care that these things are not made common knowledge."

I gazed at her in half admiration, half worry. "You mean you blackmail them."

My wife smiled at me. "Only a little."

I suppressed a shudder. "I pray you will not have to exercise your criminal tendencies. I will find Mr. Quimby and ask him to pay a call on young Colonel Isherwood."

I HAD A REPAST FIRST, WITH DONATA AND GABRIELLA, THEN went out into the gathering darkness, heading for Quimby's lodgings. On the way, I found the Quaker woman, Miss Purkis.

Or rather, she found me.

CHAPTER 19

*Y*ou are Gabriel Lacey?" A middle-aged woman in a finely-made frock of dark maroon and a high-crowned bonnet stopped me.

I did not know her, and politely bowed. "At your service, madam."

A smile spread across her face. "I hear you have been searching for me. I am Katherine Purkis. Or at least, I was. I am Mrs. Craddock now."

"Craddock ..." I blinked in amazement. I also realized that she, a Quaker woman, had not used *thee* or *thou*, and had called herself *Mrs.*

"Good Lord." I fumbled for words as she watched me with evident delight. "I beg your pardon, but you have astonished me. The bishop I met at the Pavilion is called Craddock."

Her eyes twinkled. "Indeed. And I have married him. Two days ago."

"Good ... heavens."

I thought about the few times I'd encountered the bishop,

how he'd growled and snarled about Dissenters—all Dissenters, not only Quakers. His comments on how they dismissed those who turned away from them suddenly took on new context.

I bowed again, my heart lighter. "My felicitations, good lady. I am pleased to see you are happy and well. The Friends were worried about you."

"Not at all—I have no doubt they wanted you to find me so they could stop me. Dear Ephram took me to his niece's house at Worthing." She leaned close, a scent of mint and cloves wafting to me. "I married not to kick dust on the Friends, as Matilda Farrow believes. I fell in love."

I thought about the testy bishop with his penchant for miles-long tramps along the coast, but his surliness made a bit more sense now. He might have feared betraying Miss Purkis's whereabouts. Growling about how he despised all Dissenters might have been meant to put everyone off the scent, though his disparagement had rung with truth.

"I offer my congratulations once again," I said. "How did you know I looked for you? Not very successfully, I admit."

"Matilda, once I broke the news to her, confessed that she and Clive Bickley asked a known friend of the Runners to hunt for me." All merriment left her expression. "She also told me of Joshua. The poor lad. How could something so foul happen to him?"

"It is tragic, indeed." Josh Bickley's death would haunt me for some time.

"He'd been quite unhappy about something," Mrs. Craddock went on. "Though he would not tell me what. I admit, I did not pay much attention to him, as I had my mind set on leaving without anyone getting wind of it."

"You left about a week ago?" I recalled what Miss Farrow

had said, that Miss Purkis had disappeared long before Josh had gone.

"I did. I went with Mr. Craddock to Worthing—to his sister's as I said—and we married there, by special license. I never saw Josh after I left." Sadness filled her words. "He was a truly good soul, that lad. Many join the Friends seeking what they cannot find either in their church or their day-to-day lives. Some find that peace, but others are never truly quiet in themselves. Josh was an exception. He was filled with the Spirit." Tears wet her eyes. "But even that could not save him from evil."

"The evil was in the world," I said, anger tinging my words. "I intend to find the villain who did this and see that he is punished."

"I agree you should, though it won't restore Josh to us." She shook her head. "I feel deep sorrow for Josh's father—Clive is a troubled man."

I recalled what Bickley had told me when I'd met him on the shingle, that he had hoped to find peace in Brighton, but it had eluded him.

It was time I politely ended the conversation, but another question occurred to me. "I beg your pardon, Miss Purkis—er, Mrs. Craddock. What sorts of plants do the Friends grow in their garden?"

She regarded me with bewilderment. "In the garden? All sorts of things, depending on the season. Runner beans, cabbages, courgettes, peppers when it's warm enough, onions, herbs. We have an apple tree that bears glorious fruit in the fall."

"Comestibles only?" I asked.

"The Friends raise what they need. Some of the extra is sold at market to maintain the building or fund charitable works, though that income is sparse."

"What about flowers? There is a vine ... "

Mrs. Craddock looked doubtful. "Some of the edible plants do flower. And the herbs. The vine is honeysuckle, which was on the house when it was purchased."

No poppies then. "Do they use plants for medicines?"

"Of course. Nettles, mint, valerian ..."

"Valerian helps with sleep, if I remember aright," I said, fixing on it.

"It does indeed. So does sitting quietly and contemplating the sea. I do agree with the Friends that ingesting all sorts of substances to soothe one's nerves is self-indulgent."

I barely heard her. I wondered if a large dose of valerian could have made me groggy and forgetful. I would have to ask the surgeon, if Denis hadn't already sent him away.

Mrs. Craddock watched me curiously, clearly wondering at my change of topic. I bowed to her once more.

"Forgive me. I am very happy to find that you are well."

"I am quite well. I believe marriage will suit me, even at my advanced age."

She was in her sixties, like the bishop, but her back was straight, her step lively, her hair only touched with gray. Some people aged rapidly in my experience, others hardly at all.

"I predict a long and happy life for you both," I told her. "I too found happiness late."

"Not all that late." Mrs. Craddock's eyes twinkled. "Compared to me, you're still quite a young man, Captain. But yes, I believe you are correct that I will be much happier now. I will not return to the Friends."

She was adamant. I respected the Quakers for their devotion and the kindness they showed to the downtrodden, but I could see that if one was not happy with that way of life, it could be difficult.

"Look after Bickley," Mrs. Craddock went on. "Losing his son is a terrible blow to him. He lost his wife, and a brother too, you know. Well, a half-brother."

Poor Bickley had certainly seen his share of tragedies. "He has gone to stay with his sister."

"I am glad. Much better for him. Good day to you, Captain. Well met."

I wished her a good day in return, and we parted, I with the feeling of having been put in my place.

***

MR. QUIMBY WAS OUT, BUT I LEFT HIM A MESSAGE TO CALL ON me at his earliest convenience. I next turned my steps to Denis's lodgings, not entirely expecting to be admitted.

I was, to my surprise, and the surgeon hadn't yet departed. In Denis's study under Denis's watchful eye, the surgeon listened to my questions with his usual stoicism.

When I finished, he shook his head. "Valerian root is used for sedation. Its effects are mild—you would have to take quite a lot to inebriate you."

"If it were given to me in alcohol? Such as in strong port?"

"No, Captain. My suggestion of pure opium is the most likely answer."

I saw an emotion in his eyes now. Arrogance. He wanted to be right—was certain he was right. The arrogance was tinged with scorn at me for doubting him.

Denis, who sat at his desk, clearly agreed with the surgeon. "Why would you suppose one of the Quakers wished to murder Colonel Isherwood?" he asked me.

"I am running out of possibilities," I said in frustration. "Speaking to you both now, I see it is unlikely I was fed anything out of their garden."

"I did not mean to imply they had nothing to do with it," Denis said. "The surgeon's opinion is only that what you took was stronger than valerian. They may not have made the opium concoction themselves, but could have had it on hand. If you can find a reason why any of the Quakers wanted Isherwood dead and for you to take the blame, you can send Mr. Quimby to them and be done."

"Isherwood was a career soldier," I pointed out. "The Quakers are pacifists. They refuse to take part in any war."

"A potential conflict there. Perhaps one of their members has gone a little mad about his pacifism and sought to destroy a man he thought personified war."

I considered the suggestion a moment. "Farfetched."

"But possible." Denis signaled one of his guards to open the door, indicating the interview was at an end. "Examine *all* possibilities, Captain, until you find the right one."

UPON MY RETURN, BARTHOLOMEW GAVE ME A NOTE FROM MR. Quimby that said he would call on me tomorrow. The missive indicated nothing more than that, and I was confident the man was busily investigating leads of his own.

The social whirl of Brighton continued. The death of a colonel of Preston Barracks and a Quaker lad did not affect the upper classes who'd come to the seaside to play.

We attended a ball that evening in a well-appointment mansion at an estate not far from Brighton. The festivities spilled into the gardens, where paper lanterns hung along the paths, the air warm enough for a stroll.

Comte Desjardins arrived with a young lady who turned out to be his niece. She began chattering to Gabriella, walking away with her, which unfortunately left me alone with Desjardins.

"You aren't armed tonight, are you, sir?" I asked, making a show of checking him over.

The man laughed. "No, no, my Purdeys are at home. You know I didn't shoot at you intentionally, my good man."

He spoke in French, far less awkward in that language. Or was he? Many a Frenchman of my acquaintance who'd lived in England since childhood, as Desjardins had, spoke English fluently, with little accent. I wondered if he affected the awkwardness for his own purposes.

"No?" I countered. I thought about the height and build of the figure in the park, the gleam of moonlight on a fine pistol. "What about during the fireworks in the Steine last night? Was that not you in the shadows, with another gun?"

Desjardins lost his fatuous smile. "What do you mean? You accuse me? You English—I have always been on *your* side."

"He's got you bang to rights." Lord Armitage had wandered to us, glass of champagne in hand, lantern light touching his sleek dark hair. "It was indeed the good count taking shots in the park. Again, you got in the way, Lacey."

My temper splintered. "Why the devil were you shooting away in the dark? You could have hit anyone. You could have hit my *daughter*, damn you."

"I wasn't aiming at you," Desjardins snapped.

"Who then? And does it matter? We are all lucky you are such a rotten shot."

"I spotted a traitorous *femme*," Desjardins said, his scorn rife. "As you might say, a turncoat bitch."

My hand tightened on my cane, eager to draw the sword within. "If you are speaking of Marguerite Gibbons, there is no evidence of that. Only Armitage's word."

Armitage's brows climbed. "Oh no? I know damn well she went through Isherwood's dispatches and stole papers. Who can say what else she did? And she shared your bed—everyone was rife with that gossip. Did she pass information to you? Whisper secrets while she lay in your arms?"

I gazed at him in amazement. "Why on earth should she?"

Armitage shrugged. "She recruited where she could. She will deny it—who would not? But she did spy, my dear Captain. Tried to recruit Desjardins here as well."

Desjardins opened his light blue eyes very wide. With his thick, fair hair, he looked like an overgrown schoolboy, one of the none-too-bright but bullying lads of the upper form.

"I told you, I am loyal to the British," Desjardins said indignantly. "Your country took me in when my family had to flee the Directorate. Those in power shifted every day—one day a friend, the next, they were sending you to the guillotine." He shuddered. "Terrible times. I would never betray your country, Captain Lacey. No matter what papers Mrs. Isherwood tried to hand me to leak to Bonaparte's generals."

Armitage scowled as Desjardins spluttered through this speech, as though he'd heard it one too many times.

"A moment." I surveyed the two men, the dandified Frenchman and the ramrod straight Englishman who'd watched the destruction at Austerlitz. "*You* were on the Peninsula, Desjardins?"

"Of course," Desjardins said without hesitation. "As an

advisor only. Who better to instruct His Grace of Wellington in the thoughts of Marmont and Bonet?"

"And, as you know, the French were allowed to escape when it was all over at Salamanca," Armitage put in. "How do you suppose that happened? Money changed hands, I imagine. Someone told the French where the weak point lay, and they fled."

Wellington had not been happy with that blunder—it had given the French time to regroup and join their fellows when they came at us later in Madrid.

Coldness stole over me. I'd always assumed those guarding the French retreat had been given bad orders, or was Armitage correct that information had been leaked?

"It hardly mattered in the end," I said, trying to keep my expression calm. "Wellington won Salamanca with good tactics, and Bonaparte weakened his Peninsular army by pulling out too many regiments to march to Russia."

"But Marguerite could not have known that, could she?" Armitage waved his glass. "She seized an opportunity. Likely she was paid for her perfidy. How else could she afford to make her way back to England when Isherwood cut her off?"

I had paid her way to England, but I decided not to bring that up at the moment.

"If you had evidence of her betrayal, gentlemen, why did you not give it to Wellington?" I demanded. "Or send word to have Marguerite arrested when she reached England?"

Desjardins shook his head in sorrow. "These things are difficult to prove, Captain. No doubt she passed on the papers or burned them. Plus she was, as you say, wily."

Armitage agreed. "I am certain she made certain she'd never be convicted. Marrying a nondescript Englishman must have helped her enormously. I suspect her spying days are over, but I would not trust that woman, Lacey. Not an inch."

I did not like these two, and I liked what they said still less. "Why are you warning me of her? Why bother?"

"Doing you a favor, old boy," Armitage said. "She's still a beautiful woman, and she deceived you once. She can do so again."

"I have not renewed my intimacy with her," I said stiffly. "Nor do I intend to."

"That does not mean she will not use you," Desjardins said. "Or your friendship. Depend upon it, she is up to no good. Why has she come to Brighton, do you suppose?"

"Her former husband died," I said, my patience thinning. "She came to see her stepson."

"Did she?" Desjardins opened his eyes wide. "Perhaps *he* is passing on English secrets too. Perhaps it runs in the family."

Armitage scoffed. "Do not become *too* fanciful, my friend. Isherwood's son is well thought of in his circle. Isherwood senior was a bullying churl. His son is an angel in comparison."

"You seemed happy enough to converse with Isherwood at our supper at the Pavilion," I said. "Congenially, I recall."

"Politeness." Armitage's smile was cold. "The politeness that is drilled into all of us from an early age. We sit with those we despise and do not make a scene."

Not entirely, as I'd observed. From what I recalled of the supper, Armitage had been boastfully arrogant about his role as diplomat to the Austrian court. Desjardins had been a buffoon, and had ogled Marianne repeatedly. Grenville had studiously ignored them, and Marianne had behaved as though Desjardins was not even in the room.

"Ah, well, Isherwood is dead now," Desjardins said. "And can tell no tales about his wife."

Armitage seemed displeased at Desjardins' words. He lifted his chin. "She might still tell plenty. Have a care of her, Captain. Remain with the beautiful Lady Breckenridge and pay Marguerite no mind."

Desjardins' lopsided grin moved dangerously close to a leer. "You did well there, Captain. How do you manage to draw the most beguiling women to your side?"

I bowed coldly. "I will take that as a compliment to my wife. Good evening, gentlemen."

"I meant no insult, of course," Desjardins said quickly. I imagine that with his lack of skill at shooting he did his best to stay out of duels. "Englishmen can be so quick to take offense."

I bowed again without a word and took my leave of both of them.

———————

In the morning as I breakfasted, I found not an answer to my letter to Brandon, but Colonel Brandon himself.

CHAPTER 20

*C*olonel Aloysius Brandon had never deigned call on me since I'd been married, though he'd attended Donata's soirees and suppers at the South Audley Street House with his wife, Louisa. Therefore, I was astonished when Bartholomew admitted him to the dining room.

Brandon had always been a hearty man, large without being soft, with a big voice, firm handshake, and loud opinions. I noted a bit more gray in his dark hair today and a few more wrinkles on his forehead, but his blue eyes were as bright and vigorous as ever.

"Did you ride all night?" I asked as I rose to shake his hand and gesture him to a seat.

Bartholomew, without prompting, set a place for Brandon, poured him coffee, and checked the dishes under silver covers on the sideboard. He hurried out, likely to shout at those in the kitchen to replenish the food.

Brandon sat down, lifting the cup of coffee, eyes pinching at the steam. "Left early this morning. Fine weather for riding, and I wanted to reach Brighton before it grew too hot. Easier on my horse." He spoke with the consideration of a cavalryman for his mount.

I set aside the newspaper I'd been reading, more uncomfortable with his presence than I wished to admit. My turbulent relationship with Brandon had calmed in the last year, but there remained a bit of strain between us.

"How is Louisa?" I asked, keeping my voice light. "Is she well?"

Brandon took a sip of the coffee, an excuse to not meet my eyes. "She is right as rain. Can't drag her out of the gardens most days. She loves summer in the country."

"I cannot blame her." The Brandons' large house in Kent was indeed a lovely place, the gardens lush under Louisa's care.

"And Mrs. Lacey?" Brandon asked in return. "She is well?"

"Donata enjoys the sea bathing. Has insisted we go several times a week, claiming the salt water is good for us. Gabriella likes splashing about, and Peter swims like a fish," I finished proudly.

"Excellent." Brandon's tension eased at my answers. "I received your letter, of course, and decided to come down. Easier for me to explain face to face."

Brandon had never been one for letter writing. He could agonize an entire afternoon over a single paragraph.

"Explain what?" I asked. "That Isherwood was a boor? And what of this fantastic idea that Mrs. Isherwood was a spy for Bonaparte?"

Brandon started to answer, then clamped his mouth shut as Bartholomew and a footman returned with more platters for the sideboard. Bartholomew offered to serve Brandon, but Brandon waved him away, climbed to his feet, and moved to pile food on his plate. I signaled Bartholomew to withdraw, which the young man did with reluctance, taking the footman with him.

Brandon clumped back to the table and thunked down his plate. He resumed his seat, lifted knife and fork, and attacked the mound of bacon, sausage, eggs, toast, and meat pie.

"In truth, Louisa thought I'd do better to speak to you," he said around a mouthful of sausages. "She remembers Salamanca. She was taken with the place, has suggested we return and hire a house there." His expression told me he thought Louisa had run mad.

"The warmth is nice." I recalled balmy Spain with nostalgia, particularly whenever the weather turned cold and dank in London. "The French chose well when they garrisoned in Salamanca."

"Yes, they made good use of the place." Brandon assumed the look of admiration he wore when discussing tactics and battles. "But I have not come to reminisce about the war. I need to tell you about Armitage and Isherwood. Two more self-serving gentlemen I have never met. I suppose that is the sort the Forty-Seventh Light attracts."

I nodded, sharing his disdain for any regiment but our own. "I barely knew anything about Isherwood, except for what he did to his wife. I never realized Armitage was even in the Forty-Seventh."

"Because you did not attend the senior officers' suppers and soirees and all that nonsense." Brandon tore apart his eggs. "I had the displeasure of dining with Lord Armitage, Colonel— then Major—Isherwood, and Comte Desjardins on several occasions. Desjardins was more a hanger-on. He was brought in by Armitage, who'd known him for years, to advise Wellington about the Frenchmen he fought. But Desjardins was useless, in my opinion. Most of the Corsican's marshals despised emigres like Desjardins and wouldn't have moved in his circles, but Armitage insisted. I do not know if the two men were simply old friends or Armitage owed him something. The latter, probably." Brandon paused to take a noisy sip of coffee.

"You were alarmed enough by my letter to ride to Brighton," I said.

Brandon nodded and set down his cup. "If there is perfidy, Armitage is behind it, trust me. He killed his own brother, you know."

I started at his bluntness. "A rumor, I thought. Unproven."

Brandon snorted. "He did it, all right. Lady Armitage married him quickly enough—angling for it, a few fellows who were in Austria at the time tell me. Armitage had the money, the prestige, the title, and the composure to give Miss Randolph a grand house and a soft life. His brother was a wastrel and she knew it —she chased him only in order to gain Armitage's attention."

"Lady Aline told me she was increasing at the time of the brother's death. She'd have leapt at any offer of marriage, I'd think."

"She'd had other offers to marry," Brandon said darkly. "But she wanted Armitage. They say she even encouraged Armitage to kill his brother and pretend a stray bullet did it."

I grimaced. "That is a fairly monstrous accusation."

"Monstrous is the word. Which is why I rose at an ungodly hour and rode to Brighton to tell you." Brandon finished off another forkful. "Damn fine cook you've found here, Lacey."

I, for one, had lost my appetite. "Lady Armitage had the child."

"A daughter, which was a mercy for the poor mite. No worries about the entail. She gave Armitage a son a year after that, so all is well in Armitage's world."

I drew a pattern on the tablecloth with the back of my knife. "What perfidy did Armitage commit at Salamanca?"

Brandon chewed and swallowed. "You recall that a large part of the French battalions we fought escaped during their retreat? That Wellington pursued them but had to give up?"

"I do remember chasing them, fruitlessly, over hills full of olive trees and being dead tired when I finally returned. Armitage tried to tell me last night that Marguerite caused this by passing information stolen from Isherwood to the French marshals."

"Ha. Isherwood did that himself," Brandon said. "Aided and abetted by Lord Armitage."

I froze, my lazy patterns coming to an end. "*Isherwood* did? I'd believe it of Armitage, but I thought Isherwood was a stickler for the rules, very upright. He had a long career as an officer. If his name was tarnished, I would have heard. Wouldn't I?"

"He was also head over arse in debt. His commission cost money, his fine house in Derbyshire cost money, not to mention the one here in Brighton, and the keeping of his wife cost money. Probably he wagered heavily at cards—who knows?" Brandon spoke with the virtuous air of one who'd never been in debt. "Armitage gave Isherwood money to help him pay up. They spoke of it quite openly over cheroots one night. Isherwood expressed a wish for the war to go on forever, as he was too worried about his creditors to return to England. He said it jokingly, but Armitage told him he need have no fears—Armitage would pay the debts and make an arrangement with Isherwood to return the money when he could."

"Devilish generous," I said in surprise. "From my brief

acquaintance with Armitage, I cannot believe he'd pass Isherwood money out of the goodness of his heart."

"Of course not." Brandon scraped his plate clean, took a final bite, and laid down his fork with satisfaction. "Armitage exacted a price, and I believe that price was letting the French retreat without hindrance. Isherwood was to have issued commands that day—the story is that the commands went astray or were misunderstood, but I don't believe that. Wellington doesn't either, but he had no proof that Isherwood deliberately disobeyed."

I stared at him, mystified. "I dislike Armitage intensely, but I cannot fathom a reason for him to help Bonaparte, and drag Isherwood into the mess. Armitage comes from an old lineage and a family with plenty of blunt. Lady Aline told me a bit about him, and her information is always spot on. And anyway, the tide was turning for Napoleon at that point. Russia was already going badly for him, and Wellington rode into Madrid soon after Salamanca, overturning Bonaparte's best-laid plans. Armitage had no reason to betray us."

Brandon shrugged and lifted his coffee. "I'm not certain of all the twists and turns, but the money Armitage gave Isherwood came actually from Desjardins, who has pots of it. He keeps those pots by playing all sides of the fence. He'd be all for Bonaparte one day, all for Louis the Eighteenth the next. Now, I believe, he's backing the Duc d'Orleans, reasoning that the duke is the strongest man to take over whenever Louis dies, never mind he's a few steps down in the line of succession. Desjardins does not try very hard to keep this a secret. Armitage is in his pocket, believe me. Perhaps Armitage's finances are worse off than he lets the world believe."

"So Armitage owed Desjardins, and Desjardins found a way Armitage could pay, using Isherwood. This way Isherwood would stand in the debt of both men." I laid down my knife. "If you are saying you believe the pair of them killed Isherwood, I can see them doing such a thing, though I'm not certain why they should. If Isherwood owed them, and they had him doing as they pleased, why murder him?"

Brandon swirled the dregs of his coffee. "Perhaps they feared he'd grown a conscience and wanted to confess. Perhaps Isherwood threatened them with this."

"They could easily deny everything. It was Isherwood who gave the orders." I pondered. "Or were they fools and kept a written record of all they did?"

"No idea. I can only tell you what I heard, and what I think."

I warmed with anger. "I wonder if Marguerite knew. Perhaps that is why Isherwood abandoned her. If she went to Wellington and told him what her husband had done, her accusations might be dismissed as the bitterness of a woman who'd been set aside."

"Wellington is no fool," Brandon said. "He'd have at least listened."

"If she was even allowed to speak to him." I growled. "Damnation. That is why Armitage insisted she was a spy and a liar. They feared she *had* known everything and had relayed it to me. They have been waiting for me to denounce them."

"And did she tell you?"

I cast my mind back to the warm days in Salamanca, the heady laziness inside the high stone house while I celebrated being alive after fierce battle.

"Nothing at all of this. If anything, Marguerite was happy to be free of Isherwood. If she did know what he'd done, I doubt she'd think I could help. But later, if she threatened to use the knowledge against him ..." I let out a breath. "I am happy I convinced her to return to England. That was a dangerous secret to hold."

"Still is," Brandon pointed out. "But it was a long time ago, Isherwood is dead now, and nothing can be proved. I only know of it because of overheard conversations and whispers afterward—put two and two together, don't you know. But no one has evidence of it. It would be Marguerite's word against Armitage's, and as you point out, his is an old name, and he's a trusted diplomat."

"Unless Isherwood left a confession." I tapped the table, lost in thought. "Perhaps he threatened to betray Armitage or Desjardins—both of them. They decided to lure him to the Pavilion, and there they cornered him and killed him." And tried to fit me up for the murder, in case I *did* know something about the Salamanca business, damn them. "But what if Isherwood already passed on this knowledge? To Major Forbes, his most trusted man? Or his son ..." I rose in agitation. "Good Lord. I need to warn him."

"If Isherwood left a letter about it, his son already knows," Brandon said reasonably, remaining in his seat. "He must guess they are the culprits, but how to prove it?"

"Young Isherwood asked *me* to prove it." I began to pace. "He might not know—Isherwood did not necessarily tell him, but would Armitage realize this? And Marguerite must be warned."

"Racing around half-cocked only brings you trouble," Brandon said, too calm for my taste. "As usual."

I halted, making myself think. If Armitage had killed Colonel Isherwood, wouldn't his troubles be over? Marguerite *might* know of the orders at Salamanca, young Isherwood *might* know, and I might. But as Brandon said, it would be our word against his. It would be too risky for Armitage to kill us all. He'd never cover up four murders.

He had wanted me to be found over Isherwood's body, had drugged me for the purpose. Even if I didn't go to the gallows for the murder, who would believe me when I bleated about betrayal at Salamanca? I would not have much credit after being found standing over his body.

I had shared port with Isherwood. Perhaps the dose had been in that, put there by Armitage—or Desjardins, who'd admitted he'd been in the room—starting to work as I walked in the Steine with Grenville...

But why would I have returned to the Pavilion? If I'd felt odd and unwell, wouldn't I have simply returned home and gone to bed? And why had I stopped in the public house where Captain Wilks had seen me?

Armitage obviously hadn't believed I'd be able to flee the Pavilion before being discovered, and they hadn't expected Isherwood's son to keep silent about the crime.

When I hadn't been arrested, Desjardins had tried twice to shoot me. He'd claimed accident the first time, and that he'd shot at Marguerite in anger the second. But he'd hardly confess to trying to murder me when I taxed him with it.

Marguerite, if she now attempted to tell her tale, might be dismissed as a vindictive woman. Young Isherwood, on the other hand, was highly respected, well liked.

"I am off to see Isherwood's son." I drained my coffee and clattered the cup to the table. "Will you send word to Marguerite for me? Brewster knows where she's lodging. He can tell you, or Bartholomew, if Brewster refuses to run the errand himself."

Brandon rose, a frown in place. "Have a care, Lacey. Armitage is dangerous. If you accuse him, he'll have the best solicitors and barristers on his side, and he can turn around and accuse you of whatever he wishes. At the least, he'll have you in lawsuits the rest of your life for slander, your wife along with you."

He had a point. "Then we will have to catch him without a doubt," I said fervently. "Make sure *he's* ruined if nothing else."

I had plenty of ideas on that score, none I would share with my former commander. Brandon would only try to talk me out of them.

Brewster would by no means allow me to walk across Brighton without him. He waited like a bulwark outside, and so Brandon would have to send the message to Marguerite through Bartholomew.

I also sent a footman running for Quimby, telling him to meet me at young Isherwood's home, urgently.

Except Isherwood wasn't home. He was at Preston Barracks, his footman stiffly informed me, on duty today. The footman was contemptuously surprised I would not know this.

Nothing for it but to hire a hackney to drive us north out of Brighton to the barracks.

It had been a long time since I'd been in an army camp. This one was permanent, not the temporary bivouacs I'd stayed in throughout Portugal and Spain. The barracks reminded me of the one I'd been assigned to in Kent, where I'd trained others in the lull in the war before I'd been sent to the ill-fated campaign in the Netherlands.

Long brick buildings housed both horses and men, enclosing a yard where soldiers drilled, cared for the horses, or vigorously polished tack.

I was directed after inquiries to an office above the stables. There I found young Colonel Isherwood conferring with Major Forbes on a shipment of buckles that had gone missing.

Army life was mostly this, not the excitement of battle many young men dreamed of—endless training, disciplining bored troops, and finding out what had become of a gross of bridle buckles.

The aid-de-camp unfortunate enough to announce me endured a blistering stare from Forbes and quickly retreated.

Isherwood, who was both more polite and more steely, shook my hand. "What news, Captain?"

"I believe I know who murdered your father," I said. "But I will need your help to draw him out and prove it."

CHAPTER 21

*a*bsolutely not." Major Forbes thrust himself forward, his scowl sending the ends of his mustache to touch his chin. "I wanted the murder reported, but Isherwood made me see sense in not making his father's death a sensation. Now you want to spread the tale far and wide, disgracing my friend and his family?"

"In a few ears only, Major," I said. "And let it be known I am beginning to remember events of the night."

"*Beginning* to remember?" Forbes looked confused—I hadn't related to them my entire part in the affair. "Ah, you mean you were drunk."

"Something like that."

Forbes gave me a disgusted sneer. "You were field promoted, weren't you? From nothing to captain, because you were friends with Colonel Brandon and didn't run away in the heat of battle."

"It was a decisive flanking move," I said stiffly, remembering the blood, terror, and my fury at Talavera. "My men were courageous enough to surround and capture artillery, which kept the battle from becoming a rout. The unit that was supposed to have done it was nowhere in sight. My *decision* won me my promotion, sir."

Isherwood raised a hand. "I have read Captain Lacey's record, and it is without stain. But you are saying my father's shouldn't be."

"Which is absolute poppycock," Major Forbes said loudly.

"I am sorry to report it." I broke through his blustering. "From what Colonel Brandon has told me about Lord Armitage, I believe he corrupted your father, promising him freedom from debt, and then probably blackmailed him into changing the orders to troops guarding the retreat. Mephistopheles to his Faustus."

The reference was lost on Forbes, who likely never read anything but army manuals, but Isherwood nodded.

"My father, unfortunately, could be easily influenced." He gave me the pained look of a man used to the truth not being what he wished. "Well I know this, to my regret, though he managed to cover his sins well. Lord Armitage, however, is a lofty personage. A diplomat, trusted by the king—or at least the Regent and Pitt, who sent him to Austria all those years ago. How will you make anything stick?"

I gave him a thin smile. "By letting him try to kill me, of course."

***

"Bad idea, guv."

I hadn't expected Brewster to go along with my scheme, and he did not disappoint me.

"I've heard again and again that Armitage is untouchable," I said as we left the barracks to the waiting hackney. "I do not want him to get away with either Isherwood's murder or sabotaging a battle. If Armitage is caught doing his best to stab me to death, that will be a different thing."

Brewster was not convinced. "Blokes like that don't end up in the dock at the Old Bailey. He'll say you provoked him, and he was defending hisself, like."

"No, he'll be tried in the House of Lords, which could ruin him even if it doesn't hang him. Or perhaps he will try to poison me, as he did before." I shrugged. "If none of this works, I'll challenge him to a duel. Or perhaps Desjardins. The man cannot shoot straight."

Brewster did not like my grim humor. "You're daft if you think His Nibs will let you be bait in a trap for a murderer."

"I am hoping His Nibs will help, and stand by to keep Armitage from killing me."

Whatever Brewster would reply to this was cut off by Major Forbes, who stormed out of the gate and caught us at the hackney. The driver, who leaned against the wheel, having a nip out of a flask, looked on without expression.

"I will not stand by while you smear the reputation of a great man." Forbes glared at me with the fury of a mastiff, ready to protect his master.

"If he truly gave those orders, he has already smeared it himself," I said calmly.

Forbes blustered, but I saw in his eyes desperation of a man who wanted to believe in his hero. "Whatever you accuse the colonel of doing, he'd have had good reason. And what did it matter what happened once the battle was won? The slaughter might have been immeasurable if the retreat had been blocked."

"Matter?" Brewster broke in with a laugh. He was never

one to keep his opinions to himself. "That was treason, it was. Even I know that."

"*You* are a ruffian and ignorant," Forbes snarled at him. "How can you understand the motives of one a hundred times better than you? Hear me, Lacey—I'll destroy you if you slander Hamilton Isherwood."

"I'd think you'd want his murderer brought to justice," I said. "If Armitage killed him, why would you stop me from proving it?"

I could see Forbes had no answer. He lunged at me instead, as though ready to strike, but Brewster stopped him with one hand around the lapel of his coat. Forbes tried to free himself, but Brewster held him fast.

"Let him go," I ordered.

Brewster ignored me. "Mayhap *you* did it." He gave Forbes a shake. "You were cozy with your colonel—maybe you worried he'd own up to treason and disgrace himself. Or maybe you found out about it and were in a rage at him for not being the great man you thought he was."

Forbes struggled, his grief that Isherwood had betrayed him stark on his face. "You're mad."

"Let him go," I repeated, my voice forceful. "I doubt Forbes killed him. He'd challenge Isherwood instead, let him defend his honor."

Brewster gave Forbes another shake but at last released him. Forbes straightened his uniform coat.

"Of course I'd challenge him," he said, as though angry I'd suggest anything different. He pointed at Brewster. "I'll have *you* for striking a gentleman."

Brewster had little fear of being arrested, as he had Denis's protection. He stepped back, unworried.

"Mrs. Isherwood," I said as Forbes regained his footing.

"Would she have known of Isherwood's orders to the troops guarding the retreat? Did she listen in on his conversations? Read his dispatches?"

"Good Lord, of course not." Forbes blinked in surprise. "The woman was nowhere near when Isherwood had his meetings, and he kept his dispatches locked away and not in his own tent. She had no interest in military matters."

"Then, in your opinion, she wasn't a spy for Bonaparte?" I asked.

Forbes's bewilderment increased. "Marguerite Isherwood? She was a hedonist. Loved to wear pretty dresses and dance with every gentleman in sight. The war was an opportunity for her to flirt with the officers, including Wellington himself. You know how *he* was with the ladies."

Unfortunately, his description could be used to paint Marguerite as a spy, one who used her wiles to grow close to high-ranking officers. On the other hand, she could be just as Forbes depicted, a lady who only wished to enjoy herself. She'd made the best of army life and marriage to a hard-hearted man like Isherwood.

"Thank you," I said. "Mrs. Gibbons will be entertained by your opinion of her."

"It's not opinion—it is the truth. I knew her better than anyone, including Isherwood himself."

An interesting thing to state. I wondered if Forbes had carried a tendresse for Marguerite and she'd shunned him.

I had one final question. "Why did Isherwood return to the Pavilion after the supper? Or did he ever leave it? Had he planned to meet someone there?"

Forbes gave me a look of anguish, which he tried to hide with outrage. "How the devil should I know? I did not see him at all that night, nor was I invited to the Pavilion with him. I told you, if he'd billeted at the barracks instead of taking a house in town, none of this would have happened."

He truly did not know. Forbes could have done nothing to prevent Isherwood's death, and that knowledge was killing him.

I took pity on him, and left him alone.

"WHERE TO NOW, GUV?" BREWSTER ASKED AS WE BOARDED THE hackney, the driver climbing leisurely to his box. "To see the Runner?"

"No," I answered. "To Mr. Denis."

Brewster was not pleased that I continued to impose myself on Denis, but if the man wanted this problem resolved, he would have to put up with me.

I could not simply bang my way into his house, of course. As when I visited him in Curzon Street, one of his ruffians took word upstairs, and I had to wait upon his pleasure.

Today, I was shown up almost at once. Denis rose when I entered his study, cool face concealing irritation.

I explained to him what Brandon had told me and my idea for finishing this.

"Risky." Denis rested his hands on the desk. "How can you force words of confession from their lips?"

"I have a few ideas. Desjardins is a coward. I believe he will break. Armitage will need more care."

I told him why I needed *him*—Denis specifically—and not only because of his trained fighting men. It was a favor, one he had no reason to grant me, and I knew I'd be yet further in his debt.

Denis knew it too. He considered for a time, though I knew

he'd already decided. "If I do this, you will undertake the task I have for you without argument." It was a statement, not a question.

The favor would prevent me from being arrested for Isherwood's murder and standing trial for it. Brandon was correct that Armitage was powerful.

I nodded, placing my fate in Denis's hands.

I VISITED MR. QUIMBY, CATCHING HIM IN HIS LODGINGS THIS time, and told him most of what I'd told Denis. Like Denis, Quimby was skeptical my plan would work, but agreed to help.

I went home—nothing more I could do in the meantime. Brandon had gone to visit Mrs. Gibbons, Bartholomew told me, and had not yet returned. I was curious to hear how the meeting went, but I would have to wait. Brandon, of course, would stay with us until he returned to London—no matter our past differences, it would be churlish indeed of me to deny him hospitality.

It was eleven of the clock. Donata was still abed, but Gabriella, dressed and energetic, waited for me, and we went for a walk on the shore. Peter came with us, playing near the water under Brewster's watchful eye.

My time with Gabriella was precious. I'd lost her for so many years, and now she intended to marry a young man in Lyon. I'd visit her, of course, and she us, but marriage took one's time and attention, and soon she'd bear children of her own.

"Tell me more about Emile." I named the young man who'd stolen her heart.

Gabriella softened, with a look that sent a dart of pain

through me. "You will like him, Father. He is clever, if a bit shy. Very hard-working."

What every father wanted to hear—industrious, doesn't speak much, isn't a complete fool. "He cares for you?"

Gabriella flushed. "Of course."

"No 'of course' about it. If he doesn't worship the ground on which you walk, I will thrash him."

Gabriella laughed uncertainly. "There will be no need for that."

"I only want you to be happy, my daughter. Marriage can be uncertain, and I do not want you to experience a bad one."

"You and Lady Donata are happy," Gabriella said. "You shout at each other but enjoy it, and you make it up."

I could not deny that arguing with Donata kept my blood warm and my spirits high. I doubted I'd do well with a cheerful wife who never contradicted me.

"My mama and papa are happy too." Gabriella gave me a sideway glance. "Though I know you and she were not so well suited."

"It worked out for the best," I managed to say. I always felt awkward discussing Carlotta.

The truth was, I'd been a rotten husband to Carlotta—a timid yet spoiled young woman who'd expected to be wrapped in cushions and taken care of. Following the drum was a hard life, and not a good one for her. Donata, on the other hand, had the strength of a hard-bitten general. She'd have kept Isher-wood in his place—and every other ranking officer as well—had she been on campaign with me.

We turned for home, Peter jogging at my side. People smiled at us as we passed, indulgent at my little family.

When we reached the house, Brewster went home,

declaring he'd spend time with his Em before I put my plans into motion.

I'd settled down to coffee, meaning to tell all to Donata once she'd risen, when Bartholomew handed me a note.

"Delivered a few minutes ago," he said. "By one of them Quaker lads."

I broke the seal and opened it. "From Mr. Bickley," I said in surprise, and read the short missive.

He'd returned to Brighton, reluctantly, to settle some business matters, and would like to speak to me.

This was fortunate, because I wanted to speak to him. There was a particular question I wished to ask him. I'd planned to write to him in Chichester, but this would save time.

"Tell Mr. Brewster I've set off to meet Mr. Bickley at this address." I shoved the paper at him. "He can meet me there if he has a mind to."

Bickley had listed a house on the road to Hove, which was not a long walk from our square. I took my walking stick and hat and left for it.

It had occurred to me as I read the note that Armitage could lure me to a lonely house by pretending Mr. Bickley had asked me to attend him there. However, the note had rung with Bickley's voice, and I did wish to question the man—he might know more about this business than he realized. He could be the linchpin that held the entire case together.

The house I reached was set back from the road behind a colorful garden, rife with summer flowers. A sign on the gate read, *Rooms to Let*.

Mr. Bickley was truly there, no sign of Armitage or Desjardins. Bickley met me at the door a maid opened and took me through a bright passage to a parlor in the back of the house.

Bickley looked haggard. His plump cheeks sagged, colorless, and the sadness in his eyes was difficult to witness. His son's death had taken all joy from him.

"I thank thee for seeing me, Gabriel." His voice rasped as though he'd worn it out.

The room was sparsely furnished, with only a few hard chairs, though the tall windows let out onto a green with a splendid view of the sea, no houses to block it. A person could stroll from here to the water and enjoy the solitude.

"Not at all," I said. "Are you settling in with your sister?"

"Indeed. She is most kind. She was fond of Joshua." Bickley choked off at the name and squeezed his eyes tightly shut.

"My dear fellow, I am so sorry." I went to Bickley and laid a hand on his shoulder. "There was a time when I thought I'd lost my daughter. A very long time. The days were dark. I understand."

"But there is no more light for me." Tears trickled down his cheeks. He opened his eyes and gazed at me sadly. "I am a grave sinner, Gabriel. I have asked thee here to beg thy forgiveness."

I released him, awkward. "There is nothing to forgive." We stood in uncomfortable silence for a moment, then I cleared my throat and asked my question. "Mr. Bickley, you told me that you'd lost a brother, in the war. Tell me, was he killed on the Peninsula? ... At Salamanca?"

Bickley stared at me, stricken, then his expression became one of horrible guilt. "He was a cavalry officer," he said in a near whisper. "He died as his troop charged a French one."

My heart gave a painful throb. I hated that I'd guessed correctly. "His name?"

"Ensign William March. He was my half-brother, much younger than I was. He was not Quaker—my mother remarried years after my father died, and she left the Friends."

I scarcely heard the last part of his statement. I recalled Ensign March, a young man, sandy-haired and restless, with plenty of jokes and a fondness for port and the ladies. He'd never mentioned his family beyond the usual remarks, and I could not remember if he'd ever stated where his home was. He'd had a south coast accent, and never said that his mother had once been a Quaker.

At Salamanca, we'd engaged with French cavalry, driving apart the line that had already been ragged so Wellington could make his sudden attack. March had raised his carbine, yelling and laughing, and he'd been shot out of the saddle.

"Ensign William March, of the Thirty-Fifth Light Dragoons," I said in a hushed voice. "Killed in courageous assault on Clausel's division. One of my men."

Bickley nodded, the bleakness in his eyes heartrending. "And so I was persuaded to take my revenge on thee. Anger was in my heart, opening the way to evil. Please forgive me."

"You drugged me," I said with conviction.

I had concluded that the only place I could have been given the concoction to render me insensible was when I'd halted to speak to the Quakers. Every other drink I'd taken that night had been shared with others or at a public place where someone could have seen it doctored.

"I did. They knew my grief, and fanned my anger. And I obeyed."

"I understand," I made myself say. "But I wish like the devil you hadn't."

"As do I. I thought remaining with the Friends would take the evil from me. But it did not."

"How long had you plotted this revenge? Salamanca was seven years ago."

Bickley looked confused. "I hadn't. I was angry with my brother for joining the army, but I had fixed blame for his death on no one but war itself. But then they came to me, a few weeks ago, told me thou had been William's commander and were a terrible man. They knew all about it—thee, William, that I was William's brother—and said they would help me punish thee for not keeping Will safe. I said I'd take no part in any violence, but they assured me I did not need to. All I must do was give thee a cup of tea and make certain thou drank it. They would do the rest, and thou would be hanged ..." He trailed off, his voice breaking.

I reined in my anger with effort. Bickley had been a dupe, like me—like Isherwood—used and discarded. I could argue about his actions loud and long, but for now, I needed to turn to practical matters.

"What's done is done, Bickley. But you are a witness to it. Are you willing—"

A sound behind me cut off my words. I felt a rush of air, and as I turned to meet the threat, pain exploded through my skull, sending me to my knees.

My head and left leg seared in agony, but I managed to draw the sword from my walking stick. I only needed to hold off the enemy until Brewster arrived.

I struck out but missed the booted legs that sprang out of the way. Dizzy, I pulled back, but another blow landed on my temple.

I fell back, blackness taking me. The last thing I saw was the butt of a beautifully made Purdey fowling piece, heading straight for my face.

CHAPTER 22

I woke to damp, a briny smell, and sharp air. I
shivered.

"Close the window, Bartholomew," I tried to say.

The wind took my breath away. It was cold, damned cold,
as though a gale had burst through my bedchamber. I reached
for the blankets and touched only the stiff prickle of what felt
like hemp.

I cracked my eyes open. Sunlight poured into them—I was
outside, and lying on a hard surface. The world rocked and
pitched.

A slap of cold water stunned me awake. I tried to sit up in
alarm, but found myself bound fast to something unyielding.

"What the devil!" I shouted as loudly as I could, both in fear
and the hope someone would hear.

Prying my eyes open all the way, I saw that I was in a boat,
a small one, my hands and arms lashed behind me to a board
on the bottom. My feet, I discovered as I tried to move, were
likewise bound. My boots were gone, my ankles tightly
gripped by thin rope.

"Bloody hell."

Speaking out loud seemed to reassure myself that I was still alive. I cranked my head around the best I could to take stock of my situation.

The first sight I beheld was the soles of a pair of boots. Not mine—these were thick-heeled and well worn. I levered my shoulders as high as I could and followed the boots to homespun breeches and a wool coat on a round body. The wearer had an equally round face, red now from sun and wind.

"Bickley!" I shouted.

He was bound as thoroughly as I was. We were alone in this small craft, tossing on the waves, who the devil knew where. The boat was small, old—patches and holes in the sides met my eyes—and smelled strongly of fish.

With much struggling, I managed to lift myself enough to peer over the gunwale.

I saw nothing. Gray sea met my gaze wherever I looked, land nowhere in sight.

"Damnation." I thumped back down, my head banging painfully.

Dizziness swamped me. My breath hitched, and as I tried to catch it, I recalled the gun, used as a club, that had rendered me unconscious. The hand that plied it had belonged to Comte Desjardins, his face lit with glee as he used his very costly Purdey to pummel me.

He must have trussed me up, or had help to do so, and trundled me out the open windows of Bickley's back parlor. I had admired the unbroken way to the sea—so handy for spiriting us off to a waiting boat.

I'd been confident as I'd tamely walked to meet Bickley, certain Bickley had sent for me, not Armitage. Bickley *had* written the note, but he'd obviously lured me to the house so Desjardins could strike.

What had they threatened him with this time? Had they vowed they'd see him strung up for murder alongside me? Had Bickley decided to confess all, either to me or the magistrate? Bickley had a sister—I wagered Armitage had threatened to hurt her. Bickley would not be able to bear losing any more family.

But I supposed, from Bickley's presence, that they'd decided to rid themselves of Bickley as well. They'd tricked Bickley today as much as they'd tricked me.

I also might have known that my plot—to have Denis imply he could deliver me to Desjardins and Armitage for a price— would not work. Either there hadn't been time for Denis to get word to them, or they'd decided that their trap was the better one.

"Am I correct that they killed your son because he knew?" I croaked. "Joshua must have found out you were helping them with Isherwood's murder, even if you were keeping yourself in the wings. Joshua was a good lad, by all accounts. I wager he tried to talk you out of giving me the opium. Did he vow to go to the magistrate?"

Bickley did not answer, did not move. I could not tell at present whether he was dead or alive.

I wriggled and thrashed, my left leg and head blasting pain through me in waves. I had to stop, breathe, and keep my roiling stomach from heaving up its contents.

How long had I been here? I'd departed to visit Bickley near noon, and the sun was on the horizon now. The wind was cold, but did not hold the iciness of dawn, so it must be evening, not morning. Sunset these days came about nine of the clock, which meant I'd been here nearly eight hours. I reasoned that

I'd be wetter, more stiff, or possibly dead from my head wound and exposure if a night and a day had passed.

What was the idea? I wondered as I continued trying to loosen my bonds. To send us out to sea to sink, drown, or simply die of thirst and cold?

An inefficient way to kill us, but then again, possibly a wise one. Who would know, upon finding our bodies, what hands had thrust us into the boat and pushed us out to sea?

They'd done a similar thing to Josh, I realized, except he'd been strangled before being put into the boat. He must have fought his captors much harder than Bickley and I had. Josh had been killed on Monday night, soon after Isherwood or possibly even before, when he'd threatened to reveal the plot.

"Your son knew you'd dosed me or were planning to," I told the inert Bickley. "I imagine he, an upright lad, was appalled at what you wanted to do. Then he stormed off. You weren't worried enough about him that night to refuse to help stitch me up for Isherwood's murder, so I wager you truly did believe he'd gone to visit friends in Hove. You had no idea they would kill him, no idea they were such monsters." I paused, running my tongue over my parched lips. "You wouldn't hurt me yourself, or even Isherwood, and so not violate the letter of your beliefs. But you'd be happy to see me disgraced, ruined, even hanged for murder. I deserved it, in your eyes."

Bickley lay motionless. I thought I saw his chest rise, but it could be the dazzling light and my hopes.

I continued my struggles. "Men die in wars, Bickley. Your brother knew that. The battle at Salamanca was a confusion, and your brother fought honorably. He was a good officer. I always tried to keep my men as safe as possible, but there was only so much I could do. My orders were to skirmish with the French lines, to add to the confusion, and we did that. I lost several men that day. I hated it, but I knew at every battle it was a risk."

No response. My words were taken by the uncaring wind, the boat rocking on waves I'd once thought beautiful.

"I am glad Grenville is not with me," I said with grim humor. "He is terribly sick on boats."

The thought of Grenville gave me some hope, as did thoughts of Brewster. Brewster would have reached the house where I'd met Bickley and realized I'd been abducted from it. He'd have sent word to my friends and family, and Denis.

Unless Armitage and Desjardins had waited for him and simply killed him. I prayed I was wrong about that.

The bonds around my arms began to loosen. More struggles and plenty of skin off my hands, including nearly wrenching my shoulder out of joint, broke one of the ropes.

An abler man would have thrown off his bonds, leapt overboard, and swam robustly to shore, whichever direction shore lay. *I* collapsed to the bottom of the boat, panting, wretched, and willing the feeling to return to my limbs.

"Bickley!" I shouted over the wind. "Wake up, damn you."

I heard a faint moan, which reassured me he was still alive, but he remained unmoving.

The boat heaved on a swell and ran hard down its other side. The sky above us was mostly clear, thankfully, but wind could churn up the sea in a bad way. Our little boat might founder, and I doubted either of us would make it to back to land in that case.

After a long time of lying still, during which I nearly fell asleep, I pried myself up on my elbows. My legs were well wrapped, my boots gone, though they'd let Bickley keep his. My walking stick, needless to say, was nowhere in sight.

The bottom of the boat held no tools—they'd have cleared

out any such useful items as hooks, fishing poles, the oars. A few old boards lay there, which looked as though they'd come off the hull.

I lifted a piece of board, splintery and rotted, and wedged it beneath the ropes that held my legs. I grimaced as I dug in, my trousers ripping as well as the skin beneath them. Grenville's tailor had designed this suit for me, and I imagined the tailor's anguish upon seeing its tatters.

I pulled and squirmed, fought and kicked, until the ropes loosed enough for me to begin unwinding them. I had to cease and rest from time to time, my injuries hurting like fury.

Once I finally freed myself of the ropes, I gathered them up and coiled them carefully—I might need them later.

I crawled the short distance to Bickley. He lay on his back, skin wan, but his ragged breathing told me he was alive.

I patted his face, trying to wake him, then tugged at his bonds. I was not gentle, I confess—he'd caused me the devil of a lot of trouble.

When Bickley finally opened his eyes, he blinked in confusion. Then awareness flooded him, and he tried to scramble away from me.

"Are you more afraid of *me* than our circumstance?" I asked in amazement. "God's balls, Bickley. I can't decide whether you are a coward or a fool."

"Both." His words were barely audible. "A sinner and a weak man."

"You may flagellate yourself later. First, I'd like to decide how we'll reach shore."

Bickley summoned enough strength to peer over the gunwale. He took in the empty sea then groaned and dropped back, defeated. "It is fitting. I will fall into the deep and be eaten by a sea creature, like Jonah."

"Let us hope," I said. "Jonah was belched out after three days, none the worse for wear."

"Because he was one of God's chosen. I never will be."

"I was taught as a lad that despair is a sin." I worked as I spoke, not really aware of what I said. "It shows no gratitude for Christ bothering to die in such a horrible way. Which never made sense to me. Why should *my* way be paved to heaven because the Romans crucified a man?"

"Those are unworthy thoughts," Bickley whispered.

"I am not an unbeliever, simply skeptical of interpretation," I said. "God has looked out for me before, and I hope we can prevail upon that good will again. In the meantime, it would be wise to discover where we are."

I dragged the last of Bickley's ropes from him and coiled these as well.

Around us rolled a sea full of whitecaps, the boat skimming up the crest of one wave and dropping into the trough of another.

"We can't have gone far," I reasoned. "What say you? You've lived on the south coast all your life, haven't you?"

Bickley cast another fearful look at the water and ducked down again. "I have never been in a boat."

"Never?" I asked incredulously. "I grew up on the coast of Norfolk. I was out into the North Sea many a time with the fishermen around our village. I longed to be a fisherman myself, but of course my father beat that notion out of me. Not the profession of a gentleman."

Bickley only stared, uncertain I hadn't run mad. He did not know me well enough to understand that I used bluffness and irritating humor when I was in danger, to keep myself from giving way.

"A fact our fancy gentlemen did not count on," I continued.

"They know me only as the interfering cavalry captain—a thick-headed, gullible one, in their opinion. The perfect man to fit up for a murder of a colonel who'd grown inconvenient."

"I do not know why they wanted to kill him." Bickley regarded me pathetically. "They did not take me into their confidence."

"Because he knew too much, of course. Isherwood was beholden to Armitage for paying off his debts, yes, but he might have been growing a conscience. Especially when he had a popular son who was swiftly rising in his career. What Isherwood did at Salamanca, at Armitage's instigation was, quite simply, treason. Desjardins egged Armitage and Isherwood into it, wanting to tell Bonaparte—if Bonaparte prevailed—what he'd done to help. Both Grenville and Brandon told me that Desjardins tries to play all sides of the game. But Bonaparte is gone, Desjardins wishes to remain comfortably in England, and treason is not the charge either a lordship or a wealthy emigre want to answer to."

I gazed at the horizon as I spoke. West was obviously where the sun was sinking. The coast of England had to lie to the north. If we drifted too far east or south, we'd end up in France, not so bad a thing, if we could survive the journey. West would take us to Cornwall, or, if we were unlucky, out into the Atlantic.

With no food or water and a boat that already had too many holes in it, I did not much like our chances.

I sorted through the boards until I found one that was wide and flat. "Do you think you can row?" I asked Bickley.

He glanced at the board in confusion. "I have no idea."

"One of us will have to paddle while the other makes an attempt at steering. If this boat had a tiller, it is gone now."

Bickley only stared at me dubiously. I tried to remember

how the fishermen of my youth could slide out into the sea in craft even more rickety than this, and not only make it back home but bring in a large catch behind them. I longed for one of those wiry, taciturn, unflappable men with me now.

I hauled Bickley up and thrust a board into his hands. "Try. I'll guide us."

I had to show him how to dip the board deep into the water to make any headway, and also how to move from one side to the other, as in a coracle, so we'd go in a straight line.

After Bickley's few feeble attempts, I realized he was hopeless. I took the makeshift paddle away from him and told him to sit in the stern. He fumbled his way back, nearly turning us over, but I managed to keep the boat upright.

The rope would help. I spent some time tying it to the top of the gunwale, which fortunately had a few rings for just this purpose. "Hold onto that," I told Bickley. "If you feel yourself going, just hang on and shove your weight opposite to the way the boat tips."

The keel had probably once had ropes attached for steering, hence the rings, but I would have to dive over the side to reattach them, and I'd never be fit enough for that.

The board was difficult to hold, especially when I had no gloves—my captors had taken those too—but I approximated a single oar with one hand on top, the other close to the water. It was damned awkward, but I did get the boat pointed more or less north.

"I've been piecing together events," I said as I endeavored. I did not know if Bickley could hear me, but I did not much care. "After supper I quarreled with Isherwood, who was still annoyed with me about Marguerite. I thought at first someone had added something to the port I took with him, but Isherwood poured his measure out of the same decanter I did, and others, including Desjardins, had helped themselves as well."

I paused to catch my breath, my labors rigorous. "My memories go hazy after I departed the Pavilion with Grenville. You must have accosted me soon after Grenville left me at the Steine. Appealing to me, in your sad way, to help you with a problem."

"Yes." Bickley wheezed out the syllable.

"I must rely on you for the gist of our conversation. Was Miss Farrow present when we reached the Meeting House?"

"She was. She often remains late to help clean, or prepare meals for those who need them. But Matilda knows nothing about this."

"Good." The upright Miss Farrow could remain on the moral high ground. "I like her. She was worried about Miss Purkis. You weren't as concerned about Josh at the moment—at that time, you had no idea of his fate. But Miss Farrow had noted his absence and asked me to discover what had happened to him."

I went quiet, out of breath, moving my paddle steadily. "Did you invite me in for a cup of something?" I asked when I could speak again.

"Tea." The words were bitter. "Thou didst not want it but politely drank it."

"Damn me and my good manners. I rarely drink the stuff—I prefer coffee." I might not have noticed if the tea seemed off, as most tea tasted foul to me. Brewster must have lost me when I'd stepped inside the Meeting House for the fateful drink. "What did you put into it? Opium?"

"Yes. Very strong opium, I think. I am not certain exactly what it was." Bickley coughed. "Fernand gave it to me."

"Fernand? Ah, Comte Desjardins." The man behind me had

violated most of his own principles but still could not bring himself to call a count by his title. "Then your part was over. Harmless, you must have told yourself. All you'd done was give me a substance that some physicians use for healing. I must have felt woozy immediately, because when I went into the pub not far from the Meeting House, I asked for coffee, not ale. I must have wanted to clear my head."

I ceased speaking to paddle for a time. My thoughts did not stop, however, and soon I was speculating aloud again.

"The lady who lured me out of the pub might have been Lady Armitage, though I suppose I will never know unless I ask her. I imagine she is in thick with her husband's plots, has been since she met him in Vienna. She must have told me something alarming to make me run back to the Pavilion. I wonder whether Armitage or Desjardins killed Isherwood in front of my dazed eyes, or whether he was already dead by the time I reached the spot. I remember growing disoriented at the sight of Armitage the next night, so I will believe it was he who made the killing blow. The event must have stuck in my head. After that, Clement, up and about because he's a young man with a healthy appetite, helped me leave the Pavilion. I found my way home to collapse into bed ,and remembered nothing when I woke." I gave a breathless laugh. "The evil was in *them*, Bickley, not you. They are cruel men who will do anything to get what they want."

Bickley said nothing. I risked a glance at him to find him openly weeping.

"None of that," I told him sternly. "I need your eyes clear so we don't run into anything. Even the smallest bit of flotsam might capsize this craft."

Bickley shook his head. "I am sorry, Gabriel. I did not know how good a man thou art, but that should not have mattered. I conspired to ruin a gentleman, and I had no right to, no matter what I believed about his character."

The words were broken, Bickley miserable. He'd been upset enough about his brother's death to convince himself to help Armitage and Desjardins, and then he'd been punished in the most terrible way. No wonder he'd thought his own sins had been the culprit.

"I don't mind what the bastards did to me," I said. "Even Isherwood was a cad. But I'll get them for killing Joshua."

I'd make certain I lived, if only for that.

I closed my mouth and concentrated on paddling. I thought I was moving us in the correct direction, but the truth was, I could not say. The sun continued to sink, and once the summer twilight gave out, we'd be in complete darkness. If the film of clouds that gathered on the horizon spread through the sky, I would not be able to use the stars for navigation.

I continued to paddle. The sun slipped down, turning the water golden and too dazzling.

Bickley had fallen silent. I looked over my shoulder to see him slumped against the gunwale, hands wrapped in the ropes.

I opened my mouth to shout at him to stay awake, when I caught sight of a speck on the horizon beyond him. My heart banged, my throat and mouth impossibly dry, and I prayed.

The speck grew larger. I squinted against the glare to watch it, willing the thing to be what I wished.

I was rewarded when I saw the silhouette of a spread sail. It was a small ship, with only one mast, a cargo sloop, or possibly an excise cutter. Or a smuggler—but I wasn't much bothered by that. As long as they pulled us out of this damned boat and gave us water, they could be pirates of the worst stripe for all I cared.

"Bickley." The word grated from me, barely audible. "Take

heart, my friend. There is a ship." I dropped the board to the bottom of the boat and waved my arms. "Hey! Ahoy!"

Bickley woke with a start. I felt him moving, then he was laughing in relief, waving with me. Apparently he'd decided he wanted to live.

We shouted, arms moving rapidly, our motions nearly tipping us over. I removed my coat and stuck it on the end of the board, brandishing it like a flag.

As the ship neared us, I saw that it was too small for a cargo ship but also too clean and sleek for an excise cutter. I realized as it drew ever closer, that it was a yacht, a rich man's pleasure boat.

I'd seen these small crafts sailing close to shore, and Grenville had told me it was popular for gentlemen sailors to ply the Solent, the water between Southampton and the Isle of Wight. Grenville had been asked many a time to join the fairly new Yacht Club, based in St. James's in London, for gentlemen who owned such craft, but Grenville always declined with a shudder. A man who was a slave to motion sickness was not likely to hurry out and purchase a pleasure boat.

The boat drew alongside. I was worn out from shouting and had to sink down and wait. I hoped they had plenty of water and coffee—and a keg of brandy wouldn't go amiss. I was chilled through.

The craft was lovely, the wood honed and cared for, the metalworks polished, the sails, now being furled, white and whole. A flag of the Yacht Club danced on a line.

A man appeared at the rail. Before I could appeal to him to take us aboard, he leveled a shotgun at me and fired it.

CHAPTER 23

I slammed myself to the bottom of the boat. Bickley, crying out, did the same.

The shot went wide, Desjardins always bad at aiming.

I ought to have known a man like Desjardins would have a pleasure craft. Or perhaps it belonged to Armitage, who liked to be the perfect aristocrat. They likely hired someone to sail it for them, but they must have used it to tow our boat out of sight of shore.

They hadn't intended to leave us to die, I realized. Bickley and I might survive if we got ourselves untied or could be rescued by one of the excise cutters I'd first imagined this ship to be. They'd wait until we were weakened by sun and thirst, and then return to make an end to us before letting us drift into the darkness.

Desjardins leisurely reloaded the gun and fired again. He missed of course.

But it was only a matter of time before he got in a lucky shot, or before Armitage took the gun away from him and

finished the deed. We were bobbing in the water with nowhere
to go.

"Bloody hell," I yelled up at him. "At least challenge me. If I
kill you, you'll go out with honor. If you kill *me*, that will be an
end to it. Let Bickley go home—you've already hurt him
enough."

Desjardins only fired again. I felt the scatter of that shot,
hot pain in the fleshy part of my arm. My shirtsleeve showed a
crimson streak.

I took up my board, disentangled my coat from it, and
returned to paddling. I'd never outrun a well-rigged sloop, but
the devil if I'd sit and tamely wait for Desjardins to pot me.

Lord Armitage appeared at the rail alongside his friend. He
too had a fowling piece, another Purdey, I guessed, but he held
it upright, waiting. When Desjardins tired of his sport,
Armitage would kill us.

Desjardins chuckled, the good-natured laugh of a man
enjoying himself. "We are only dispatching a murderer," he
called in French across the space. "You ran that sword through
Isherwood. Took it from him and killed him."

At the moment, I could not stop and muse whether he told
the truth. I continued dipping my paddle desperately into
the waves.

Armitage's voice rumbled to me. "We witnessed it, Lacey.
Someone told you he would harm your daughter in revenge
for taking his wife. You went mad."

Coldness burned my heart. What if the woman outside the
pub, probably Lady Armitage—I doubted they'd risk hiring a
woman—had told me this? That Isherwood had been boasting
of his plans, and was now at the Pavilion, alone?

Such a threat would certainly have made me dash there and
confronted Isherwood, especially if I'd not been in my right

senses. Perhaps the confrontation had turned into a brawl, and I'd managed to seize Isherwood's sword. Armitage and Desjardins would have made themselves scarce and let me condemn myself.

No memories came. However, at the moment, I did not have time to speculate. Desjardins leveled his gun and shot again.

Our boat was no longer in his line of fire. I drove us straight at the larger craft, hugging its shadow as I turned to follow its hull.

I saw Desjardins and Armitage hurry along the rail as I made my way to the stern. There, I heaved myself up, grabbing the gunwale of the rocking sloop, and slithered over the side to the deck.

I hurt—devil take it, I hurt. I knew I'd never have the wherewithal to fight even if I could stand up, but I intended to do plenty of damage before they killed me.

The pilot in the stern gaped at me, and roaring, I charged him. He stepped determinedly from the wheel to fight me off, and I dodged around him, grabbed the wheel, and gave it a wild crank.

The ship jumped and spun hard to port, slamming straight into a rising wave. I grabbed a sheet, easily slipped its knot, and let it fly free. I did it to another line, and another, blessing those fishermen of my youth who'd taught me about ropes and sails.

Desjardins was cursing in French as he came at me, the pilot in English. Armitage, angrily silent, balanced the best he could on the rocking deck and aimed his gun at me.

I dropped into a hatch that led below as his shot echoed above me. They'd corner me down here, but I scarcely cared.

The berserker anger that had let me live after I'd been hung by my heels on a hot day in Spain, and again helped me kill a deserter who'd threatened the woman and children who'd rescued me, made me yank a chair from the floor and start breaking the windows that lined the hull. Water would flood in, and this pretty sloop and her be-damned yachtsmen would wash away.

Desjardins came below first, luckily for me. He flung aside his weapon to run at me and fight. I fended off his blows, landing a few of my own, but he was strong, and I was already flagging. My advantage was that Armitage, who more slowly descended the stairs, couldn't shoot me without hitting Desjardins.

A deafening roar filled the cabin. Desjardins screamed and spat blood as he fell limply from my grasp.

I'd been wrong. Armitage had been prepared to shoot right through his friend to get to me. Desjardins collapsed to the floor, cursing and moaning, and Armitage calmly reloaded.

A startled shout from up top made him pause, and in that second I slammed into him, fighting for control of the gun. Armitage's hands slipped on it, but he could afford to let it go, as its shot was already spent. I brought up the gun like a club, at the same time Armitage unsheathed a long knife.

I spun away from him, but what I saw out the window as I did made me stop in amazement. The shouting from the sailors outside increased, their cries now edged with panic.

Armitage saw what I did, and his eyes widened.

Another ship, squat and thick-bodied, charged at us across the waves. No sails propelled it, but thick black smoke poured out of a metal chimney poking high behind the pilot house. The last of the evening sun touched it with red-gold light, tinging the smoke a faint pink.

Steamboats were a new phenomenon of the last dozen

years, and now a few plied up and down the Thames, carrying curious passengers from dock to dock. More boats, I'd heard, moved along the Clyde and across firths in Scotland. Some steam vessels worked in harbors as tugboats, pulling in larger ships to docks or shipyards.

This was a tug, I realized, as it came closer, an interesting meld of steam power, paddle wheels, and ingenuity.

It was also heading dead for us, no swerving. It was set to ram us.

Armitage bolted. He was above and at the side, yelling at the tug, calling them bloody fools, threatening them with the law. I chuckled with wry humor at the sight of a murderer claiming the law as his ally.

I grabbed the bleeding Desjardins and hauled him up the ladder to the deck. I fell there, Desjardins half on top of me, and watched in fascinated horror as the belching tug bore down upon us.

The yacht's pilot had caught the wheel, desperately trying to turn us. The lines I'd loosened whipped overhead, and the sails, half unfurled, jerked hard at the mast. The yacht listed heavily to port, and in that moment, the tug rammed it.

Board hit board, the pleasure craft breaking open with a tearing screech. I pulled myself up and stared at the tug as I balanced on the gunwale, and at the sturdy body of Brewster at its bow. Behind him stood Colonel Brandon, a look of grim satisfaction on his face.

That was the last I saw before I dove sideways, overboard, away from the path of the giant wheel. The small boat, with Bickley still in it, had drifted off, and I swam hard for it.

I'd never make it. My arms and legs were cramped with exhaustion, my right arm stinging where Desjardins' shot had scraped it. Bickley, eyes wide, watched me swim, feebly holding out a board for me to grab.

The beautiful face of Donata flashed through my mind, followed by that of Gabriella and then Anne. Then Peter's grin that transformed his rather stern countenance into a light-hearted boy's.

I wanted to be with them one more time.

Something splashed beside me. A rope, with a loop tied in it.

I looked up at the tall side of the tug, to see Brewster, his mouth moving as he shouted at me. I could hear nothing over the roar of the engine, the waves, and the shattering boards of the sloop.

Brandon leaned next to him, and beyond Brandon, Grenville hung on to the rail with both hands. Brave man, was Grenville, to come out here in that boat.

I caught the rope and dragged it around myself and under my arms. Immediately, it tightened, and I was pulled, like a large fish, to the aft hull of the tugboat.

A ladder of rope and wood slats dropped down from the side, and I realized I was meant to climb this. I clung to the ladder, trying to move my legs to make my feet find the steps.

The rope tightened. I was half-dragged up the side as I fumbled with the ladder, until I spilled over the gunwale and landed, sodden and gasping, in a heap on the deck.

"Brewster," I whispered, my voice a thin rasp. "Tell Denis to give you a rise in wages."

The crowd that had gathered around me drew back in relief.

"He's all right," Brewster said to the others in his slow way. "Daft bastard."

THE TUG WAS A TERRIBLE PLACE. IT STANK OF SMOKE, COAL, AND oil, the air inside the pilot house barely breathable.

I leaned back on a hard wooden bench, which was a long way from the elegance of the chair I'd used to bash out the window on the yacht, and thanked God for delivering me. I was out of the wind, the sun, and the water. A hot mug of coffee, laced with Grenville's best brandy, warmed my hand.

"How is Bickley?" I asked after a few more sips of fortified coffee.

The man had been fished out of the small boat and hauled aboard. He was now in a cabin in a deck below this one.

"Ill and unhappy," Brandon said cheerfully. He sipped deeply of the dark coffee. "But he'll mend. He was already chattering to the magistrate about all the things Lord Armitage did and threatened to do."

Brandon gestured with his cup to the portly magistrate, Sir Reginald Pyne, huddled on a bench in the stern. He looked as miserable as Grenville. Grenville manfully sat across from me at the table, holding on to said table while he imbibed directly from his brandy flask.

We were now clanking and bumping toward shore. The wind tore at the boat, and the waves heaved her, but the tug moved unwaveringly.

"Desjardins?" I asked after a time. I'd not seen anyone brought up but Bickley and the yacht's pilot.

"Bleeding from a nasty wound." Brandon's delight was unnerving. "Surgeon's sewing him up. He'll be fine, in my opinion, and soon sent back to France, leaving all his money and assets here. He's safe to live there again—unless the French king objects to him trying to aid Bonaparte."

"Desjardins is not very bright," I remarked, drawing warmth from the coffee cup. "But he has managed to grow wealthy and influential on cunning. Perhaps he'll learn to do that in France as well."

"No matter what, he'll be leaving our shores," Brandon said, his delight turning to determination. "I'll make certain of it. Poxy bastard made that damned war harder on us, and we lost good men."

"Where is Armitage?" I asked. "Cowering next to Desjardins? Or washing his hands of the fellow?"

Grenville lowered his flask. "He's dead, I'm afraid."

"Oh." I thought of fighting the man, how strong he'd been, how he'd nearly killed me. He'd seemed indestructible. "Drowned? Or run down by the tug?"

"Killed hisself, didn't he?" Brewster broke in. He too had a flask, no diluting his spirits with coffee. He stood near the front of the cabin, watching the land come at us.

"Killed himself?" I blinked. "How on earth did he do that?"

Brewster turned, taking a pull of his flask. "Had a knife. Plunged it right into his own throat. Bled fast, dead before we pulled him out of the water."

I gaped. "Good Lord."

"A swifter and easier death than he'd have been given as a traitor and a murderer," Colonel Brandon said. "He'd have faced ignominy and then execution, his lands and title taken back by the crown. He knew it."

"He'd have to be tried first," I argued. "Easy for him to claim he was falsely accused. Isherwood is dead, Desjardins is a foreigner. Even Bickley's testimony could be dismissed as one of a grieving man. We can't prove orders Isherwood might or might not have given seven years ago. I know bloody well

Armitage killed Bickley's son, to eliminate another witness, but there is no proof. Why did he not believe he'd have a chance?"

"Because he'd be tried in the Lords," Grenville said, his voice calm and quiet to my angry one. "And so many lords can't stick him. Armitage went over heads to gain that posting to Austria, and the rumor that he killed his own brother is credible. He'd have been convicted, I'm willing to wager. He's made himself that many enemies."

"His wife had better claim complete ignorance and innocence," Brandon said. "Or she'll be dragged down herself."

"I could pretend I remember that it was Lady Armitage who assailed me outside the pub and tricked me into going to the Pavilion." I thought of what Desjardins and Armitage had claimed—that it had been my hand that had dealt Isherwood the fatal blow. Was it the truth? Or the pair still trying to shift the blame for their deeds? Unless my memory returned, I could never know. I sighed and returned to my coffee. "But I'd have to swear that in court, and I am not very good at lying."

"You aren't that," Brewster agreed.

I ignored this. "How did you find me?" I asked the general company.

"Went to the cottage you'd been summoned to," Brewster answered. "You weren't there when I arrived, and none had seen you go. But then I spotted a gentry cove's sailing ship putting out to sea, towing a little boat behind. I nabbed a spyglass from a bloke and had a butcher's. Couldn't see anything, but I wagered it were you out there."

"So you commandeered a steamboat?"

"His Nibs did. I ran back and told him. He went down to the docks himself. Had to finagle, and the colonel here had to help, but His Nibs paid a large amount of money for the tug captain to set off after the boat. It were slow, but finished the task."

"You plowed it into a yacht owned by a count," I said, impressed. "Or a viscount if it's Armitage's."

Brewster wiped his mouth. "Accidents do happen at sea."

"Indeed they do." James Denis had seen to that.

The shore came up fast, as did the jetties that stuck out from below West Street and Middle Street. Just as I swore we'd run straight into them, the engine stopped, and in silence, we glided gently to the dock.

"Much easier than a sailing ship," Brewster said as the world ceased rocking. "It belches like a stevedore, but it moves as sweet as kiss your arse."

CHAPTER 24

I managed not to collapse until I made it to the small white house I currently called home.

Donata, Gabriella, Peter, and most of the servants met us at the front door, all wild with worry. My arm had been bandaged by the surgeon—not Denis's surgeon, who could not very well show himself with a magistrate about—but a competent man from Brighton. I showed all my sling.

"Nothing to worry about. Just grazed me. I'll be closed up in no time."

Gabriella and Peter let themselves be reassured. Gabriella hugged me hard and Peter clasped my hand, manfully gulping back tears. They escorted me upstairs, but left me with Donata by my chamber door, Gabriella leading Peter away.

I turned and made for Donata's bedchamber instead, she following, because hers was soft, comfortable, smelled nice, and would contain her. Donata hovered while Bartholomew undressed me.

"Damnation," she declared when my battered and bruised torso came into view. "Gabriel, you must cease this."

I tried not to wince as Bartholomew began scrubbing off my back with a large, sopping sponge. I stood in under-breeches and nothing else, my cold skin prickling in the stuffy chamber.

"Indeed," I said as Bartholomew worked to remove all traces of my adventure. "I am growing too old to be blamed for a murder and then nearly killed. I am supposed to be on holiday."

"Blast you, Gabriel," Donata growled, and then she came at me.

Bartholomew tactfully stepped back as my wife enfolded me in a clutching embrace, burying her face in my shoulder. Her body shook, but she tried to muffle her sobs—she did not like to be seen giving way.

I stroked her hair and kissed the top of her head. "We've let the house for another few weeks," I said soothingly. "The holiday isn't lost. We'll go for walks and bathe in the sea and attend insipid soirees as much as you like."

Donata remained silent. Bartholomew quietly returned the sponge to the basin and withdrew, sending me a grin before he noiselessly closed the door.

Donata lifted her head when the latch clicked. Her eyes were red-rimmed, tears on her lashes.

"We won't stay here," she said sharply. "I cannot bear this place any longer."

"London will be hot," I said. "The stench fearsome." I recalled my years living in Grimpen Lane, with the Thames not far enough away to mitigate the stink.

"No, Oxfordshire," she said. "We'll spend the remainder of the month at my father's house and then go to Norfolk, before we return Gabriella to France. You'll have to see to the harvest."

My cousin would see to the harvest quite well without me, but I nodded. "We'll go, love."

I thought of Oxfordshire and the seat of the Pembrokes, the long avenue that led to the house of golden stone, the gardens that were the pride of Donata's mother. I could ride with Peter through the fields, or walk with Gabriella along paths by the river. I would carry Anne on my shoulders and show her the lands of her ancestors.

Then Norfolk where Peter and I would dig for clams and picnic in the abbey ruins, ride for miles along the salt flats. I longed for the wide lands, the huge sky, the sea stretching like a gray sheet to the north.

"We'll go, love." I repeated.

I raised her face to mine and sealed the bargain with a gentle kiss. Donata retrieved the sponge, and she and I finished wiping grime and blood from me. Once I considered myself clean enough not to mar the sheets, we took to bed.

"HIS NIBS WANTS A WORD."

Brewster's voice came mournfully around the packing crates in our downstairs hall, the boxes waiting to be loaded onto the wagons outside.

"His Nibs is still here?" I asked in surprise. A week had passed since the day I'd been forced to sea. I'd healed my hurts but did not like to think of how close I'd come to dying.

Desjardins, though he'd taken a heavy shot to the thigh, was mending. Brandon visited him every day, as did Mr. Quimby, who took plenty of notes. The comte was doing his best to save himself by blaming everything on Armitage, but Brandon remained of the opinion he'd be sent to France as soon as he could travel.

Young Isherwood had visited and thanked me. I was not certain what for—I could bring no one to justice. Still he was gracious, with the right touch of acknowledgment. I predicted he'd go far as an officer.

Marguerite Gibbons and her husband finished their business in Brighton and returned to Portsmouth. Isherwood had left her a bit of income, she'd told me when she came to say good-bye, which indicated to me that the man might have felt some remorse for how he'd treated her.

Marguerite was more of the opinion that her stepson had persuaded Isherwood that leaving her a token amount would look better for him than ignoring her altogether. In any case, she had finished with Isherwood's man of business and looked forward to going home.

She and her husband had said their farewells to Donata and me both, Marguerite giving me a warm smile. The smile told me she was grateful for what I'd done for her in the past, but that it would remain in the past. Mr. Gibbons was congenial throughout, as though he had no fears about his wife's former lover. And he did not. I wished them well.

Mr. Bickley left for his sister's in Chichester once more. He'd offered to testify against Desjardins and take the blame for his part, though the magistrate said it probably wouldn't come to that. Bickley had done nothing more than put opium in my coffee, and no jury would believe he masterminded the plot, or even understood all it entailed. Unless someone prosecuted Bickley, he'd remain quietly with his sister.

I thought it brave of him to offer. Bickley would have had to stand in the dock and tell the world how his actions had caused death of his own son. Yet he'd done it, possibly to ease his conscience, though I could see he was a broken man.

Armitage must have worked on his grief, feeding him stories of my life, happily married to a wealthy woman, while his brother had died under my watch in Salamanca. But Bickley's punishment for participating in Armitage's scheme had been dire indeed. I pitied him.

Brewster nodded at me now, unhappy. "Mr. Denis is waiting until you're safe in Oxfordshire before he goes home. Says he needs to pack you in cotton wool."

"Amusing." I took my hat from Bartholomew and stepped out onto the street. "Nothing for it, I suppose."

We walked the short way to the house Denis had let. Around us families enjoyed the summer air, moving down to the promenade or carrying baskets to picnic at the Steine. A few pleasure craft drifted offshore, sails full.

Work continued on the Pavilion. Clement had showed Grenville and me through it this past week, he an elegantly liveried and knowledgeable guide. He'd demanded the entire story of the end game, of course. I liked the lad and hoped I would be able to visit him and his mother again one day. They were refreshingly kind people.

Denis received me in his upstairs study, with its view over the fields behind it. A brush of sea air touched the close room, and wind bent the grasses under a cloud-dotted sky.

"I'm off," I said as I entered. "As you know. This afternoon, in fact. Direct any missives to her ladyship's father's house in Oxfordshire."

Denis only looked at me. "I called you here to remind you that I expect you to perform a task for me."

We remained standing, which told me the interview would be brief.

"I remember," I said. "Though, in the end, I never needed your help to trap Armitage."

"While that is true, you agreed to the bargain." Denis's eyes were cool.

I gave him a nod. "You did, however, commandeer a boat to rescue me. For which I am grateful."

"It was expedient. Can I hold you to this promise?"

"Yes." A bargain was a bargain, and I'd honor it. Without Denis, I would now be dead, and we both knew it.

"I will not ask the mission of you now," he went on. "You will travel to Oxfordshire, Norfolk, and France as planned. Afterward, I will send for you."

"You could have stated this in a note." I said, a trifle impatiently. "I have much to do today."

"I have more to say that I did not wish to write. Such as the fact that Comte Desjardins insists that you actually did stab Colonel Isherwood to death. He has told this to the magistrate, but it is clear that his word is not believed."

I swallowed, my throat dry. "He claimed this, yes, when he was trying to pot me in the boat. Do you think he is lying?"

"It does not matter." Denis gave me a level stare. "I have made certain that this statement will be taken as a falsehood— the comte's effort to move the blame to another. The belief at the moment is that Lord Armitage struck the fatal blow. Colonel Isherwood's son, who well knows Lord Armitage, accepts the explanation. Armitage strangled Joshua Bickley as well, Desjardins was quick to add." He paused a moment. "Comte Desjardins will be ejected from England, Armitage is dead, and that is the end of it."

I listened in stillness. I could demand Denis to tell me how he knew all this, but I had no need. Denis would keep himself informed about the magistrate's every decision, and he would arrange to speak the right word into the right ears at the right time.

Uneasiness sat disagreeably on my stomach. "If my memories do not return, I will never know for certain whether I murdered Isherwood."

"As I say, it no longer matters. The episode is finished." Denis's voice was hard, final.

It would always matter to me, but I would have to find a way to live with this. "Is that all?" I asked, keeping my voice steady. "As I said, I am much occupied with trying to extricate myself from Brighton."

Denis's expression grew icy. "I also wish to inform you that Mr. Brewster will no longer be accompanying you. I have assigned another man to this task."

My gaze swung to Brewster. He kept his head up, but moroseness flowed from him. Now I understood the unhappiness he'd exuded since he'd come to fetch me.

"Why?" I demanded. "Brewster ordered that tug to ram the boat, and he fished me to safety."

"The fact that such a thing was necessary indicates Mr. Brewster is not up to the task of looking after you. He also did nothing to prevent you from being drugged and nearly accused of murder, not to mention you being trussed up on a boat and floated out to sea." Denis closed his mouth, the line of it flat.

"It is hardly Brewster's fault I manage to get into scrape after scrape," I said, trying to curb my anger. "It is my way. Another minder will fare no better."

"That remains to be seen."

I began to grow alarmed. Denis was not kind to those who displeased him. "Brewster is a good man," I said. "I ask you to leave him be."

Denis's brows drew together the slightest bit. "I intend to leave him be. But he will no longer work for me."

"You're sacking him?" Denis had done this to Brewster before, or at least had pretended to for his own reasons. "Rather unfair, I'd say."

"It is *not* for you to say." Denis's voice turned hard. "I decide my business in my own way, and I have no intention of consulting you. I wish you good day."

He said this to both of us. Brewster swallowed, but he'd already accepted Denis's decision, knowing he could not fight it.

Denis waited, the room growing silent. The men stationed at each window watched Brewster and me, alert.

Arguing would not change the situation, I saw. I gave Denis a curt nod and left him standing in the middle of the sunny room.

Brewster followed me down the stairs. Outside, he adjusted his hat. "Well, that's that. I'm off."

"Wait." I stepped in front of him, planting my walking stick on the pavement. "What will you do?"

Brewster shrugged. "Retire, most like." From his look, the thought of that appalled him.

I could guess what might happen if Brewster found himself idle. He had once been a very good thief, and left on his own, he might well return to his old ways.

"You're out a place because of me," I said. "You worked for me before. Do so again."

Brewster's eyes narrowed. "As what? Your footman?" He curled his lip.

"Doing what you do now. My wife would be pleased to have you follow me to keep me out of trouble. Who knows what will happen in Oxfordshire? Or during whatever this errand Denis has in mind for me?"

Brewster studied me a bit longer, his long-suffering look returning. "I can barely keep you out of trouble *now*. How am I supposed to manage without His Nibs and his lackeys to help me?"

"I imagine Mr. Denis would step in if things grew too dire." I had no doubt he would send another to watch me, and little doubt he would learn every word of this discussion.

Brewster removed his hat. He crushed it between his big hands while he considered, then he heaved a long sigh and jammed the hat back on his head.

"I'll have to talk it over with Em. But all right. I'll work for ye. *If* the wage is high enough." He sighed again then turned away and began the trek back to the house.

"Lord help me," I heard him mutter. "What am I in for?"

THANK YOU FOR READING!

Captain Lacey's adventures continue in *The Customs House Murders* (Captain Lacey Regency Mysteries, Book 15). Sign up for my newsletter to be informed of releases in this series here: http://eepurl.com/5n7rz

HISTORICAL NOTE

I had the great fortune while researching this book to visit the beautiful walled city of Salamanca in western Spain, not far from the Portuguese border. The land is hilly and dry, with stretches of flat plains filled with olive groves, farms, and cattle. I could easily imagine the French and British armies winding along the ridges, watching each other warily until Wellington made the decision to strike.

The battle of Salamanca took place to the south of it, near the small town of Arapiles. It was a short, brutal battle that lost the French more than 13,000 men and won Wellington great aplomb. The battle was never supposed to have happened—Wellington was keeping an eye on the French lines, and he'd planned to leave and march back to Portugal, when he saw an opportunity for attack. Acting immediately and decisively, he surprised the French and wreaked plenty of havoc.

A contingent of the Spanish army was supposed to have guarded a bridge that would prevent the French army's escape. But for some reason, the Spanish commander had word that he was to let the French through, or at least not try very hard to hinder them. Pursuit failed to capture the retreating French.

Wellington was furious—he'd never given the order, and to this day, there is speculation that the orders were misunderstood or simply never reached the Spanish commander. I decided to put my own interpretation on the matter.

The battlefield at Arapiles is one of the most intact of those Peninsular War, with guided tours offered.

Salamanca itself was fortunately not much damaged in the battle, and the city is largely unchanged. The cathedral is immense and stunningly beautiful. I spent a long time wandering about inside it, in both the old and new structures, admiring the architecture and art.

Back streets slope from cathedral to river, quiet and enchanting. Here the Roman bridge, its arches and stones intact, crosses the Tormes. On this end of Salamanca lies a wonderful Art Nouveau museum, the Casa Lis. While it hails from a hundred years later than Lacey's time, it was well worth a visit, and became one of my favorite places in Salamanca.

Yachting

The Yacht Club—now the Royal Yacht Squadron—was founded in 1815 in St. James's, London, as a place where gentlemen who owned pleasure sailing craft could meet and discuss the sport. The Prince Regent was an honorary member. The club took on the "Royal" designation when the Regent became George IV in 1820, and was renamed the Royal Yacht Squadron by George's successor, William IV. The organization, now based on the Isle of Wight, is still going strong.

Steamboats were in use for passenger and cargo service on

the Thames as early as 1815, and in 1816, tugs began working to guide large sailing vessels through the waters.

I hope you enjoyed Lacey's adventures in Brighton.

ALL MY BEST WISHES,

ASHLEY GARDNER

ALSO BY ASHLEY GARDNER

Captain Lacey Regency Mystery Series
The Hanover Square Affair
A Regimental Murder
The Glass House
The Sudbury School Murders
The Necklace Affair and Other Stories
A Body in Berkeley Square
A Covent Garden Mystery
A Death in Norfolk
A Disappearance in Drury Lane
Murder in Grosvenor Square
The Thames River Murders
The Alexandria Affair
A Mystery at Carlton House
Murder in St. Giles
Death at Brighton Pavilion
The Customs House Murders

Kat Holloway "Below Stairs" Victorian Mysteries
(writing as Jennifer Ashley)
A Soupçon of Poison
Death Below Stairs
Scandal Above Stairs
Death in Kew Gardens
Murder in the East End

Leonidas the Gladiator Mysteries
(writing as Ashley Gardner)
Blood of a Gladiator
Blood Debts (novella)
(More to come)

Mystery Anthologies
Past Crimes

ABOUT THE AUTHOR

USA Today Bestselling author Ashley Gardner is a pseudonym for *New York Times* bestselling author Jennifer Ashley. Under both names—and a third, Allyson James—Ashley has written more than 100 published novels and novellas in mystery, romance, fantasy, and historical fiction. Ashley's books have been translated into more than a dozen different languages and have earned starred reviews in *Publisher's Weekly* and *Booklist.* When she isn't writing, she indulges her love for history by researching and building miniature houses and furniture from many periods, and playing classical guitar and piano.

More about the Captain Lacey series can be found at the website: www.gardnermysteries.com. Stay up to date on new releases by joining her email alerts here: http://eepurl.com/5n7rz

Made in the USA
Middletown, DE
15 March 2020